Thrusting CarlyAnn
the tangled pile of
These are her clothe
medicine. This is her num-num cup; these are extra lids."

"Num-num?" Sean looked at CarlyAnn. He was feeling a little num-num himself.

"Yes, and these are her yum-yums, her binkie, her wa-wa, her dolly, her boo-boo bear, her googie cloth, her yucky wipes, her mushy treats . . ."

Stepping to Sean, she nuzzled her daughter's soft cheek. "Be good for Uncle Sean, okay?" Suddenly tears sprang into her eyes, and her throat sounded tight. "And . . . *snnfff* . . . do what he . . . *snnifff* . . . says. *Ohhhh,"* she wailed. "I've never been away from her for more than a few hours at a tiiimmmmeee. Oh dear . . . *snnifff* . . ."

Sean rolled his eyes. *Good grief.* Had he asked for this? He was supposed to be on his way down to the dinner table, hopefully mustering up enough courage to ask Julia on a date.

"Bap," CarlyAnn shouted and smacked her delirious mother on the nose.

"Thank you, sweetie," Kathleen sighed. "I needed that. Thank you, too, little brother. I owe you one." She glanced at her watch. "Good heavens, it's 5:45! I'm beyond late. Gotta run!" Yanking open his door, Kathleen rushed out into the hall, leaving her daughter and brother in the dust.

Following his sister out into the hall, Sean watched Kathleen's retreating form as she skipped backward down the hall, still issuing some last-minute instructions.

"Say bye-bye, CarlyAnn," Sean sighed.

"Bap," CarlyAnn shouted uncertainly after her mother. Her small face began to pucker.

Our **Giggle** Guarantee

We're so sure our books will make you smile, giggle, or laugh out loud that we're putting our "giggle guarantee" behind each one. If this book fails to tickle your funny bone, return it to your local bookstore and exchange it for another in our *"A Time for Laughter...and Romance"* line.

Comments?

We'd love to hear from you!
Write to:
Lisa Bergren, Executive Editor
WaterBrook Press
5446 N. Academy #200
Colorado Springs, CO 80918

Say Uncle...
and Aunt

Suzy Pizzuti

WATERBROOK
PRESS
COLORADO SPRINGS

Say Uncle . . . and Aunt
Published by WaterBrook Press
5446 North Academy Boulevard, Suite 200
Colorado Springs, Colorado 80918
A division of Bantam Doubleday Dell Publishing Group, Inc.

ISBN 1-57856-044-6

Printed in the United States of America.

1998—First Edition

1 3 5 7 9 10 8 6 4 2

For my daughter Madeline.
No career could ever hold a candle to you, my love.

And thanks,
dear Lord, for giving us
laughter with which to face
life's valleys.

1

Are you . . . uh, oh . . . are you going to . . . ," Julia Evans stammered uncertainly, ". . . be all right? Oh, dear . . . can I . . . help . . . ?" Grimacing, she rushed forward to offer Mrs. Hattie Hopkins her arm as the elderly woman proceeded to lurch up the porch stairs. "Mrs. Hopkins? Uh . . . can I give you . . . some help?"

As she hovered at Hattie's back, Julia trailed the boarding-house landlady up the steps, her arms outstretched, ready to catch this tiny dynamo should the need arise. I . . . uh . . . okay, I guess you . . . have it under control. I'll just stand back . . . here."

Oblivious to Julia's concern, Hattie swayed wildly and snagged a porch post with the hook of her walking cane. Regaining her balance, she continued her precarious trip up the steps, never once breaking her informative monologue.

". . . and the house was built in 1864—or was it '65? Gracious sakes," Hattie twittered with laughter. "I can never remember . . . and of course, back yonder are the rose gardens and gazebo. Nice place to sit, on a midsummer night, yes, my, my, my. Lovely view of the lake, don't you know. In the fall the trees really put on a show. It's stunning, I'm telling you. Well, you'll see for yourself in a few weeks. October is always spectacular, I say."

Once they had safely reached the top of the steps, Julia dropped her arms and allowed her gaze to travel slowly around the front porch as Hattie—owner and proprietress of Hattie Hopkins's Boarding House—continued to lead her on an interesting, if somewhat wobbly, tour of the facilities.

Covered with corbels and fish scales, spindles and spokes, and an abundance of ornate gingerbread from a bygone era, the aging Victorian reminded Julia of her own grandmother's house. Only Hattie's place, sitting atop a gentle hill at the edge of a lake in McLaughlin, Vermont, was even lovelier. It was uncanny how at home Julia felt, considering how far away from home, and her grandmother's house, she actually was.

"Well," Hattie warbled, "that's the whole place, inside and out. Come on back inside and tell me what you think," she instructed, beckoning Julia with a shaky wave of her cane.

Julia followed Hattie into the quaint parlor and perched on the springy, buttoned-and-tufted loveseat the little landlady indicated. From the smell of lilacs and lemon furniture polish to the way the afternoon light filtered through the voluminous lace curtains, from the porcelain knickknacks to the musty old books, yes, and even the elderly woman who slowly settled onto the antique settee across from her—everything reminded Julia of home. Of family. "I *love* this place," Julia breathed.

Yes, she decided firmly. She would take the room, regardless of what it looked like.

"You *love* his face . . . hmmm." Hattie bunched her lips into a thoughtful wad as she pondered Julia's words. "Oh!

My, my, yes. Why, thank you, dearie. Yes, I love his face too."

A puzzled frown marred Julia's brow. *Whose face?* Had she missed something?

The elderly business owner waved a gnarled finger back at the black-and-white picture of a smiling man on the fireplace mantel. "That's my dear late husband, Ernest. Ernie went to be with the Lord about ten years ago, and I'm sure he's up there having a fine time chasing the angels around till I arrive to cuff him upside the head. Hee-hoo-hoo-hoo!" Sapphire-blue eyes twinkling, her laughter yodeled up and down the scale. Tucking a snow-white tendril back into her droopy bun, Hattie sobered slightly. "I surely do miss him."

"Oh, I can imagine," Julia murmured. Brows arched, she attempted to keep track of the erratic conversation.

"So," Hattie trilled in her birdlike falsetto as she slowly grasped a stack of papers that had been lying on the coffee table and moved them to her lap, "are you going to take the room?"

Julia nodded. "Yes, ma'am. As soon as possible. In fact, the sooner, the better." As often as she had been transferred on her climb up the corporate ladder, Julia didn't have much in the way of personal effects. Everything she owned was crammed into her car, now parked at the curb. Though Julia considered renting an apartment right away, Hattie's boarding house seemed like a much less complex, much less lonely, answer to her housing needs. For now, anyway. After she'd had time to discover McLaughlin's rental possibilities, she would undoubtedly move again. Until then, Hattie's place was surely a godsend. "I hate to disrupt your Sunday afternoon, but I'd like to get settled today and explore the town tomorrow. So, if it's all right with you, I'd like to move in right away."

"Oh, no, don't worry, I haven't given the room away. Now then," Hattie fingered the delicate cameo broach at her throat, "when will you want to move in, honey?"

Julia blinked. "Uh, right away," she repeated, "if that's okay." Smoothing her skirt over her knees, she smiled expectantly.

"Not today?"

"Oh." *Not today. Hmm.* Was the old woman asking or telling? In the short hour she'd been here, the conversation had taken more turns than a spinning ice skater. Perhaps it would be easier to work within Hattie's schedule. "What would be good for you?"

Looking pleased, Hattie nodded. "Ah, yes. Well, that's just fine."

What? What was fine? Julia studied Hattie's sunny face for a clue. "Um, Mrs. Hopkins, what exactly is, uh, fine?"

"Good. Good, then it's settled." Reaching forward, Hattie patted Julia's stocking-clad knee. "Breakfast begins at 6:30 every morning. You're on your own for lunch, and I start serving supper at 6:30 every evening, except for the Lord's day. Sundays after church, we all lie around, eat sandwiches, play games, and rest. In the afternoon, everyone is on his own." Peering at Julia, she winked. "Just remember 6:30, and you'll be fine."

Okay. Six-thirty is mealtime. That much she comprehended. Julia smiled and gave her head a slight shake. This was certainly the answer to her prayer, she thought gratefully and heaved an internal sigh of relief. Being transferred to a new city was always such a hassle. Having dinner prepared every night was a bonus she hadn't counted on. "That's really lovely."

"Oh yes, we have laundry facilities in the basement."

Hattie tapped her orthopedic shoe on the hardwood floor to emphasize her point.

Julia cocked her head. Laundry? Now they were discussing laundry? Well, good. That had been her next question.

This was perfect. Aside from the rather frustrating style of Hattie's conversation, Julia was sure she'd stumbled into a little piece of heaven. And even though her new landlady at times seemed a bit dotty, Hattie was a doll. Julia loved her already.

"Hattie!" a male voice bellowed from the top of the basement stairs at the end of the hallway. "Hattie? Where are you?" The insistent hollering continued to fill the parlor.

Ignoring the ruckus, Hattie extended toward Julia the rental agreement that had been lying in her lap. "Now then. If you will just sign here, dear," she chirped, pointing to the dotted line at the bottom of the page.

"I think someone is calling you, Mrs. Hopkins." Julia inclined her head toward the doorway as she scribbled her name at the bottom of the agreement.

"No, I'll fill out the rest, honey." Hattie smiled placidly.

"Hattie!"

Julia looked up in surprise as a young man carrying several overflowing baskets of laundry stumbled into the room, leaving a trail of socks and underwear as he went.

"Hey, Hattie, Rahni left a bunch of stuff in the dryer again," he said, shouting at her. Then he noticed Julia. "Oh, hi," he said, lowering his voice and smiling appreciatively. "I'm sorry. I didn't know Hattie had company." Turning, he deposited the mountain of clothing in front of the fireplace, his smile fading to a frown.

Gesturing to the laundry, his voice rose again as he announced loudly, "Rahni forgot the laundry again."

Startled, Julia clutched uncertainly at the overstuffed arm of the small loveseat.

"Bonnie forgot the sundries again?" Hattie frowned. "I will speak with her."

"The *laundry!*" he shouted, then turned and grinned at Julia. "Rahni is an exchange student who helps out around here with the cooking and cleaning when she's not in class learning English."

"Bonnie is from the Midwest," the beaming landlady put in.

"Middle East," he corrected, biting back a smile.

"Don, dear, this is Beulah."

"Hi, Beulah." Smiling easily, the handsome young man moved to Julia and extended his hand. "Nice to meet you."

"It's, uh, *Julia,*" she murmured as his large, warm hand enveloped hers. "My name, that is—Julia." What was her last name? Oh, yes. "Evans." *Mercy!* Julia thought, her heart picking up speed as she stared up into his mischievous green eyes. *He sure is cute.* "Nice to meet you, Don."

"Sean," he corrected with a wink, lowering his voice to a normal level. "Sean Flannigan. Nice to meet you too. You've probably noticed by now that Hattie is a little hard of hearing."

Hattie smiled benignly at the two as they conversed.

"Ahhh, so *that's* it," Julia murmured, returning his smile.

"Sit, sit, sit, Don," Hattie ordered. "Don is a director of films over in England." Beaming, she motioned for him to squeeze in next to Julia on the minuscule loveseat.

"Rooms," Sean murmured as he took his place next to Julia. "I'm director of rooms for the New England Inn."

Julia could feel a warmth radiating from him and couldn't be sure if it was from his lanky body as he wedged it into the remaining space on the tufted loveseat or from the light of his compelling personality. Something about Sean was simply irresistible.

Clearing her throat, Julia tore her eyes away from his and studied her shoes in embarrassment. Could he tell she was blushing? *How silly.* He couldn't read her mind. He couldn't have any idea how appealing she thought the little cleft in his chin was. His thigh rested lightly against hers. Swallowing, she tried shifting away to allow him extra room, but the ancient springs beneath her legs thwarted her best efforts, making it uncomfortable to rest anywhere else.

"The New England Inn? Ah, yes," Julia nodded, attempting to bring the erratic timpani of her heartbeat under control and exude a cool, sophisticated demeanor. "I love the New England Inn. I stay there quite often when I travel on business," she said, finding herself staring at the small cleft in his chin. Julia quickly looked away. *Goodness.* She was practically sitting in his lap.

"Yes," Hattie interjected happily, following the gist of the conversation, "Beulah is a nurse."

"Nursing-home medical equipment," Julia whispered for Sean's benefit and glanced up at the dimples that created deep crevices in his cheeks. *Have mercy!* They were sitting so close his face was nearly out of focus. Fighting the lumpy cushions that held her captive, she leaned slightly back and continued. "I work for Gerico Industries. We sell medical equipment to . . . ahhh . . . nursing homes." Her gaze traveled over his nose, across his cheekbones, over his slightly unruly, chestnut-colored hair, back down his forehead, and finally collided with his glowing, green eyes.

He certainly wasn't handsome in the classical sense. So,

considering she didn't know him from Adam, what on earth was it about him that made him so . . . *interesting*? No, Sean Flannigan wasn't just another pretty face, but his rugged good looks coupled with the twinkle in his emerald eyes made him an attention grabber. The quiet strength he exuded was also very compelling.

Eyes darting in confusion, Julia looked away and struggled to don the mask of professionalism that had gotten her this far in her career.

"In that case," Sean deadpanned, "next time I'm injured or bleeding, I won't bother you, Beulah."

"Not unless you want to see me faint, Don," Julia returned.

Sean grinned. "So. You're moving in?"

Clearing her throat, she wondered briefly if he was married. *No ring.* Not that it mattered to her, of course. She was simply curious. At this point in her increasingly successful career, Julia didn't have time for regular social relationships, let alone the romantic variety. A long time ago she'd made up her mind to follow her career path instead of the paths of the heart. It had been a good decision. Already she was senior vice president of the sales division of Gerico Industries and only twenty-seven years old. She'd lived in almost every state on the East Coast so far and had traveled extensively on behalf of her company. She had no regrets. In respect to her career, she'd been blessed.

"Yes," she said, proud of the cultured note she was able to inject into her voice. "I think this boarding house will suit my needs as I get the lay of the land, so to speak. It's close to my new office and to shopping. I just arrived here in Vermont. I was transferred." She exhaled slowly. "Again."

"Oh yeah. I've been transferred a time or two myself.

Always seem to end up back here though." Sean's lopsided smile was empathetic. "Well, that's great. Welcome to McLaughlin."

"Thank you," she murmured, trying to ignore the little tingles that danced down her spine at his kind words.

"Need any help moving in?"

His voice was like chocolate, rich and smooth. Julia decided she could listen to him recite the greater McLaughlin area phone book all afternoon, it was so soothing.

"Oh, no," she demurred quickly, once again catching herself staring in a most unprofessional fashion. Generally, Julia's heart didn't go all atwitter this way at a mere offer of assistance. "I don't have much to move, being transferred so often and all . . . just a suitcase or two and some light boxes." It was important that she travel light. Surely she would be transferred again before a year had passed. She sighed. Relocating was always so bothersome.

"Don," Hattie trilled, "when you have a moment, give Beulah a hand moving, will you, dear? Her room is next to yours on the tower side." To Julia she said, "Don's always loaning me his muscles."

Julia's eyes bounced to the biceps that bulged beneath the fabric of his ratty football jersey.

"You heard the lady," Sean said with an easy grin. "I guess you're stuck with me."

"Oh. I . . . well. Okay then." Secretly pleased, Julia focused on her hands and tried to keep her growing attraction in its proper perspective. She didn't know anything about this man. Maybe his easy countenance and affable charisma were simply part of an act. She glanced up into his eyes. *Hmm. No.* Some gut feeling told her that Sean was a genuinely nice person.

"Here, Beulah," Hattie warbled, plunging her hand into

the valley of her generous bosom—where Julia noticed that the older woman tended to store various items—and extracted a key ring. She removed a single key. "This is yours. Run up and make sure the door is unlocked before Don begins bringing your things in from the car."

"Thank you." Julia took the key and attempted to stand up. Unfortunately, wedged as she was so tightly between Sean and the arm of the little loveseat, she merely succeeded in becoming more acutely aware of her new neighbor's solid build. "I'll just . . . uh . . . run up and do that," she huffed and smiled.

Once again, she leaned forward, gathered her momentum, and attempted to stand. With no luck.

Face now crimson, Julia gripped the overstuffed arm and tried to gracefully work her way out of her slot without inadvertently touching Sean's firm thigh any more than absolutely necessary.

"*Ooph!* I . . . uh . . . ha! . . . ," she puffed, inching her way forward on the springy cushions that tended to work against her best efforts to leave.

Darting a quick glance at her new neighbor, she noticed he was—much to his credit—trying not to grin. The telltale crimson flush that stained her cheeks now crawled to her neck and left her entire head feeling as if it were engulfed in flames. Her groping feet barely touched the floor, and she felt like a high-centered car revving her engines but going nowhere fast.

Waving an airy hand, she strained to appear graceful. "Excuse me," she murmured in what she hoped was a well-modulated, breezy tone of voice—and not the grunt she suspected it was. Clutching at the hem of her skirt, she tugged it back down around her knees as she alternately worked her hips back and forth. She felt like a complete and total idiot.

"Of course," Sean said, leaning over to his side of the loveseat in an effort to give her more room. Creaking and popping, the springs in the cushions responded, creating a dip in his direction that suddenly sent Julia sprawling against his side and pinning one of her hands beneath her. Mortified, she dared not look up.

Time suspended for a moment as she wondered what to do. Other than the shoulder her cheek was now flattened against, there didn't seem to be a single thing she could grab hold of for a boost. Slowly, she brought her eyes to his. His brows were arched in surprise.

"Uh . . . ha! Oh, dear," Julia warbled. *Now don't go and get all flustered,* she warned herself, attempting to exude an attitude of carefree abandon. "I'm so sorry," she chirped, gripping Sean's arm with her one free hand as she tried to find purchase on the floor for her airborne feet. *Oh, this is just awful,* she thought wildly.

"I'm really sorry," she apologized again, her legs flopping about like the tail of a freshly landed fish. *Gracious!* Some impression she must be making. She'd only just met him, and now here she was, trying to tear the sleeve off the poor man's shirt.

"No problem," he assured her as the grin he'd been holding in check finally split across his face.

Eventually, they managed to sort themselves out.

"Oh, thank you," Julia said. She could feel Sean supporting her lower back with his hand as he helped her over to her side of the seat. "Thank you," she repeated, battling her way to her feet. Once standing, she pushed her skirt back down around her knees and patted her falling chignon back into place. Her cheeks still felt like twin spots of molten lava.

"Any time," Sean assured her in that chocolate voice of his.

Taking a giant step back, Julia fought a burst of hysterical laughter as she darted a glance at the nearest exit. "All right, then," she said with a lilt to her voice. She laughed brightly, hoping to belie her mortification. "I'll just go unlock the door, then I'll . . . be back." Unless of course, she died of embarrassment before she could return.

"I'll be here," Sean assured her.

Turning, Julia waved good-bye then promptly bolted into a tottering wall of buttons, military bars, and medals.

Will this hideous embarrassment never end? she wondered as she slowly peered past a pair of wire-framed bifocals and into the quizzical, watery-blue eyes that stared back at her from the surprised face of the ancient man she'd almost knocked to the floor. Wispy gray hair sprouted crazily from his spotted and balding pate, and his sagging lips opened and closed rhythmically, reminding Julia of a goldfish.

"At ease!" the aged commander commanded, his thin, reedy voice cracking as he reached out to pat Julia on the arm.

"I'm so sorry." Julia's apology was breathless as she backed into the parlor to make way for the older man.

Nodding, he continued to stare at Julia for a moment as if trying to remember where they'd last met; he thoughtfully sucked and clicked his ill-fitting dentures, then giving up, shuffled into the room. Shoulders stooped under the weight of a good century on this earth, he stopped in front of Sean and waited.

Sean shot a glance at Julia, who still hovered near the doorway. Blushing as he attempted to maneuver his lanky frame from the depths of Hattie's man-eating loveseat, he grunted, "Good afternoon, Colonel, sir," as he finally found his feet. Coming to attention, he crisply saluted.

Pleased, the Colonel returned his salute and nodded. "At ease," he rasped, then slowly turned and smiled. "Afternoon, Hattie," he said and cackled dryly. Swinging his gaze back to Julia, he hiked a curious brow. "Afternoon, miss."

Uncertain as to whether she was expected to salute this superior officer, Julia lifted her hand to her brow, scratched a little, and decided to let him do the interpreting.

"Hello." Straightening her spine, Julia brought her hands stiffly to her sides.

Sean's dimples exploded into bloom. "Colonel," he said, crossing the room to stand between Julia and the older man, "I'd like to present our newest boarder, Julia Evans. Julia, this is Colonel Milton Merryweather."

"So nice to meet you," Julia murmured.

"Likewise," the Colonel said with a bob of his head and an illusive twinkle in his pale-blue eyes. Snatching his gaze from her face, he unsteadily surveyed the rest of the room. "Anyone seen the Ross sisters?" At the blank faces that greeted his question, he shook his head. "I told them thirteen hundred hours," he muttered as he fished his timepiece out of his coat pocket. "They'd never have made it in the army."

At this ominous pronouncement, a throbbing ballyhoo down the hall filtered into the parlor.

"Have you lost what's left of your senses? I'm simply telling you it's not proper at this station in life, Glynnis!"

"Who says?" a snappy voice replied.

"Are you *trying* to get us thrown out of the senior center?"

"Really, Agnes, you are such a kill-joy."

"I am *not-t-t-t!*" the first voice shouted, mindless of the fact that her words carried farther than a foghorn on an ocean liner.

"You are too!"

"Why? Because I do not think you should consider a swimming costume that reveals the midriff? Especially a midriff that looks as if it could use a good ironing."

There was an audible gasp. "I beg your pardon! I'm in fine shape. Besides, I'm not planning on wearing it to . . . to . . . *to church!*"

"Not yet, you're not! I don't care, Glynnis. Call me a pooper and start the party without me."

Suddenly the Ross sisters rounded the corner and came sternly toward Julia and Sean as their argument continued. "The senior waterobics class would never withstand the shock." Raising a finger, the first sister—Julia quickly figured out it was Agnes—gestured at the Colonel. "Oh, he's in here. Come on, Glynnis," she screeched as though the other woman were a half-mile away instead of following closely behind her. Agnes beckoned to her sister with one of her long, bony arms.

"Oh, *here* you are," Glynnis twittered girlishly, spotting the Colonel and pushing in front of her elderly older sister.

"I'm precisely where I should be," the Colonel hollered, then coughed and wheezed for a frightening minute. "It's . . . thirteen hundred hours." He flipped open his watch and held it open to prove his point.

"You see," Agnes said with a smug look at her elderly

younger sister, "I told you thirteen hundred hours was one o'clock, not three o'clock."

"You did not."

"Glynnis, I distinctly remember . . ."

Hattie smiled blandly as the sisters squabbled.

Deciding to interrupt before Monday arrived, Sean stepped between the bickering ladies and charmed them with his smile. Julia watched in amusement.

"Oh, hello, Sean, dear," Agnes groused. The frown lines between her brows furrowed. The slighter and more dignified of the two sisters, Agnes still had a commanding presence that Julia feared could be formidable when the situation warranted.

Glynnis, taller, plumper, and most obviously—by her clashing clothing choices—less concerned about style than her sister, laughed flirtatiously and patted Sean's cheek.

"Miss Agnes and Miss Glynnis, I'd like you to meet our newest boarder, Julia Evans."

"Well, hello," Agnes sniffed. The older woman slowly about-faced, taking several dozen tiny steps, and squinted up at Julia through the thick lenses of her trifocals. "Do you play bridge? We are looking for a fourth . . ."

"Actually," Glynnis crabbed, correcting her sister, "we are looking for a third too. Sean, do *you* play?"

Sean took a step back toward Julia, and they exchanged befuddled glances.

"I—" Julia started to say.

"You know, Miss Glynnis, bridge was never one of those games I learned to—" Sean began, but before he had a chance to reveal his hopelessness at the art of bridge, a large, black Doberman pinscher came bounding into the parlor.

Ears back, teeth bared, fur at attention, the dog sniffed the air.

Terror-stricken, Julia unconsciously reached out and clutched Sean's strong arm.

"Nobody move!" came a harried and breathless shout from down the hallway. *"Sweetpea! Stay! Sit, boy!"*

Eyes wild, clothes rumpled, and hair standing on end, a man swung around the doorcasing and into the parlor. Sweetpea, an ominous growl emanating from deep in his throat, crouched low and surveyed the room's terrified occupants.

"Freeze!" the man needlessly instructed the frozen faction and, holding his palms up, slowly inched his way toward the dog.

"Please what, Brian, dear?" Hattie wondered. Obviously not having heard the dire instructions, she laboriously made her way to her feet.

Swinging his head in Hattie's direction, Sweetpea bared his teeth. Saliva slowly dripped from the animal's jowls. Eyes narrowed and filled with suspicion, the dog crouched low, and it seemed to Sean to be eyeing Hattie's jugular. He was sure his heart had stopped beating.

"Sh-Sh-Sean?" Julia whispered, paralyzed with fear.

Sean covered her fingers with his own. As he mentally sized up the animal, he rolled his eyes and could only hope that he wasn't going to have to resort to mortal combat with this devil dog.

"Don't worry. It will . . . uh . . . ," Sean swallowed, ". . . be okay," he asserted manfully under his breath to Julia. *Yeah. Right,* he thought, moving slightly between Julia and the dog. Everything would be okay, provided this devil's spawn didn't rip out their throats before he could remember his basic karate. Unconsciously, he began to pray. *Oh, Lord. Oh, Lord. Ohhhh, Lord. Hellllpppp!*

"Hattie!" the dog's compatriot hissed. "Don't move!

And whatever you do, don't make eye contact with the dog. That will only serve to incite him."

Julia tightened her grip on Sean's arm as five pairs of eyes shot to the floor.

Adjusting her glasses, Hattie peered into the dog's eyes. "Well, of course you can invite him in, Brian, dear," she warbled and clutched her cane for balance. "Hello, darling puppy. Come here." She held a shaky hand out to the dog's viselike jaw.

Everyone gasped.

"Nice doggy," she crooned.

As if in slow motion, the dog leaned forward and tentatively sniffed Hattie's fingers. Then, apparently deciding she was to his liking, Sweetpea flopped docilely at her feet.

A collective sigh of relief filled the air.

Moving purposefully toward the dog, the man who'd been chasing him slipped a muzzle over his mouth and deftly fastened the buckles. Straightening, he cast an apologetic glance around the room.

"Sorry if he scared you. We were in the middle of his first session when he decided to . . . uh—the dog began to thrash in an attempt to cast off the unwanted muzzle."

"He went AWOL!" the Colonel cried with a look of disdain at the crazily swaying dog. "Look out, Ryan, old man; he's going ballistic!"

Leaping forward, Ryan barely managed to keep one of Hattie's vases from toppling over. "Uh . . . yeah," he panted, "but I can . . . promise you . . . it won't . . . happen again."

Clipping a leash on Sweetpea's collar, Ryan tugged the violently flailing dog to his side. Anxious to regain his freedom, Sweetpea growled and strained against the leash.

Ryan grunted, attempting to maintain his balance, "I'm

. . . s-s-sorry for . . . *uff!* . . . the bother. Sit, Sweetpea!" he roared. "Stay!"

In an effort to soothe the alarm he saw in her eyes, Sean patted Julia's hand as it still clutched his arm. "Ryan, I'd like you to meet our newest neighbor, Julia Evans. Julia, this is Ryan Lowell."

Though rather disheveled, Julia could tell that when Ryan wasn't chasing renegade dogs, he was a handsome man. Although not, in her humble opinion, as handsome as Sean. Tall and dark, he exuded a certain kindness and sensitivity that Julia responded to immediately.

"Nice to . . . meet you," Ryan huffed as Sweetpea proceeded to circle his legs, tightly winding the leash around his knees.

"Nice to meet you too, Ryan." Julia glanced up at Sean, then at Hattie. Adjusting her glasses, the landlady gazed fondly at Ryan as he grappled with the hyperactive and decidedly unhappy Sweetpea.

"Brian works with dogs from the Colombian rain forest," she told Julia with pride. "The poor things seem to have an inordinate amount of problems, for some reason. Must be the humidity," she mused, oblivious to the whirling dervish at her side.

"Actually," Ryan grunted as he struggled to disentangle the leash from his legs, "I'm a . . . *canine behaviorist.*" Arms waving in broad circles, he fought to remain upright and tossed a feeble smile at Julia. "And, uh . . . most of my dogs . . . are . . . *sit, Sweetpea!* . . . from . . . right here in McLaughlin. Sometimes . . . as far away as . . . Montpelier or Barre, but mostly right around here. SWEETPEA! SIT!" Having issued the order, he dove to the floor and pinned the writhing and growling Sweetpea beneath his body.

Seemingly used to such unusual behavior, the little

group in the parlor relaxed and began to make small talk among themselves.

Julia sent a questioning look at Sean.

"Dogs are pack animals," he explained with a shrug. "Ryan tells us that pinning the dog with the . . ." He frowned thoughtfully, "What do you call that hold, Ryan?"

"Alpha s-s-stronghold," Ryan panted.

"Oh, yeah. The alpha stronghold. Anyway, this shows the dog who's boss."

"Oh," Julia said dubiously.

Sweetpea issued a vicious snarl from somewhere beneath Ryan's chest.

"Well, ladies," the Colonel said to Agnes and Glynnis as he impatiently clicked and sucked at his dentures, "if we are going to make it to waterobics, we are going to have to march."

Amid much dissension and hullabaloo, the Ross sisters each took a proffered arm and proceeded to battle for the Colonel's attention.

"I've got a new swimming costume," Glynnis informed him as they shuffled into the hall.

"It's disgusting," Agnes snapped.

"Why, Agnes! What a meanspirited thing to say!" Then to the Colonel, Glynnis groused, "I think she's jealous."

"Of what?"

"Of my new swimsuit. *And* my new bathing cap. Next to me, she'll look positively frumpy."

"Better a frump than a strumpet. Colonel, you should see the undignified thing she stretches on over her addled brain. All that gaudy fruit. Carmen Miranda wouldn't have been caught dead in such a getup."

Their voices faded as they argued their way to the front door.

"It is *not* gaudy."

"Yes, it is!" reverberated down the hallway until the Colonel herded them onto the porch and slammed the door behind him.

Once Sweetpea was suitably subdued, Ryan rose to his feet and dusted himself off. "All right then," he said with a quick peck on Hattie's temple, "I have to get back to work myself." With a sheepish smile at Julia, he bade everyone good day and was summarily yanked into the hallway by the dog.

The room was silent for a moment as Hattie, Sean, and Julia stared after him. Julia glanced around, shifting awkwardly from foot to foot as she groped for something to say.

"Well, Julia," Sean's voice finally broke the hush, "the only person—aside from Rahni, our exchange student—that you have yet to meet is Olivia."

Julia smiled weakly. "There's another one?"

Sean grinned. "Don't worry. Olivia is very quiet. No pets either."

Heaving a grateful sigh, Julia glanced at the key in her hand. "Okay. Well, I suppose I should . . . you know . . . go open my door." Waving the key in a little circle, she took a tentative step back. She looked both ways before she ventured into the hallway and then turned. To Sean she said, "I'll be back in a moment to unlock my car if, you know, you still want to help."

"I'll be right here."

His eyes stayed on the empty doorway for a moment after Julia had eased herself out of the room.

"Nice girl," Hattie informed him, snapping him out of his reverie. "You should invite her out on a date, Don. She's single. Twenty-seven years old. Never been married." The old woman narrowed her gaze at him.

She's single? he thought jubilantly, feeling Hattie's hawk-like gaze studying him. He tried to look blasé. *Yes!* He'd wondered about that, considering she wasn't wearing a wedding ring and all. Playing it cool in front of Hattie, he decided he'd wait until he was alone to do a little end-zone victory jig. Carefully, he filed this information away in his mind, where he hoped it would someday come in handy.

So, at twenty-seven, she was a year younger than he was, huh? She was sure pretty. Sophisticated. Cultured. She reminded him of that perky anchor on the local six o'clock news. He liked her voice. He liked her smile. He liked the shiny lights in her strawberry-blond hair and the way she wore it in that little knot at the back of her head. And he liked the way she blushed and got so embarrassed over a silly thing like getting stuck in a chair. But most especially, he liked the sweet countenance she projected.

There was a lot to like.

"That's a nice idea, Hattie," he said loudly, referring to her suggestion that he ask Julia out. Although, with his busy schedule, finding the time for a date presented a problem. On the other hand, the fact that she lived next door was a plus. Saved valuable commute time. He was a busy guy.

He smiled at Hattie. "A date with Julia might be fun. At any rate, I'll keep it in mind."

"Oh no, no, no. I don't think she'll mind. No, I think she's probably lonely. Invite her to church, honey. She was asking about that. Said she might attend with me next week. After she settles in."

"Really?" Sean's pulse kicked up another notch. He was really beginning to like this girl. *Careful, old boy,* he cautioned himself. *Find out if she has a boyfriend before you start thinking about the dating scene.*

That was a laugh. He was lucky if he had time to shop for socks, let alone start going out to dinner and a movie and whatever it would take to keep the relationship going. Shaking his head at this ridiculous train of thought, Sean looked at Hattie.

Aside from the occasional church social, Sean rarely dated. He simply didn't have the time. Not with his killer schedule at work. Especially now that he was working overtime on a regular basis, trying to build points for the big promotion.

Which reminded him. He needed to ask his landlady a favor.

"Listen, Hattie, the reason I stopped by is—aside from Rahni's laundry—I've been meaning to ask you," he raised his voice to be certain she understood, "to remember me in your prayers."

Hattie was a real prayer warrior. Everyone who'd known her for more than a day knew that she liked to talk. Especially to the Lord.

"Why of course, sweetheart. What's the problem?" Hattie's brow knitted as she affectionately patted his arm.

"No problem, really. It's just that I need your prayers," he said, raising his voice again, "because I'm in line for a big promotion at work."

Adjusting her glasses at the tip of her nose, Hattie peered at him and made mental notes, nodding earnestly. "Uh-huh. Cruise line. Big vacation. Uh-huh," she muttered under her breath.

"I've been working for this for so long now I feel pretty confident. But any assistance you could give me in the form of prayer would sure be appreciated." He grinned, feeling kind of silly for asking but serious about his request nonetheless.

"Oh, why, of course, honey. You know what I always tell the Lord. 'Lord,' I say, 'if something is meant to be, please fling those doors wide open. But if it's not meant to be, Lord, slam 'em shut.' " Hattie nodded sagely. "I'll begin speaking to him about it right away." Clasping her hands to her bosom, the older woman beamed. "My favorite little verse goes like this: 'Whatever you ask for in prayer with faith, you will receive.' Isn't that comforting, Don? Eight decades now, I've taken that one to heart."

Sean grinned. Everything would turn out fine. Already, he could see himself on the fast track to success. Hattie claimed that her prayers were always answered.

Hattie patted him with a loving hand. "Give your troubles to God; he'll be up all night anyway. Hoo-hee-hee-hoo!" she trilled, amusing herself.

"Thanks, Hattie. You're the best." Leaning forward, he kissed Hattie on the soft, paper-thin skin of her wrinkled cheek.

"You're welcome, Don, dear. Now, run along and help Beulah move in."

"Oh, Lord," Hattie whispered, bowing her head after Sean had bounded out of the room in search of Julia, "Don has been working so hard lately."

She sniffed. "Too hard, if you want my opinion, but I'll keep my nose out of it. Anyway, Lord, Don tells me that he wants to take a cruise line, on a vacation, and he wanted me to put in a good word with you on this matter. Lord, if you want my opinion, I think this is a wonderful idea. Don needs some time off—to smell the roses, so to speak. He is far too wrapped up in his career.

"So, Lord, if you could see your way clear to give Don the vacation he so desperately needs and deserves, well,

Lord, I would appreciate it. And, I know Don will too. Such a sweet boy.

"And, Lord, while I have your ear, thank you for sending me a new boarder for the room next to Don's. Beulah seems like a lovely girl, one of your flock. How wonderful. Thank you for your time and, most especially, for answered prayer, Lord. And in case I haven't mentioned it in the last hour or so . . . I love you."

2

Monday evening—the next day and shortly before dinner—found Sean slumped dejectedly at the edge of his bed. Head cradled between his hands, he fumbled for the ringing phone and managed to wedge it between his shoulder and his cheek.

"Hello." His mumbled greeting was barely audible.

Sean sighed, thankful that it was his older sister, Kathleen, and not another one of his sympathetic coworkers. "Hey, Kath. What's up?"

Sean winced as her voice buzzed into his ear, asking the inevitable question. "No, sis," he groaned on a slow exhalation of breath. "I didn't get the promotion."

Settling in for a chat, he listened to his sister's indignant squawk.

Sean snorted. "You think *you're* bummed." He laughed derisively. "Man! And I was so sure, you know?

"No, Kath. You don't know him. They gave it to a guy from out of state. Can you believe that? No. To be honest he was more qualified than I am." *A lot more,* Sean thought, dragging a weary hand through his hair.

"I don't know. Midthirties, I guess. He's starting to lose his hair." Sean laughed. "Thanks, Kath, but a full head of hair doesn't impress the fat cats upstairs. Yep. Ha! I'll tell 'em you said so.

"Thanks. Uh-huh. Yeah, I heard that one before. And don't forget, 'When God closes a door, he opens a window.' " Sean chuckled. "I guess he has something else in mind. Vows of poverty? I hope not. Uh-huh. Well, I'll just have to stay meek and look forward to inheriting the earth."

Sean laughed. Kathleen always could make him forget his troubles.

"Yeah, well on the bright side, for some strange reason, I ended up with two extra weeks of vacation. Ha! Yeah, a consolation prize. That's rich. No, I don't know why. But hey, I'm not gonna argue. Any time I want, they said. I just need to find something fun to do.

"Yeah, right. So, anyway, why'd you call? To say good-bye? Okay. Good-bye," Sean quipped.

"Really? Where to this time? Florida? What's going on down there? Oh. Another seminar, huh? Two seminars? When are you leaving? *Tonight?* Man! That's quick. The red-eye, huh? How long are you going to be gone? Two weeks? Wow, that's a long time to be away from the baby. I thought this was supposed to be a part-time job. When is your boss coming back? Oh. Things will slow down then."

Settling back against the headboard, Sean tucked the phone between his cheek and shoulder and closed his eyes. It was good to talk to Kath. She was his closest living relative. If anyone could make him feel better about losing out on the promotion, Kathleen could. He knew she would do anything for him, and the feeling was mutual. Just hearing her voice was a soothing balm.

"So, what are you going to do about the baby while you're gone? Is Martin gonna pull a Mr. Mom with CarlyAnn? A baby-sitter? Neighbor? That's handy. So,

Martin's off on business too, huh? Two weeks? Really? At the same time? That's weird. Where's Martin going? *Alaska*? Why Alaska?"

Sean allowed his head to loll backward against his headboard and stared unseeing at the ceiling as he listened to his sister fill him in on her family's busy life.

"Man! That is nuts. You guys better slow down before you have a stroke or something. Yeah, yeah, yeah, I know. Look who's calling the kettle black, right? It must be in our genes. I bet that had a lot to do with why Dad died so young. Uh-huh. Well, just take care of yourself, okay? You're all the family I've got left. Sure. Okay. Yep. Hey, no big deal. I'll live. Love you too. Kiss the monster for me. No," he said dryly, "not Martin. Yeah. Bye."

Hanging up, Sean exhaled noisily and returned to his pre-call pity party. He was still in denial. Or shock. Or some kind of really bad nightmare.

He simply couldn't believe it. He didn't get the job. What a loser. He looked around at his charming little—if somewhat messy—room. Twenty-eight years old and still living like a kid. He'd only planned to live here until he'd saved up enough money to buy a big house, then fill it with a loving wife and a passel of kids. But with his schedule, one day just seemed to lead to another, and before he knew it, he'd been living here for several years now. And without a mortgage or wedding date in sight. What was wrong with him? he wondered morosely. Most of his friends already owned nice homes and had wives and children and high-paying jobs.

Not, of course, that those things made them any better. But here he was, living in Hattie's Boarding House with nothing but two extra weeks of paid vacation to show for all his toil and trouble. What was *that* all about, anyway? In all his years with New England Inn, he'd never heard of a two-week vacation being given to anyone out of the blue that way.

Vaguely, he knew he should crawl off the bed to his knees and ask the Lord to give him strength and peace, but he was too depressed. *Man!* He must be bummed if he was too wrecked to cry on God's shoulder. Sighing heavily, he rolled onto his side and stared out the window. He was tired of examining his pathetic life. He didn't want to think about it, let alone discuss it.

Not even with God.

Wasn't there something in the Bible about God answering prayer when the person was too bummed out to pray? He thought he remembered something like that about groanings and utterings being made in intercession. Yep, that was about all he could handle at the moment.

He groaned. Loudly. He groaned again and waited for peace to fill his soul. Nothing. Perhaps he wasn't the one who was supposed to be groaning.

Next door, he could hear Julia humming in her room.

Listening to the pleasant tune, he wondered what she was doing. Most likely unpacking. For someone who boasted about her meager material possessions, she'd sure crammed a whole lot of stuff in that car of hers. She had more clothes than a department store, and shoes . . . *Good grief!* Claimed she needed all those things for her job.

Yeah, he could believe it. Listening to her talk as they'd trudged back and forth to her car, he'd gotten the feeling she liked to work almost as much as he did.

Forgetting his own troubles for the time being, Sean allowed himself to feel for Julia. With the exception of a few of the folks here at the boarding house, she didn't know anybody in McLaughlin, and unfortunately, she wouldn't even start her new job for another couple of weeks. She seemed at loose ends. Maybe he should take Hattie's advice and ask her out. It wasn't like he had more pressing responsibilities at work. Even though he'd only known her for a day now, he could tell she was very special.

Far too special to go out with a loser.

So he guessed if he wanted to attract her attention, he should stop feeling sorry for himself. Leveraging himself off the bed, Sean stretched, took a deep, cleansing breath, and looked up at the ceiling.

"Thank you, Lord," he breathed, attempting to exhale his trouble away, "for help getting off the bed. And as much as it kills me to admit this, I know that you have a better plan for my life than this promotion. So, thank you for the trial, and I hope I'm passing the test. Amen."

Bounding into his tiny bathroom, he turned on his shower and looked in the mirror. "I didn't want that dumb job anyway," he said to his morose reflection. He forced himself to smile and, stripping his shirt off over his head, polished off the fog that was beginning to form on the glass.

If he was lucky, Julia might be up for taking in a movie tonight. *Okay, then!* It sounded like a lot more fun than sitting around moping.

Steam billowed, the shower roared, and Sean, his spirits returning to normal, belted out an off-key rendition of "Blue Suede Shoes" as he lathered his body with his microphone.

This exuberant cacophony must have accounted for the fact that Sean did not hear his phone ring. And ring.

And . . . ring.

Julia smiled at the comical noises that filtered through the dividing wall between her and Sean's rooms. Obviously,

Sean could not hear his phone ringing over the racket he was making in the shower. Wrinkling her nose, she decided he was no Elvis. As she folded her clothes to fit into the dresser drawers and listened to him thrash around inside his small fiberglass shower enclosure, Julia decided his style more closely resembled Weird Al.

Julia wondered if he was getting ready to go out on a date. Hattie had mentioned that "Don" was unmarried when her delightful new landlady had checked on her after she'd moved in yesterday afternoon. But any information that came from Hattie was, at best, rather unreliable. And coming right out and asking Sean if he was married was out of the question. He would no doubt think she was some kind of husband hunter and run the opposite direction. Not that she had her sights on Sean, of course, Julia thought with a chuckle and a shrug. She was simply . . . curious.

In any event, the pragmatic portion of Julia's mind knew that anyone as truly nice and charismatic as Sean Flannigan had to have at least one girlfriend.

Lifting a stack of freshly folded T-shirts off the quilted fourposter bed, she moved over to the bureau and glanced at her wall clock. *Five o'clock, an hour and a half to kill before dinner,* she thought as she opened a drawer and dropped the shirts into place.

Would Sean be there? Maybe she would wear her new blue sweater. Did Sean like blue? Perhaps she would shampoo her hair and put on a little makeup too. What was Sean doing after dinner?

Oh, for pity's sake! Who cared what Sean was doing or what Sean thought? She was really losing it. Give her a few days off work, and what did she do? Go and get a crush on the boy next door.

Shaking her head in disgust, Julia quickly put away the

rest of her clothing. If there was one thing she could not afford at this juncture in her life, it was a personal relationship. Especially considering how often she was transferred lately. No. She had to concentrate on her career. To prove herself worthy of this exciting new territory. Thanks to her hard work, Gerico Industries was growing and building a solid reputation. She had no time for distractions like the affable boy next door.

When she'd finished putting away her things, she glanced at her watch: 5:05 P.M. Julia's cheeks puffed as she looked around the room and wondered what to do with herself. Maybe she should call her grandmother. Certainly that would help her feel a tad less homesick. It always worked wonders whenever she was transferred.

Crossing the room, she perched on the edge of her new bed and pulled the phone off the nightstand.

"Two for the shoowww. Three to get ready, now go, cat, goooo!"

Sean's impromptu concert filtered through the wall, lifting the corners of Julia's mouth. He must have gotten that promotion he'd been telling her about as they'd transported her boxes up to her new room yesterday afternoon. He sure sounded happy about something. Well, good for him. In a way, Julia was relieved that he seemed to be such a workaholic. That would certainly keep them from getting too chummy as next-door neighbors. Yes. It was for the best. Absently, she hummed along with Sean's enthusiastic caterwauling as she stared at the wall that divided their rooms.

The small suite was covered in a wonderful, old-fashioned sandy beige wallpaper blooming with giant rose blossoms. White, lacy curtains adorned her windows, and the furniture was an eclectic collection of amazing, highly polished mahogany antiques. Gilt frames surrounded pictures of what had to be Hattie's ancestors on the walls, and the floor—a hardwood oak—was scattered liberally with area rugs.

Julia adored her new home. Long-forgotten memories of visits to her own grandmother's house had come flooding back in great waves of nostalgia as she glanced around her room. Cradling the phone in her lap, Julia suddenly realized just how much she missed her grandmother. The sugar cookies, the knitting lessons, the old songs, the Bible stories, the love. Hattie and her house brought back those cozy feelings.

Feelings of family. Of a spiritual closeness with her Creator. Of friends and good times and lazy Sunday afternoons on Grammy's front porch. Feelings that the workaday business world had steamrolled into oblivion years ago.

Where has the time gone? she wondered absently. Life just seemed to get away from her these days. With a heavy sigh, she dialed her grandmother's phone number and waited for the cheery voice to answer.

"Grammy? It's me. Have you got a minute?"

Julia smiled. Unlike herself, Grammy always had time to chat.

"Oh, no, everything is just fine. I just called to tell you my new phone number. Uh-huh. Yes, it was quick. Love at first sight, really."

Chuckling, Julia kicked off her slippers and settled back against the generous stack of pillows that ornamented her bed.

"No, Grammy, not with a man, with a house! No, just a room. It's a boarding house. Actually, it reminds me a lot of your house. An old Victorian. You'd love it."

With a contented smile, Julia answered her grandmother's curious questions.

"An older woman. Hattie Hopkins is her name. She's a real cutie. A little older than you, and unfortunately she has no idea that she desperately needs a hearing aid." Julia giggled. "So when you call, ask for Beulah. Yes, really. Oh, no . . . she has help. An exchange student named Rahni. Rahni. R-a-h-n-i. Yes. An exchange student. From the Middle East. I met her at breakfast this morning. No, only a few words of English. She is taking some classes though. But you know what's really strange? She and Hattie seem to be able to understand each other. It's weird.

"Uh, let's see . . ." Julia held up her hand and began to count on her fingers. "There are two ladies about your age. The Ross sisters, Glynnis and Agnes. They are Hattie's cousins, which is why Hattie knows their real names. It's the same with the Colonel. He was a childhood friend of Hattie's late husband, Ernie. The Colonel? The army, I think. Very nice. I think he's kind of miserly though. Well, for one thing he turned off the lights while we were eating this morning. Said the natural light coming through the windows was plenty. Yes!" Julia giggled. "I could barely find my coffee. Then he gathered up everyone's dirty old napkins. I'm not sure. Something about using them to make a rug. And, he looked positively horrified when I couldn't finish my toast."

Her grandmother's lilting laughter bubbled across the line accompanied by another barrage of loving inquiries.

"No," Julia explained, "the others are closer to my age. Who? Well, let's see, there is a guy named Ryan, who trains dogs. Problem dogs. Problem dogs, Grammy. Not rabid dogs. No, don't worry. He . . . well, he seems to be in control. . . . I will be careful. I promise. Don't worry. Really."

Quickly changing the subject, Julia described Olivia in a more hushed voice. "She seems so sad and lonely,

Grammy. I understand that she lost her husband and daughter about four years ago in some kind of terrible car accident. She was the only survivor. Yes. She keeps to herself a lot. I met her at breakfast, and she seems very nice . . . just so . . . so melancholy.

"There's only one more. Uh, Sean. Yes, Sean. Well, I don't know! What do you mean my voice sounds funny? I do not. You're hearing things." Julia giggled. "I did not! Gram! Quit it. You *know* what! Matchmaking! You are too. Yes, he is nice. Okay, very nice. Yes, if it will make you happy, he's handsome too. Clark Gable handsome? I don't know about that. I think more Patrick Swayze handsome, with browner, sort of chestnutty hair with little gold highlights. What do you mean, he has beady eyes? Oh, *puhleeezze*. Do you mean to tell me that if someone who looked like Patrick Swayze asked you for a date, you'd turn him down? Aha! I rest my case.

"So," she asked, hoping once again to change the subject, "how are Mom and Dad? Of course they're busy. Where? Singapore? I thought they were going to be in Hong Kong for another two weeks. What are they doing in Singapore? Oh. Right. Will they be back in time for Christmas? Oh."

Deflating some, Julia closed her eyes. Her parents were always so busy. Not that she could blame them, of course. After all, if anyone understood the career-driven mind, she did. It was just that once in a while, she wished she had normal parents. A mom and dad who washed the car and barbecued and mowed the lawn on weekends, not the jet-setting, high-powered investment brokers her parents were. As far back as Julia could remember, they'd never been home.

Thank God for Grammy. If it hadn't been for her mother's

mother, Julia would have no concept whatsoever of a normal home life.

After another few minutes spent bringing her grandmother up to date, Julia—with a growing lump in her throat—wound up the conversation. "I sure miss you, Gram. Uh-huh. Yeah." Julia sniffed and wiped at her eyes with the back of her sleeve. "Yes," she whispered. "I love you too. I will. Thank you. Yes, you are in my prayers too. Okay."

Sniffing, Julia placed the phone back on the nightstand, then glanced at her alarm clock: 5:20 P.M. Still more than an hour to kill.

Julia sighed.

There were some interesting brochures on fun things to do in Vermont in her car. Maybe she could do a little light reading before dinner. At the very least, it would give her something to add to the dinner conversation.

But first, she would take a quick shower.

Swinging her legs to the edge of the bed, Julia padded across her room toward her small, utility bathroom. The little bathroom was surprisingly functional, and it, too, matched the style of the house with an old claw-foot tub, a pedestal sink, and a toilet with an elevated tank. The only concession to this century was the shower enclosure. Yanking open the door, Julia turned on the water.

As she stepped out of her clothes, she began to mumble lyrics. "One for the money . . ."

"What?"

"I'm as serious as a heart attack, Sean," Kathleen cried, her voice nearing hysteria. Nine-month-old CarlyAnn bobbed and drooled haplessly against her mother's hip as Kathleen barged past her brother and into his room. Sleek and sophisticated in her business suit and upswept hairstyle, Kathleen, with her chestnut hair and sparkling green eyes, was the female version of her brother. "Why didn't you answer your phone? I tried to warn you."

Sean yanked the cotton swab out of his ear to make sure he'd heard correctly.

"What exactly do you mean, *your sitter canceled?*" Turning, he followed his sister into his room and watched in dumbfounded fascination as she proceeded to dump a stroller full of baby paraphernalia into the middle of his floor.

"Just what I said, Sean!" Kathleen's cry was plaintive. "She canceled. Like that! No warning! I'm as surprised as you are."

"Now, wait just a doggone minute here, sis. What makes you think *I* can take care of CarlyAnn while you're gone? Ha! No way!" Adjusting the sash of his robe more tightly around his waist, he tried to exude a measure of authority over his older sister.

"Sean, you are my only living relative. That, and the fact that the other gajillion people I called were all out of town or busy—*that's* what makes me think it. Listen," she cajoled, hiking the baby higher on her hip, "you told me yourself that you have two extra weeks of vacation coming, right? You can use them whenever you want, right? So, use them *now*! I can't stand here and argue with you about this. My plane is leaving in three hours, and I still have a *four-hour drive!"* she shrieked, her eyes wild. "I *have* to be at both of these conferences over the next two weeks. I'm the keynote speaker, for heaven's sake, not to mention the classes I'm scheduled to instruct every day."

Thrusting CarlyAnn into Sean's arms, Kathleen rushed

to the tangled pile of baby supplies. "Okay, here's the deal. These are her clothes, diapers, sleeper suits, diaper rash medicine. This is her num-num cup; these are extra lids."

"Num-num?" Sean looked at CarlyAnn. He was feeling a little num-num himself.

"Yes, and these are her yum-yums, her binkie, her wa-wa, her dolly, her boo-boo bear, her googie cloth, her yucky wipes, her mushy treats . . ."

Staring at his sister as she yammered on and demonstrated techniques for dislodging small objects from the baby's throat, Sean could only wonder where Kathleen had learned to speak this second language. What the devil were yum-yums? A googie cloth? He frowned at the chubby baby in his arms as she smiled passively up at him. How hard could it be?

"Bap," CarlyAnn said, and slapped him on the nose.

"You and me both, kid," Sean sighed.

"Just press this button here, and the stroller balloons into a portable crib. Isn't that neat? Got that for my baby shower. Bedtime is at eight, dinner and a bath before that. She loves books and singing of any kind. Even yours, brother dear."

"Gee, thanks," Sean drawled sarcastically.

Kathleen began to relax, now that she was starting to regain control of the situation. "Well, that just about does it. Here is the number for her pediatrician. She just had a round of shots at her well-baby checkup yesterday. And, oh, before I forget, these are her liquid vitamins and the baby Tylenol. Okay then."

Stepping to Sean, she nuzzled her daughter's soft cheek. "Be good for Uncle Sean, okay?" Suddenly tears sprang into her eyes, and her throat sounded tight. "And . . . *snnfff* . . .

do what he . . . *snnifff* . . . says. *Ohhhh,*" she wailed. "I've never been away from her for more than a few hours at a tiiimmmmeee. Oh dear . . . *snnifff* . . ."

Sean rolled his eyes. *Good grief.* Had he asked for this? He was supposed to be on his way down to the dinner table, hopefully mustering up enough courage to ask Julia on a date.

"Bap," CarlyAnn shouted and smacked her delirious mother on the nose.

"Thank you, sweetie," Kathleen sighed. "I needed that. Thank you, too, little brother. I owe you one." She glanced at her watch. "Good heavens, it's 5:45! I'm beyond late. Gotta run!" Yanking open his door, Kathleen rushed out into the hall, leaving her daughter and brother in the dust.

Following his sister out into the hall, Sean watched Kathleen's retreating form as she skipped backward down the hall, still issuing some last-minute instructions.

"Say bye-bye, CarlyAnn," Sean sighed.

"Bap," CarlyAnn shouted uncertainly after her mother. Her small face began to pucker.

Meanwhile, next door, Julia fastened her jeans, tugged on her favorite blue sweater—the one that everyone said brought out the color of her eyes—stuffed her feet into her tennis shoes, ran a quick towel over her head, and shook her damp hair over her shoulder. She still had forty-five minutes to kill. Might as well run to her car and get the brochures on fun things to do in Vermont. She could peek at the different flyers and brochures while she dried her hair and applied her makeup.

Opening her door and stepping out into the hallway, Julia nearly collided with Kathleen. "Oh, excuse me."

"My fault," Kathleen excused herself, then turning,

barreled down the hall, taking the stairs two at a time. "Bye-bye!"

Julia stared after her for a moment then allowed her gaze to travel back to Sean. Why was he standing in the hallway wearing a bathrobe? she wondered, unable to control her gaze as it skimmed over his knobby knees. Not that she minded the view, of course.

And why was he holding that baby? Hattie must not have heard or understood when Sean told her the part about his wife and child.

Julia sighed, suddenly melancholy, then gave herself a mental shake. How ridiculous. She didn't care one way or another whether he was single or not. After all, she wasn't looking for a romantic relationship. But still, it had been kind of amusing to think that he was single.

Oh well.

3

Sean froze as the rapid-fire clicking of Kathleen's heels ricocheted down the stairs. Shifting his gaze to Julia, he watched as she paused in her doorway and bestowed a curious smile on him and CarlyAnn.

He sighed. It figured. She *would* choose this exact moment to step out into the hall and catch him with his proverbial pants down . . . Glancing down at his naked knees, he felt himself color. For pity's sake. He wasn't even *wearing* pants. Slowly and sheepishly, he lifted his eyes back to hers.

Man! She was even prettier than he remembered. Blue was really her color.

Deciding to ignore the fact that he was clad in only a ratty bathrobe, Sean hefted CarlyAnn a little higher on his chest and returned Julia's smile. Awkwardly, he patted the baby's back and hoped he looked like he knew what he was doing.

"Hi there," he said, attempting to exude a friendly confidence, even as a sudden draft flirted with the hem of his short robe. Kathleen must have left the front door open in her haste to catch her flight.

"Hello," Julia responded, a hint of laughter sparkling in her eyes.

He felt like a first-class idiot. Crossing his legs at the ankles, he leaned against the wall and tried to effect a manly pose. "On your way to dinner?"

"Not just yet." She glanced at her watch. "It's a little early. I was just on my way to my car for a couple of things." Taking a step closer, she held her finger out to CarlyAnn. "Hi there, sweetie," she cooed to the baby, then darted an interested glance at Sean. "Your daughter? She looks just like your . . . uh," Julia gestured toward the staircase, "wife I guess?"

Sean frowned. His wife? His daughter? A light dawned.

"My daughter? Ha! Oh no! She's my *niece*. I'm going to be taking care of her for the next two weeks while her mommy and daddy are on business trips," he asserted masterfully, hoping he looked more confident than he felt. CarlyAnn began to whimper, so he patted her back and jostled her up and down the way he'd seen Martin do. "No, no, no, that woman who just left was my older sister, Kathleen. No, I'm not married."

He was glad to get this cleared up now. It wouldn't do to have her thinking he was married. Especially when he was hoping to invite her to a movie or to church this coming Sunday.

"What's her name?"

"Pardon?" Sean flushed guiltily. He'd been staring. But he had to wonder if she had any idea how blue her eyes were in this light. "Whose name?"

She gestured to the baby. "Your niece?"

"Oh," he said with a laugh, "CarlyAnn. Her name is CarlyAnn Peterson."

"That's pretty." Julia looked at the baby. "You're sure a cutie pie. Where'd you get all those beautiful gold curls?"

Feeling suddenly bashful, CarlyAnn buried her head in

her uncle's chest. "Yeah. She's a pretty great kid. Aren't you, CarlyAnn?"

CarlyAnn whimpered again and thrust her lower lip out. "Bap," she cried and smacked him on the nose.

"Ha. She likes to do that," Sean explained, donning his best professional-uncle tone of voice that hopefully said, *"Hey, I'm great with kids." "Hey, kids love me."* And, of course, *"Hey, I'm in control."*

Which he wasn't.

With the exception of Kathleen's hasty, last-minute instructions, Sean knew absolutely nothing about taking care of a nine-month-old baby. But shucks. How hard could it be? He'd spent an afternoon or two in the last nine months, during his rare spare time, playing with CarlyAnn. It had been a piece of cake. They were buddies, he and old CarlyAnn here.

Yeah, the way Julia was looking at him, so impressed with his abilities as a sensitive-male-daycare-type-provider, well, he knew it wouldn't be long before she agreed to go out with him. After all, considering he didn't get the promotion he'd hoped for, he had some time on his hands for the first time in years. Time for a little social life. He grinned rakishly down at her and, in a fit of sudden self-confidence, forgot his half-dressed state and winked at her.

"Your baby is leaking."

"What?"

"Your baby. CarlyAnn. She is leaking."

A warm rush oozed from the southern region of CarlyAnn's diaper, and Sean realized too late what Julia was saying.

"Do you have a towel?" Julia asked, looking concerned.

"Yeah," he grimaced, looking down at his chest and slowly up toward his door, "in the bathroom." *Good grief.*

Was it possible to feel any more idiotic? This had certainly been a world-class day. First, he'd been overlooked for the promotion of a lifetime, and now this.

Julia's eyes flitted to the growing damp spot on his robe, and she grinned. "So I see. Well, maybe I'll catch you two down at dinner?"

"Uh . . . yeah. Sure," Sean muttered as CarlyAnn began to wail an ear-piercing screech that he feared might just shatter the windows.

This was definitely not his day.

"So, we meet again," Sean said and attempted to inject a note of easy charm into his voice. Julia was just closing the door to her room as he stepped out into the hallway from his own room. He only hoped that his freshly laundered polo shirt would put earlier images of him in his soiled, ratty robe out of her mind. Held tightly in his arms, CarlyAnn—her face streaked with tears—was clutching as much of his collar as she could grasp in her pudgy little hands.

"So it would seem," Julia said with a laugh as she secured her lock with her key. Turning, she smiled at them. "I see you managed to get yourselves all cleaned up. Very nice," she said with appreciation.

Sean flushed, unsure whether she was talking about him or the baby. *Must be the baby,* he decided as Julia held her finger out to CarlyAnn. It had taken him all of forty-five minutes just to figure out the myriad Velcro fastenings, snaps, tapes, pins, and buttons that finally had CarlyAnn presentable again. He hoped everything at least matched.

It was amazing how much mess could come out of one tiny little kid. He'd considered simply throwing her soiled outfit away. But after giving it some consideration, he figured Kathleen would probably have a cow, so he tossed it into his laundry with his robe and decided to let Rahni deal with it tomorrow.

The baby clutched Julia's finger and brought it to her mouth for a taste. "Hi, sweetie," Julia crooned. "Are you guys on your way down to dinner?"

"Yeah," Sean answered. "I brought her bottle, and I'm hoping maybe she'll eat a little something off my plate."

Julia frowned. "Do they eat regular food when they're this little?"

Sean lifted and dropped his shoulders. "I don't have a clue. Kathleen was in and out of here so fast my head is still spinning. Hattie will probably know. She had six kids of her own."

"Oh," Julia agreed with a nod, "then she would know."

Inclining his head toward the top of the stairs, Sean said, "Shall we?"

"We shall," Julia said, a smile in her voice.

As she extracted her finger from CarlyAnn's mouth, the baby's face twisted into a puffy pucker of insecurity. Lower lip protruding, brow furrowing, she glanced back at Sean, and then, cutting loose with a wail that even Hattie would have heard, CarlyAnn held her arms out to Julia.

"*Maaamaaaam,*" she bleated, screeching and squealing and pounding on poor Uncle Sean's arms as if he were her executioner rather than her dinner date.

At a complete loss, Sean turned and stared at Julia. "I . . . I . . ." He shrugged helplessly.

They exchanged baffled glances as CarlyAnn's obvious dismay rose to a fevered pitch. Cheeks now an angry shade of red, the baby's face became a fountain as liquid literally squirted from her eyes and mouth.

"I think maybe she wants you to hold her." Sean cast an apologetic look at Julia.

"Me?"

"Uh-huh. I think maybe you, being a woman and all, remind her of her mother."

"Oh." Julia's eyes widened with surprise.

CarlyAnn's shrieks became more frenzied as she strained toward Julia.

"Do you mind?" Sean asked, feeling increasingly idiotic with the passing of each torturous second. *So much for leading her to believe that I'm great with kids. That kids love me. That I'm in control.* He cleared his throat. "Normally I would never impose on you this way. It's just that she seems to want you, and I, quite frankly, don't know what else to do."

"Well, of course, but," Julia said, unable to keep the note of uncertainty from her voice, "you should probably know that I, uh, well, I don't have much experience with this sort of thing."

"Oh, that's okay. I'm sure she won't mind in the least," he encouraged.

"Okay then." Julia shrugged, wondering how to best accomplish the trade-off.

Sean held the squealing baby away from his chest. "Here you go."

Awkwardly, Julia scooted next to Sean and made a cradle of her arms. Attempting to assist the best he could, Sean angled the baby on her side and thrust her toward Julia. Julia stared at CarlyAnn with a perplexed frown.

No. That wouldn't work. Quickly stepping to the other side, Julia lowered her arms and made a seat out of her hands for CarlyAnn. Meanwhile, Sean shifted the child around and held her right-side up. Gripping her chubby thighs, he prepared her to straddle Julia's impromptu seat. Julia surveyed this new arrangement. "Hmmm. No. That won't work either."

Sean tried a new attack. Arms up. Baby down. *Uh, no.*

Try one arm up, one down, baby up, legs to the side. No. Baby facing in.

Aha! Baby facing *out.*

"Uh . . . no. Not like . . . that . . ."

Grabbing Julia's carefully styled hair into her fists, CarlyAnn—whose wails were building to a crescendo—attempted to haul herself out of her uncle's arms. These silly adults were taking far too long.

"Eeeyee . . . oucchhh," Julia squeaked, her face plainly showing her surprise at the strength in CarlyAnn's hands. Blowing a puff of exasperation, Julia looked up at Sean with a wide-eyed shrug as she gently tried to pry ten little fingers out of her hair. "I'm really sorry. I wish I was better at this."

"No, really, it's my fault. Usually she's not like this with me. It's almost like she knows Kathleen won't be back for a long time or something."

"Well, maybe she does." Grimacing, Julia slowly turned her head and looked up at Sean. "Hold still," she commanded. "I have an idea."

Sean shrugged. What did he have to lose?

Ever so slowly Julia wriggled and squirmed and inched her way under Sean's arm and finally worked her way into position between him and the baby. Impatiently, she pushed her hair out of her eyes and over her shoulder.

"Okay, then," she huffed, surveying the situation.

"Now *this,*" Sean joked, finding his lovely neighbor in his arms far sooner than he'd anticipated, "is a great idea."

Julia grinned. "Don't make me laugh. This next move is critical."

"Gotcha," he said soberly. "I mean, Roger."

"And don't call me Roger," Julia quipped.

"Okay," Sean agreed as a grin spread across his face, "Beulah."

CarlyAnn stopped crying and watched them with curiosity.

Whether it was the proximity or the situation or the tension, neither Julia nor Sean would ever be able to say. But for some reason they were both struck by the humor of the moment and began to laugh. And laugh. And laugh.

For the longest time they stood there, clutching each other and CarlyAnn, howling with laughter.

"Stop!" Julia gasped. "I'm afraid we're going to drop the baby."

"Ahh," Sean sighed, his eyes damp, "Kathleen would never forgive me if we did that."

"Okay now," Julia said, finally regaining control. Turning around, she presented her back to Sean. "I'll put my arms around her middle and when I say ready, you let go. Okay?"

"Okay."

Reaching around the baby's warm and chubby middle, Julia locked her arms over the top of Sean's. For a moment, she lingered, thinking this must be what it felt like to have a husband and a baby to love.

It wasn't so bad, actually. Not so bad at all.

"Okay, ready," she finally said, reluctant to lose this special closeness she'd missed for . . . well, forever, really.

"Here goes," Sean murmured, his voice low, his breath warm in her ear. Slowly, he released his grip on CarlyAnn and took a step back.

Now dangling in Julia's arms, CarlyAnn squirmed around and peered into the face of the person who held her.

She smiled. "Bap!" she squealed and began to probe Julia's nose with her little fingers.

"Shall we?" Julia asked, pulling the baby's hands away from her face.

Sean grinned. "We shall."

Once they reached the bottom of the steps, Sean guided Julia into the enormous dining room. An ornate hand-painted chandelier—day lilies on roseglass—dominated the middle of the room, presiding over the long mahogany table and numerous chairs like a queen over her subjects. Against the far wall stood a magnificent china cabinet, overflowing with cups and saucers, goblets and glassware, and all nature of bric-a-brac. A fire crackled merrily beneath the extravagantly carved fireplace mantel, warding off the autumn chill and giving the room a cheerful ambiance. Oriental rugs of all sizes and patterns adorned the gleaming hardwood floor.

"Looks like nobody's here yet," Sean observed, poking his head into the room and looking about. He checked his watch. "We *are* about ten minutes early."

Blessedly, CarlyAnn had snuggled into Julia's arms and, for the first time since Kathleen had left, seemed content.

"Hello, dearies," Hattie warbled, spotting them as she hobbled into the dining room, a salad bowl in her arms and Rahni hot on her heels. "You're a little early. Why don't you wait in the parlor? Bonnie will be happy to get you a cup of coffee. Okay, Bonnie?"

Rahni nodded. "Okay."

"Sounds heavenly," Julia said with a smile. "I take decaf."

"Same here," Sean put in.

Turning, Rahni cast Hattie a troubled glance. "Thee-calf?" She raised a questioning brow and put her lips together. "Moo?"

"Certainly," Hattie nodded. "Bring the cream. You'll find it in the refrigerator."

Her brows knitted, Rahni shrugged and stepped slowly to the kitchen. "Okay."

Setting the salad bowl down on the table, Hattie moved up beside Julia. "So, Beulah, dear, who have we here?" Slowly, she reached with her blue-veined hand to pet the golden floss at the back of CarlyAnn's head.

"Isn't she divine?" Julia beamed, peering down into the cherubic face.

"Yours? Really?" Hattie asked, clearly surprised. "I must not have noticed her name on your application. My eyes aren't what they used to be, though, don't you know."

"Oh, no, I didn't put *her* name on my application," Julia said loudly, suddenly filled with alarm. It wouldn't do to have Hattie think there were more people living in her room than there actually were. She glanced worriedly at Sean.

"Oh," Hattie warbled, "well, that would explain why I didn't see your name. What is your name, dear one?"

"CarlyAnn," Sean supplied.

Laughing heartily, she chucked CarlyAnn under the chin. "Ah, Caroline. That's a lovely name. Just like Caroline Kennedy. Or the Princess of Monaco. I bet you're Daddy's little princess, huh?" Hattie shot a curious glance up at Julia, then turned her attention back to the baby. Excited, CarlyAnn bestowed Hattie with a gaping, drooling smile. "Why, aren't you a little darling? You remind me of my little girl so many years ago. Aren't daughters fun?"

"Actually, CarlyAnn is Sean's baby," Julia gestured to Sean.

"My niece," Sean amended.

"Oh? Hmm . . . Oh! Yes. It *is* . . . nice." Hattie looked back and forth between the two for a moment as realization apparently dawned for her. Then she slowly bobbed her head as if this explained everything.

"I'll be taking care of her," Sean told Hattie. "Her mother had to go away for a while, but she'll be back."

"Yes, yes, yes. I see. Goodness gracious. Well, be thankful for your problems, for if they were less difficult, someone with less ability would have your job."

"That's true," Sean nodded, mulling over her whimsically sage words.

"But, the good Lord above wants to see how we handle the various trials and tribulations that fall into our lives. That's how he can tell what we're made of, right?"

"Yes ma'am," Sean agreed, looking fondly down at his niece as her chubby cheek lay nestled against Julia's shoulder.

"Well," Hattie sang, "you three just make yourselves at home here in the parlor. Bonnie and I will have dinner on the table shortly. Everyone should begin arriving in a little while. Bonnie will be in momentarily with your libations."

"Thank you," Julia called after Hattie as the elderly woman made her way back into the dining room.

Placing his hand lightly against the small of her back, Sean guided Julia over to the sitting area. For a moment, they stood regarding the minuscule old loveseat until Julia looked up at him and grinned.

"Nah," they both said in unison, then laughed.

"Why don't I take the loveseat, and you take the recliner since it rocks," Sean suggested.

"Good idea," Julia agreed as she settled in and arranged CarlyAnn across her chest. As she began to rock, the child's eyes grew heavy and her lips fell slack. "We're losing her," she observed. A lump lodged in her throat as she was suddenly overcome by the poignant sight. Tucking in her chin, she smiled down at the angelic bundle she held. She wrapped her arms more firmly around the cuddly body.

"Probably a good thing. She's had a big day."

"I know the feeling," Julia sighed and slowly allowed her gaze to travel to the door that led to the dining room. "Do you think Hattie heard anything we had to say?"

"Oh, she heard something all right. I can't tell you if it's what we had to say or not."

Julia giggled. "It must be terribly confusing for her."

Lifting his shoulders, Sean shrugged. "I can't tell. She honestly believes she's hearing what you are saying most of the time. And," he cocked his head and regarded her, "some of the time, she actually is. But the strangest thing of all is, almost all of the time things manage to work out for Hattie."

"Amazing," Julia murmured.

"I think it's her faith in God."

"You think so?"

"Oh, sure. Since I've moved in here, my faith has been restored and reaffirmed over and over again."

"How?"

"Oh, by little things. Hattie's strength, her belief in prayer, and the miracles that seem to happen around here with startling regularity."

"Really?"

Sean chuckled. "You'll see for yourself soon enough. Hattie is a regular saint."

"Saint?"

"A prayer warrior. She talks to the Lord all the time as if he were sitting right here with us," grinning, Sean looked around, "which he is."

"Well, if he's sitting in the loveseat with you," Julia joked, "he's gonna need a miracle only he can perform to get out of it."

Sean laughed. "He's up to it."

"I know," Julia murmured. "I just tend to forget at times."

"Me too. But it seems to me that Hattie never does."

"I envy that."

"I do too."

"Sometimes I think I tend to let life get in the way of my relationship with God. That makes me sad." Slowing the rocker, Julia peered at Sean. "You know what I mean?"

"I know exactly what you mean." Sean smiled fondly at Julia as she cradled his niece in her arms. "I'm sure it must make him sad too."

"Well," Julia sighed, "I have the next two weeks to relax and get back in touch with the things that really matter."

They stared at each other a moment, understanding and communicating silently.

Sean's glance drifted to CarlyAnn's sleeping face. "Yeah, I ought to do that too," he said with a bemused shrug, "since, for some strange reason, I just happen to have two weeks off myself."

"Yoo-hoo! Pssst! In here," Hattie's urgent whisper ricocheted around the dining room as she beckoned the bickering Ross sisters and the Colonel to join her in the kitchen.

"Come on, troops; step lively," the Colonel wheezed and, slowly spreading his arms, herded the older women like so many waddling geese into Hattie's old-fashioned kitchen. "What's going on?" the Colonel demanded after he'd managed to gather everyone in front of the old cast-iron oven.

"Shhh!" Her eyes bright, Hattie hushed them, holding a gnarled finger to the pucker of her lips.

"Oh, dear, *now* she has my curiosity up," Glynnis squealed.

"Shhhh!" Agnes noisily shushed her sister and elbowed her in the ribs. "Can't you ever follow directions? She wants us to *be quiet!"*

"*You* shush," Glynnis crabbed. "You make far more noise than me with your bossy SHHHUSHING!" Spittle flew as Glynnis parroted her older sister.

"Silence, ladies!" the Colonel cried and, poking the whistle that hung around his neck between his lips, gave it a deafening blast.

Startled, Rahni nearly lost the tray she carried. It contained two steaming cups of coffee and a large pitcher of milk. Passing Hattie, she moved to the door and murmured, "I serve thee-calf."

"Very good, Bonnie, dear," Hattie said, preoccupied with her startling news. "Listen, everyone," she began, gathering the Colonel and the Ross sisters into a geriatric huddle, "I wanted to brief you on a situation that could potentially cause us all a great deal of embarrassment."

Agnes gasped. "Glynnis! Tell me you're not going to wear that revolting two-piece swimming costume to supper!"

Glynnis snorted. "Don't be ridiculous, Agnes. Besides, it's not one bit revolting." She turned toward the Colonel and hissed, "She's simply jealous."

Blithely, Hattie ignored the sisters and continued. "It

would seem that our newest boarder, Beulah, has a little one."

"Great galloping galoshes!" the Colonel hollered, then frowned. "A little what?"

"A baby."

"Oh, gracious!" Agnes's eyes bulged. "And where is the father?" she shrieked, her operatic falsetto straining for the balcony.

"Well," Hattie said with a puzzled frown, "that's the part that surprised me. It's our Don!" She nodded amid the gasps of shock. "Yes, Beulah told me so herself. Said the baby is Don's. Then Don told me that Beulah had been gone for a while, but now she's back."

"Hmmm," Glynnis hummed, pursing her brightly colored lips and pondering Hattie's startling announcement. "She was gone . . . and now she's back. What could it mean?"

"Just that. It means she was gone, and now she's *back,*" Agnes snapped.

"Well, I guess that's neither here nor there," Hattie mused. "The reason I wanted to tell you all is so that you will make an extra-special effort to make her and the baby feel welcome. I'm sure it must be difficult enough to be a single parent these days without a lot of gossip and snoopy prattle going on behind your back. The Lord would want us to be good shepherds and welcome these new little lambs into our flock without judgment or censure."

Beaming, she clasped her hands together and looked tenderly at her oldest and dearest friends. "So just act normal. Obviously, Beulah is very sensitive about her predicament. Why, she didn't even mention it on her application form. Perhaps she was worried that I wouldn't accept children."

"You could have her court-martialed for perjury," the Colonel suggested, setting his chin and narrowing one eye.

"Well, technically, she wasn't under oath when she signed, Colonel, dear," Glynnis reminded him.

"True," he harrumphed.

"In any event," Hattie prattled on, oblivious to the suggestions around her, "don't make any overt statements regarding the parentage of the baby. And don't question Beulah or say anything to her that might make her feel awkward about the child. I'm sure she and Don have a lot of things to work out between them. We must be supportive. Simply accept little Caroline as a miracle from God. And remember, everyone, to pray for them." She smiled at their wrinkled faces. "Even the feeblest knock is heard on heaven's door."

"Who is little Caroline?" the Colonel wondered.

Glynnis waved an airy hand. "The baby."

"Quite frankly, I'm shocked at Sean," Agnes barked. "Abandoning his wife and child in such a callous and unfeeling manner."

Glynnis rolled her eyes. "Hattie, you didn't say Sean did that, did you? And, besides, he's here now, and that's what counts."

"I hope they're not using those paper diapers," the Colonel grumbled. "Biggest waste of money I ever heard of."

Hattie patted them all on their wrists. "I knew I could count on you all to make their little family feel welcome. And I'm counting on you to tell Brian and Olympia when they come in, as well. Can you do that for me?"

"I'll do it," Agnes sniffed.

"Good," Hattie said, summarily dismissing them. "Don and Beulah are in the parlor enjoying a cup of coffee. When

Brian and Olympia arrive, give them the word then call Don and Beulah in for supper. We'll join hands in prayer once everyone has arrived."

After everyone had left the kitchen, Hattie quickly bowed her head.

"Oh, Lord, how I do thank you for bringing Don and Beulah and their darling little Caroline into my life. Lord, I pray that you will bless this little group with your abundant love and help them to realize what a gift their little family truly is. I've surely missed the pitter-patter of little feet around the house. I shall enjoy what time I have with the baby.

"You always know our every need before we do ourselves. You are so wonderful, my Lord. Thank you, Jesus.

"And, oh! Just in case I've neglected to mention it in the last few minutes, I love you, Lord. Amen."

4

Dear Lord," Hattie began, her head bowed, her blue-veined hands clasped tightly together, "for what we are about to receive, make us, each and every one, truly grateful. Thank you for this bounty and for the loving fellowship of another meal together with good friends. Amen."

"Amen," came the whispered chorus from around the table.

The reverent, post-prayer silence did not last long.

"Hattie told us all about your baby," Agnes, under her breath, informed Sean—and, at the same time, the entire group of boarding-house diners. From across the table, she focused her hawklike eyes on Sean's. Brows arched, she smiled the tiny, secret smile of one who is in the know.

Soupspoons paused halfway to mouths as everyone wondered what Agnes might get it in her head to say next.

The Ross sisters flanked the Colonel, Hattie presided at the head of the table, and Olivia, Ryan, Sean, and Julia took up the other side. Rahni sat by the door nearest the kitchen so she could help Hattie serve.

Lowering her heavy glasses to the tip of her pointed nose, Agnes swung her gaze to where Julia sat next to Sean. CarlyAnn was snoozing contentedly on Julia's lap. Deep in thought, Agnes scrutinized the baby for a moment before pinning her gaze back on Sean.

"The child looks just like you, young man."

Pleased, Sean beamed. "Thank you, Miss Agnes."

A collective sigh heaved 'round the table as the diners resumed sipping their soup.

The Colonel leaned forward and, with a great, rattling breath, blew out the candles in the table's centerpiece. "Waste not, want not," he quoted. "Winter's a-comin'."

Miss Agnes was still zeroed in on Sean. "Too bad some parents don't seem to give a flying fig about the welfare of their children these days. Not," she paused and shook her head dramatically, "at all the way it was back when I taught the three Rs! Why, today's parents are running off here and there, leaving the poor children to fend for themselves without so much as a how-do-you-do."

Spoons froze in midair.

Always easygoing, Sean decided to let the comment about his sister's parenting skills slide. However, Kathleen was a wonderful mother, and he felt a responsibility to say so.

"Miss Agnes, CarlyAnn's mother didn't want to leave her. She simply had to leave for a while," he explained with a patient smile.

"Who's CarlyAnn?" the Colonel demanded as he pulled the candle stubs from the centerpiece and tucked them into his breast pocket. "I'll take these," he informed Hattie, "since you were just gonna burn 'em up."

Drawing her chin back into her neck much the way a chicken preparing to peck would, Agnes stared at Sean. The frown of a largemouth bass tugged at her thin lips. "I'm not referring to the child's *mother,*" she said testily. "It seems to me that these days, the *father* is the first to neglect his responsibilities as *you* obviously well know! Why, back when I taught school—"

"Oh, Agnes," Glynnis groaned, "give it a rest."

"I will not!"

Sean frowned. What did Miss Agnes know about Martin and his Alaskan trip? Glancing at Julia, he lifted and dropped a shoulder and was relieved to note that she looked as confused as he was. Sean felt duty-bound to defend his brother-in-law's honor.

"No father could love his daughter more than CarlyAnn's father loves her," he explained. "Sometimes circumstances take parents away for short periods of time. No harm done."

Julia smiled warmly at Sean over the top of CarlyAnn's head, and he felt his chest swell with some emotion he couldn't quite name. She was such a special woman.

"No harm that *you* know of," Agnes drove home her point by brandishing her soupspoon at Sean. "Back in the days when I was shaping young minds—"

"Agnes, for once, will you mind your own business?" Glynnis bristled.

As the sisters bickered, Julia twisted in her seat and, leaning toward Sean, murmured, "Don't let her bother you. She doesn't understand about your sister's and brother-in-law's careers."

"Thanks," Sean whispered back, filled with gratitude. "You're sweet to say that." Just knowing that she was on his side made all the difference.

For a moment they studied each other. The warm glow of the rose-colored light fixture bathed Julia and the baby in a wonderful, ethereal light, and Sean sat transfixed by the picture. Too bad Julia didn't have any children of her own, he mused. Sitting there, with CarlyAnn snuggled contentedly in her arms, she was the picture of tenderness and motherhood.

Cheeks pink, Julia smiled a bashful smile then ducked her head and fussed with CarlyAnn's sweater.

"Colonel!" Agnes suddenly roared, her eyes round with shock as she stared at the old man seated next to her. "I'll thank you to keep your . . . your . . . *feet* to yourself!"

Clearly befuddled, the Colonel's brows knit into a furry line. "Come again, madam?"

Bunching her fist, Agnes whapped him on the arm. "Your feet, sir. Keep them to yourself! And," she added with a narrowed glance, "for pity's sake, put some socks on. Your toes are ice cold."

"Madam," the Colonel cried excitedly then fell into a death-defying coughing fit, "I'll . . . have you know," he continued when he could finally speak again, "I'm wearing *regulation* footwear."

While the Colonel and Agnes heatedly discussed the merits of light versus heavy wool socks, Olivia, who sat on Julia's other side, reached out and stroked the baby's silky curls.

"Isn't she an angel?" she murmured wistfully.

Leaning slightly forward, Sean looked across Julia and nodded at Olivia. "Yes, but just wait. This kid has a set of lungs you wouldn't believe." He couldn't control the touch of pride that tinged his voice.

"CarlyAnn?" Olivia feigned surprise. "I can hardly believe you'd ever hear so much as a peep out of this little dolly."

Sean snorted.

"CarlyAnn?" the Colonel repeated tiring of his argument with Agnes. "Who is this mysterious person?"

Casting an inquisitive glance around the table, he tugged at the floral centerpiece in front of his plate and began to harvest seeds for his window box. "Spring's a-comin'," he explained to those who stared.

Hattie smiled benignly as the Colonel tore her plastic flower arrangement from stem to stern.

As everyone finished the bowls of thick and fragrant vegetable soup, a basket of fresh-baked bread was passed around followed by the butter dish and tureens filled with various types of salad dressing. Dishes clinked, and silver clanked, and the fire in the fireplace crackled and popped merrily. In the background some light baroque chamber music tinkled.

Sean glanced at Julia. For some reason he couldn't fathom, the evening meal seemed somehow . . . *cozier* with her seated at his side. It had been a long time since he'd felt this wonderful sense of home and family. And, he thought, allowing his gaze to travel around the table, though this little family was rather kooky at best, he cared for each and every one of them as if they were his own relatives.

Suddenly, the fact that he'd lost out on his job promotion paled in comparison to the riches he already enjoyed right here in this room. Why hadn't he noticed that before? he wondered as his gaze came to rest on the top of CarlyAnn's fair-haired head. Perhaps it took a child to give him a different perspective on things. His eyes wandered to Julia's face. Or a woman, he reflected.

Like a dog with a juicy bone, Agnes brought the conversation back to modern parents and the lack of social responsibility exhibited by this generation of ne'er-do-wells.

"Unfortunately, I never married, so I was never blessed with children of my own, but I thought of all of my pupils as if they were my own flesh and blood. And let me tell you, I could spot the ones whose parents did not care a mile away!"

Glynnis rolled her eyes. "Agnes, I hardly think young Caroline is neglected, if that is what you are implying."

"Oh! Goodness gracious! What on earth?" Julia cried and stamped her feet. Reaching out, she clutched Sean's arm.

Sean grinned. He loved her spunk. It seemed nobody would besmirch his family's good name with her around. Loyalty was a quality he really admired in a person.

"No need to get huffy, dear," Agnes declared, pursing her lips. "I'm simply stating the facts."

"No, no . . . I . . . there's something under the table, and it's . . ." Julia pulled a funny face. ". . . *licking* my ankle."

"Moondoggie!" Ryan shouted and brought his fist down on the tabletop with such force he made the china rattle. "Moondoggie! Stop it right now! Lie down!"

A pitiful groan emanated from beneath the table as Moondoggie did as he was told. After making several unwieldy turns that had the ladies gasping, Moondoggie finally found the perfect spot and, with a heavy grunt, flopped to the floor. Several more groans and snorts wafted from below as Moondoggie made known his dismay with the seating arrangements.

"Sorry about that." Ryan shot Julia a sheepish glance. "Moondoggie is a golden retriever who is problematic at dinnertime. We have been working on his begging. Three weeks ago he would have been in a chair eating from our plates."

"Really?" Julia asked incredulously.

"Yes. Actually, Moondoggie has come a long way. Good boy," Ryan called, bending low and peering under the table.

Moondoggie groaned, and his tail hopefully thumped the floor.

Unconsciously, Julia's hand still rested in the crook of Sean's arm. Covering her hand with his, he gave it a friendly pat.

Rahni stood—straightened out the gauzy, white wrap-around dress that her native culture dictated—and caught Hattie's eye. "Main . . . course?" she asked, groping for the proper words over the sounds of dining and conversation.

"Of course, what, Bonnie, darling?" Hattie wondered with a smile.

"Okay." Rahni nodded and disappeared into the kitchen.

With a shake of her head, Hattie returned to buttering her bread.

Sean leaned forward and peered at his niece's cherubic face as she lay slumped against Julia's chest.

"I guess we don't have to worry about feeding her," he said, bringing his head next to Julia's.

"Not yet, anyway." Julia's expression softened as she gazed down at the sweet face cradled in her arms. Reluctantly slipping her hand from the crook of Sean's arm, she shifted the baby to a position that better allowed her to reach her salad.

"Maybe, if we're lucky, she'll stay asleep all night long," Sean said hopefully.

"Maybe." Julia glanced at the clock. "It's seven already. What time is her usual bedtime?"

"I think it's around eight." For a moment, Sean racked his brain trying to remember what instructions Kathleen had given to him. "I'm not sure, but I think I'm supposed to give her a bath and sing to her first. It will be well after eight if I do all that." A worried frown knit his brow.

Antennae tuned to their conversation, Agnes tsked. "Surely by now you would both know what time a child of this age should be put down for the night."

Glynnis glanced at her watch. "Aggie, dear, I believe you should be the one heading off to bed. You seem a little crankier than usual tonight."

"I most certainly do not!"

"You do too!"

"I beg your pardon!"

As the sisters nattered on, Olivia pushed her long, sandy-colored hair over her shoulder and leaned closer to Julia to get a better look at CarlyAnn. "I seem to remember my daughter snoozing through dinner at this age."

"Would she eat when she woke up?" Julia wondered.

"Oh, sure. I'd fix her some warm milk or maybe a little juice. Sometimes she would eat some finger food, like Cheerios or banana slices. Then we'd play for a while before I rocked her back to sleep." Olivia's smile was nostalgic. "If you need any help with her while you're all getting settled in, just let me know. I've . . ." She paused and swallowed. ". . . missed holding a baby."

"You're on," Sean sighed gratefully.

Olivia nodded. "CarlyAnn is such a pretty name." She paused reflectively. "My daughter's name was Lillah."

"Oh, that's a beautiful name," Julia said.

"Would someone mind telling me who CarlyAnn is?" the Colonel harrumphed, sending his watery gaze around the table.

"CarlyAnn is the baby in Julia's lap, sir," Sean informed him as he placed a casual arm around the back of her chair.

"Then who's Caroline?" the Colonel demanded.

"I don't know, sir."

Agnes clucked like a ruffled hen. "That figures."

"Agnes, be still," Glynnis snapped.

Slowly, Agnes's face puckered, her nostrils flaring, her lips pursing, her eyes bulging. "Ryan," she gasped, "will you please be so kind as to get that slobbering beast out of here?"

"Moondoggie!" Ryan shouted. Flipping up the tablecloth, he dove under the table.

"Main course," Rahni announced as the table bounced and swayed, achieving a credible facsimile of a seven on the Richter scale.

"Alpha stronghold?" Julia wondered, scooting back her chair to better shield CarlyAnn from sliding cutlery.

"Yep," Sean said with a grin. Whether or not she knew it, Julia was beginning to fit in quite well at the boarding house. Something wonderful took wing in his stomach, giving him a sense of expectation about the future that he hadn't had in years.

Julia put down her book in futility and glanced at the clock next to her bed. It was after 10 P.M., and CarlyAnn had been crying for a solid hour. This particular go-round anyway. Already the baby had slipped in and out of several crying jags that seemed to go on endlessly. Luckily, theirs were the only two rooms at this end of the house on the second floor, or Julia was certain there would have been a riot by now. Sean was right. CarlyAnn had a very healthy set of lungs.

Her heart went out to Sean. She could hear him through the wall that separated their rooms, talking to CarlyAnn, pacing, singing, making silly noises, trying to distract her, but to no avail it seemed. CarlyAnn would not be pacified.

From what she could tell—based on her limited knowledge—he was doing everything right. It was probably simply the strange surroundings that had CarlyAnn in such a dither. Soon she would wear herself out and fall asleep.

Wouldn't she?

Propping herself up against the headboard of her four-poster, Julia listened to the incessant crying and had to fight the urge to hop out of bed and run next door to lend a hand. Sean had it under control. If there was one thing she had noticed about him as he'd carried his niece back to his room that evening, it was that he seemed great with kids and totally in control. Obviously, he and his niece were buddies. CarlyAnn was lucky to have such a competent uncle.

Julia, on the other hand, knew absolutely nothing about taking care of babies. Not that she would mind learning someday, it was just that with her busy, fast-track-to-success lifestyle there had been little room left for family life of any kind. As an only child herself, she didn't have the opportunities that Sean did with CarlyAnn to learn the ins and outs of childcare with a niece or nephew.

As she listened to Sean croon an off-key rendition of "Love Me Tender" through the wall, she became suddenly and acutely aware of the vacant spot in her heart that she knew only a family of her own could fill. Try as she might to placate this void with her career, at moments such as this she was reminded that she was not getting any younger. Many of her friends were already married with children of their own. Not that they were any more successful or satisfied than she was, of course, but still . . .

It was odd how the baby's cry made her arms feel so empty. Julia picked up one of the fluffy feather pillows that adorned her bed and cradled it against her chest. Holding

CarlyAnn at dinner that evening had felt so natural. How amazing it was that a little child could sleep so contentedly in the arms of a stranger. Such innocent trust, Julia reflected, remembering the child's sweet face as she slept.

"Love me tenderrrr. Love me truuue." Sean's muffled song filtered through the wall. He had a repertoire limited to Elvis it seemed.

CarlyAnn's shrill cry escalated.

Julia fidgeted under her heavy pile of quilts. Across the room under the windows there was a small, antique rocking chair. She wondered if Sean had a rocker in his room. If he didn't, maybe hers would come in handy. Babies liked to be rocked, didn't they?

CarlyAnn had seemed to enjoy the rocker in the parlor before dinner that evening when she and Sean had shared the coffee that Rahni had brought. Flinging back the covers, Julia reached for her robe and slippers. Maybe she would just hop next door and offer her rocker. It wasn't like he was in bed, asleep.

A little shiver of anticipation skipped down her spine. She wouldn't contemplate the fact that this was the perfect excuse to pay a visit to her charming neighbor. She would, however, run a quick brush through her hair and put on a touch of lipstick.

"Oh, man. I'm sorry. Did the baby wake you up?" Sean pushed his door all the way open and stepped into the hall.

"No, no. Really. I was up reading. I just—" Feeling suddenly foolish, Julia gestured to the rocking chair she'd dragged from her room out into the hall. "I wondered if you had a rocking chair in your room and thought if you didn't, maybe mine would come in handy."

Joggling the red-faced CarlyAnn up higher on his

shoulder, Sean smiled in relief. "Yeah. I mean, no. I don't have a rocker in my room. I bet that would help a lot."

"Good." Julia grinned and looked sympathetically at CarlyAnn. Tears were streaming from the child's eyes. "Poor baby," she murmured and, reaching out, awkwardly stroked the sobbing baby's back for a moment.

"I think she wants her mama," Sean attempted to explain CarlyAnn's discomfort.

More for his own benefit than hers, Julia thought.

"Mmm. I'm sure you're right." She gestured to the chair. "Here, hold the door," she instructed, grasping the rocker by its arms. "Your hands are full, so if it's okay, I'll just bring it into your room."

Looking eternally grateful, Sean moved out of the way and held the door for Julia and the rocker. Once she scooted past, he closed the door behind her.

"Gee, thanks," he called above CarlyAnn's frantic wails. "You're sure we didn't wake you up?"

"No. Honest. But even if you had, no big deal. I don't have to start setting my alarm for another two weeks. I can sleep in as long as I want." She shrugged and glanced around the cluttered room that was similar to hers in size and decor. It looked like a bomb had gone off in the baby's section at a major department store.

Sean followed the path of her eyes with his own forlorn gaze. "I haven't had time to straighten up the stuff Kathleen left. I'm sure there must be some valuable things in there, but CarlyAnn won't let me set her down."

"Do you want me to hold her while you explore?" Julia studied his harried expression in the dim light of his room, and her heart went out to him. The baby's plaintive wails were beginning to jangle her nerves, and she'd only been in the room for a moment. Obviously, Uncle Sean had the patience of Job. For a moment she allowed her eyes to leave his face and inspect the rest of her exhausted neighbor.

Barefooted, his clothing consisted of a pair of gray, ripped sweatpants and a T-shirt that had probably been reasonably clean before CarlyAnn woke up. A cloth diaper straddled his shoulder, and his thick, chestnut hair stuck out at odd angles and looked as if CarlyAnn had been clutching it for support. "I don't mind holding her. You look like you could use a break."

"Would you?" Not waiting for her to change her mind, Sean thrust the wailing CarlyAnn into her arms.

Awkwardly, Julia adjusted the howling, wriggling child against her chest. *Heavens*. Holding CarlyAnn when she was awake and freaked was a different matter altogether. It was like trying to cuddle a hyena. A hysterical hyena.

"Thanks," he breathed, taking a step back. "I owe you."

"Sure," she replied, suddenly uncertain as to what she'd gone and gotten herself into. She should be back in the relative peace and safety of her own room, staying out of this mess. This wasn't any of her business. Then again, she thought, changing her mind as she darted a glance at the pensive lines that shadowed the corners of Sean's mouth, maybe it was her Christian duty to give the poor guy a hand, unskilled though she was at motherhood. It was obvious he was in over his head here.

Frantically clutching a fistful of Julia's bathrobe, CarlyAnn hauled herself up and shrieked in Julia's already-ringing ears. *Ouch*. Yep, the least she could do was lend poor Uncle Sean some moral support. Stiffly, she held the baby out in front of her and tried to find a comfortable grip.

"There, there," she said, bouncing up and down and hoping she sounded more sure of herself than she felt.

Rushing around Julia, Sean dragged the rocker the rest of the way into the room and settled it near his window. "Here," he said, patting the wicker backrest. "Have a seat."

"Thanks," Julia murmured gratefully. Returning his tired grin, she stepped toward the window. As he dazedly moved past her and the baby, Julia paused and, with a puzzled frown, turned and lifted her eyes to him. "Sean?"

"Yeah?" He'd reached the edge of the massive pile his sister had deposited in the middle of his floor and was standing, scratching his head.

"Have you changed her diaper recently?" Julia tentatively probed the baby's bottom with her fingertips. The paper diaper was bulging like a water balloon and, according to the foul whiff that suddenly assailed her nostrils, something was rotten in Denmark.

"Not since she soaked my bathrobe before dinner. Why?"

Julia grimaced. "I think you probably need to do it again." Thank heavens it wasn't her niece. She had no desire to delve into that particular unappealing chore. Already the odor was enough to churn her stomach. CarlyAnn kicked her chubby legs in fury. *No wonder I chose career over family,* Julia mused. *It's much easier on the nerves.*

Groaning, Sean plunged a hand through his hair. "Again?"

"Uh-huh. I think she might have an upset stomach or something," she offered lamely.

"Ahhh, man!"

Julia glanced up at him. *Nuts.* What was it about his lost and somewhat depressed expression that brought out the squishy, pushover side of her nature?

"Yep. Where's her diaper bag? I'll . . . uh," she wrinkled her nose, "give you a hand." Wincing, she reared back as CarlyAnn took a swing at her face. "At least," she muttered under her breath, "I'll try."

5

Together, as CarlyAnn attempted to shatter the windows with her discontent, they finally unearthed the diaper bag and the myriad accoutrements needed to clean, cream, and powder her little behind. Bent over the edge of Sean's bed, they clumsily removed her soiled diaper.

"Eeeuuuooo!" Sean said, screwing up his face. They laughed together and made a game of pushing the rolled-up diaper back and forth into each other's unwilling hands. Sean finally won, and Julia held it in her fingertips at arm's length.

"Uh-oh," Sean warned. "Stand back. She's not done."

Julia tossed the diaper on the bed and laughing, they jumped back.

"She's a regular little fountain, isn't she?" Julia asked, amused. "Hey, too bad about your comforter there. I guess we should have put down a towel or something." She giggled.

"Yeah. Now you tell me." Sean rolled his eyes good-naturedly. He seemed too relieved that CarlyAnn had stopped crying—for the moment anyway—to care about his damp bedding.

"Don't worry. I'm an expert with a blow dryer. When we're done, I'll get you all fixed up," she assured him. "Let's just hope she doesn't . . . uh . . . oops." Julia glanced down at the smiling baby. "Now, *that* I can't fix." Holding her sides, Julia looked at Sean's forlorn expression and rocked with laughter.

"Great," he muttered. "Just great. Remind me to tell you what a great day this has been."

Julia gasped and swiped at her watering eyes. "Oh, man!" she squealed. "If it was me, I'd just throw that poor old comforter away."

"Hattie's gonna kill me," he lamented.

Julia shook her head. "I doubt it. She's had kids. She's probably seen it all." Awkwardly, she picked up and folded the diaper into a ball, sealed it with the still-sticky tapes, and handed it to Sean, who quickly lobbed it across the room and into his wastebasket.

"Good shot," Julia praised in mock admiration.

"Practice," Sean bragged, feigning great pride in his ability to sink the diaper from the three-point zone.

Her bottom free of the offensive diaper, CarlyAnn attempted to insert her foot into her mouth. The silence was a blessed relief. While she played, they tucked a fresh towel under her.

"Nurse Beulah," Sean barked, becoming suddenly businesslike. "Diaper," he ordered, holding out his hand in the fashion of an operating surgeon. Spellbound, CarlyAnn watched them work.

"Diaper," Julia parroted and slapped a fresh diaper into his hand.

"Wet wipe."

"Wet wipe."

"Rash cream."

"Rash cream."

"Googie cloth."

"*Googie* cloth?"

"Don't ask."

Julia giggled and handed him the terry-cloth towel. She watched in fascination as he cleaned his niece and his bedding, alternately tickling her ribs, chucking her under the chin, and prattling to her in nonsensical baby talk.

"Legs up, pat her on the po-po!" Sean chanted as he slid the fresh diaper under her bottom. "Let's see her laugh!"

"Yaa-yaa!" CarlyAnn's squeal was gleeful.

"Where'd you learn the chant?" Julia asked, watching as he lovingly, if not expertly, diapered his niece.

Sean frowned. "I don't know. I guess I heard Kath saying it all the time or something."

"She looks happier."

"Yeah." Shooting her a grateful look, his mouth curved ruefully. Slowly, he straightened and, placing his hands at the small of his back, he stretched. "Thanks. I don't know what I'd have done if you hadn't come over."

"Me?" Julia laughed. "I didn't do anything. You'd have been fine. And remember, there's always 911," she teased. "Has she eaten yet?"

"I gave her some juice and offered her a small chunk of the pizza I had in my little fridge, but she didn't seem too interested." Lifting his shoulders, he looked askance at Julia. "Think she's hungry?"

"I don't know. Maybe." Leaning over the edge of the bed, Julia helped Sean stuff the baby's legs into her fresh sleeper. "I didn't know you could give babies pizza. I thought they had to eat stuff like Olivia was saying. You know, Cheerios and bananas or scrambled eggs and mashed potatoes."

Sean lifted his shoulders. "Kathleen said something about her mushy treats in that big flowered bag over there. Want to go check it out?"

"Mushy . . . *treats?*" Julia lifted a skeptical brow.

Sighing, Sean lifted CarlyAnn to his chest. "Don't ask."

Julia grinned and glanced at her watch. Maybe she'd stay for another minute or two. After all, the night was still relatively young. Plus, it wasn't like she had to be at work in the morning. No. She still had two long weeks to kill before she took over her new position. Drawing her lower lip between her teeth, she tried to ignore how much she enjoyed the idea of prolonging her time in Sean's company.

"Okay." She shrugged loosely. "Mushy treats coming up."

An hour later CarlyAnn was once again announcing her indignation at life's injustice to the world at large. And, unfortunately, the mushy treats did nothing to assuage her foul mood. Turning her nose up at the tidbits that were lovingly—if not expertly—prepared, CarlyAnn slapped them away and cranked up the volume on her squeals of protest.

"I don't know how much more of this I can stand," Sean confessed, looking blearily at Julia as he paced the room with the red-faced CarlyAnn in his arms.

"Maybe you should call your sister," Julia suggested, stifling a yawn.

Sean paused and stared at her as she sat in the rocking chair. Considering her suggestion, he glanced at the clock. "I don't know," he called over CarlyAnn's ragged sobbing. "It's awfully late. Kath would probably have a heart attack if I called her already. Besides, I don't even know if she's checked into her room yet."

"Oh." Julia's nod was thoughtful. "Good point." She finally gave in to her yawn.

"Hey," Sean said, suddenly realizing that he was taking Julia's desire to help for granted. "Listen. I'm really sorry.

I'm being pretty selfish, imposing on your good nature and all. If you need to get back to your room and get some rest, I'll understand."

Arching her back, CarlyAnn brayed furiously at the ceiling.

Julia smiled and dragged a weary hand across the back of her neck. "Oh, I don't mind. Really. I doubt that I would be able to sleep until CarlyAnn settles down anyway. Besides, I want to stay and make sure you don't try to, you know, jump out the window or something." Her eyes twinkled with sympathy and humor.

Tiredly lifting a brow, Sean grinned in spite of himself. "Don't give me any ideas."

A loud pounding at the door startled CarlyAnn, and she shrieked loud enough to disturb folks sleeping in the next zip code.

Jumping from the rocker, Julia glanced worriedly at Sean and rushed to the door. On the other side, wearing a rumpled nightshirt that revealed spindly white legs and slippers over his bare feet, stood the Colonel. In one hand, he clutched his timepiece. In his other, he clutched the doorframe for balance. He gave his throat a good, noisy clearing. "Evening, ma'am. Would Sean be home?"

With a murmured greeting and a nod, Julia stepped back, admitted the Colonel, and gestured at Sean. Slippers slapping noisily as they clung to his feet, the Colonel pushed past Julia and lurched into the room. Coming to a stop in front of Sean, he waited expectantly.

Fumbling with his irate niece, Sean bent awkwardly and touched his hand to his chin in a botched attempt at a salute. "Colonel, sir."

"Sean." The Colonel saluted back. "Son," he cried, his high-pitched voice cracking dryly, "I was wondering if you were aware that it is now past twenty-three hundred hours."

Nodding, Sean closed his eyes and sighed. It felt as if he'd been holding CarlyAnn for at least twenty-three *thousand* hours. Maybe longer. "Yes sir."

"Good," he cackled. "Then you are aware that lights-out was an hour ago."

"Uh, yes sir." Sean joggled CarlyAnn, who was now hiccuping and trying to relocate his nose to a different spot on his face.

"You are also aware that you are wasting electricity."

"Uh, yes sir."

"Good. Then may I suggest that you and your . . . uh, Miss, here," he pointed stiffly at Julia, "put little CarlyAnn and Caroline to bed. Between the two of them, they are making more racket than a pair of air-raid sirens."

"Yes sir. We've been trying to do just that."

"Is there a problem, son?"

Yes, there is a problem, Sean thought in irritation. Kathleen's neck was too far away, at the moment, to wring.

"I'm—uh," Sean glanced at Julia, "—we're not sure exactly what the problem is, sir."

The Colonel's brows beetled as he reviewed the possibilities. "Have you tried discipline? Set a curfew and stick to it," the old man screeched. "Ground rules! Without them? Chaos!"

As the Colonel pontificated about the necessity of running a tight ship, Agnes threw open the door and burst—as fast as she could given her age—upon the scene.

Taking what seemed like a hundred tiny steps, Agnes finally reached the edge of the bed and set down the load she carried. At first Julia thought she'd come prepared for a picnic when she spied the basket loaded with goodies. But then, upon closer inspection, Julia could see that the basket contained a veritable cornucopia of elixirs, various medicinal potions, and sleeping drafts.

"Agnes!"

"I'M IN HERE, GLYNNIS," Agnes shrieked churlishly.

"I know where you are, Agnes," Glynnis snapped as she stepped into the room.

Slowly straightening, Agnes scowled at Julia. "We've come," she shouted above the hubbub and gesticulated wildly with her frail arm, "to see about getting this child to sleep."

Peering more closely into the basket, Julia studied the vast array of different medications, both prescription and non, then shot a worried look to Sean. "Oh, thank you so much for your generosity, Miss Agnes, but CarlyAnn is far too young to take these medications."

"They're not for the child," she barked. "They're for *me*. I've tried everything modern science has to offer in the way of sleeping aids, to no avail. Your child is keeping me from my nightly allotment of rest, and I'll thank you to have her stop immediately, if not sooner!" She cast a peevish glance at the squalling CarlyAnn.

"Have you tried burping her?" Glynnis wondered sweetly, trying to smooth things over.

"Yes," Julia said with a tired nod.

"Changing her?"

"Uh-huh."

"Feeding her?"

"Yes ma'am."

Agnes's sigh was churlish. "Putting her up for adoption?" she groused.

"Ignore her," Glynnis advised with a narrow look at her

sister. "Agnes is even grumpier than usual when she's tired."

"Honestly, nothing seems to work" Julia sighed and glanced over at Sean as he plowed a frustrated hand through his hair. "We've tried everything we can think of."

As she spoke, Moondoggie bounded into the room just ahead of Hattie, who tottered in sporting a head full of hot-pink sponge curlers. Skidding to a stop on the hardwood, the golden retriever sat down in the middle of the floor and, with a puzzled look wrinkling his furry brow, cocked his head from side to side and watched CarlyAnn with concern. Then, as if he'd finally gotten a handle on the tune, joined in with a full-bodied howl, creating a soulful duet that had everyone grimacing in pain.

Agnes fumbled in her basket until she located the aspirin.

"Moondoggie!" Ryan shouted, swinging around the doorway and leaping into the room. "I'm so sorry," he apologized, tugging on the reticent Moondoggie's collar. "I think the baby's piercing cry has him on edge."

"I know how he feels," Sean muttered.

"Come on, boy!" Ryan urged.

"Ooo-oooo-ooooo!" Paws outstretched, Moondoggie lowered his head, dug in his heels and refused to budge. *"Ooo-oooo-ooooo!"*

Sean looked around in disbelief at the three-ring circus that had once been his room. Somehow he suddenly found himself an unwilling participant in a kooky slumber party from somewhere in the southern region of Hades, the only bright spot being Julia's sunny disposition. When had his life taken such an unfortunate left turn? he wondered despondently.

Only yesterday morning, he'd had high hopes of becoming the assistant general manager of the McLaughlin New England Inn, realizing a nice little hike in his pay, and perhaps, in his spare time, flirting with the pretty new girl next door.

Today, however, the bleak reality was, for all his time and trouble he was doomed to spend the next two weeks covered in drool and undoubtedly going deaf. Dazed, he watched with bleary eyes as the Ross sisters quarreled over the practicality of flannel versus satin nightwear. Then he felt his jaw drop as the spry, bandy-legged Colonel hiked his nightshirt and began an unsteady climb over the foot of Sean's bed. Reaching the mattress, the Colonel slowly straightened and, gripping the bedpost for support, began to issue instructions.

"Why me, Lord?" Sean whispered, casting a martyred glance at the ceiling.

Julia took an uncertain step toward Sean. "Sean? Maybe he should come back down."

Shrugging helplessly, Sean handed the baby to her. "I know. But he's made it through more than one war, so I guess he knows what he's doing."

"Organization!" the Colonel insisted. "That's what we need. Someone set up a command post—" he wheezed then proceeded to cough like a backfiring Model T, sharply shouting at the ceiling from the depths of his reedy lungs. Suddenly he stopped coughing and, after a chilling moment of silence, Julia looked from Sean to the red-faced Colonel and back to Sean again.

"Colonel?" she asked in a tiny, fearful voice.

Lowering his head, the Colonel looked at her through bleary eyes. "What are you waiting for?" he shouted, then saluted her with a wild hand. Fighting his way off the bed, he dropped to the floor and shuffled back into the mayhem, issuing orders as he went.

"Sweetheart," Hattie called, tapping Julia on the arm, "I know you have tried everything you can think of, and I'm sure you're doing a marvelous job. But I can see that you need some help, and I was just wondering. Have you tried prayer?"

"Prayer?" Julia shouted back.

"Yes, darling, prayer. Used to work wonders with my brood. Prayers," she quoted wisely, "can't be answered unless they are prayed."

"True. And, that's the one thing we haven't tried." At this point a miracle was definitely in order.

"Life's road is rough, but you can make it: Hold out your hand, and God will take it." Hattie, who seemed to have a proverb to fit every occasion, inclined her head toward the door and, leading with her cane, thumped into the hallway. Julia followed with CarlyAnn in her arms. When they'd arrived in the relative quiet of the hall, Hattie hooked her cane over her arm and, reaching out, patted the still-sobbing baby soothingly on the back. Exhausted, CarlyAnn closed her eyes against the bright hall lights and burrowed her flushed face into the cool crook of Julia's neck.

"Dear Lord," the elderly woman began, bowing her head and covering one of Julia's hands with her own, "we step into your awesome presence, full of wonder at your mercy and your unending love. And we know, dear Lord, that you want us to bring even the most trivial problem to your attention. So," Hattie paused as CarlyAnn shuddered and sighed, "Lord Jesus, it is with that in mind that I bring this child to you in prayer. Oh, Lord, I ask that you give this little lamb a special peace and sense of contentment in her new surroundings. And, Lord, I know that you care about every tear that falls from every eye, no matter how young or how old, and that whatever is upsetting little Caroline is of concern to you. So, Lord, we pray, on her behalf—and on behalf of *all* of us here at the boarding house—" she added with a beleaguered sigh, "that you would please, oh, *please*, Lord, comfort young Caroline."

CarlyAnn hiccuped and heaved another great, shuddering sigh. Her eyes still squeezed tightly shut, she burrowed even more firmly into Julia's neck.

"Thank you for your kind attention to this small detail," Hattie continued, "and all these things, we ask in your sweet name, dear Lord, Amen. Oh, yes, and remember . . . I love you."

Ever so slowly Julia opened her eyes and lifted her head to peer at CarlyAnn. Miracle of miracles, the child's breathing, though still ragged at times, was becoming even and deep. She could feel the baby relaxing and becoming heavy in her arms. Julia looked incredulously at Hattie.

"Do you think he did this?" she asked, casting a reverent glance at the hall ceiling.

Hattie winked. "I don't know why not. In the Good Book he promised to answer our prayers. And I, for one, like to take him at his word. I know he probably thinks I'm a nag, as much as I ask of him. But my philosophy is, you don't ask, you don't get." Her lilting laughter shot up the scale. "Well, my dear, it's far past my bedtime, so I'll just carry myself off now."

"'Night, Hattie," Julia said. "And thank you."

"Oh, now, don't thank me," Hattie warbled with a smile and pointed heavenward. Then, making an unwieldy turn, she proceeded to thump and lurch her way down the stairs.

"In that case," Julia whispered and, closing her eyes, bowed her head, "thank you, Lord."

• • •

Julia shifted the sleeping CarlyAnn in her arms and watched as Sean struggled to convert the stroller into a crib.

"Kathleen said all I have to do is push a button, and the stroller explodes into a crib or bassinet or whatever," Sean grunted, grappling with the unwieldy contraption. Perspiration began to bead at his temples, and—if the veins that popped out on his neck were any indication—he looked more likely to explode than the stroller. "Trouble is," he gritted out through his tightly clenched jaw, "she neglected to show me where the blasted button is hiding."

Already on his hands and knees, Sean rolled over onto his back and inspected the underbelly of the apparatus. Unable to locate the mystery button, he moved back to his knees and decided to try shaking it into shape.

It was now after midnight, and everyone had finally cleared out of Sean's room, leaving them to themselves once again. Smiling down into the baby's angelic face, Julia couldn't help but think how lucky this little girl was to have an uncle like Sean to love and care for her while her parents were away. She glanced up at her new neighbor as he gripped his bedpost and dragged himself back up to his feet. The man was practically a saint, she thought, in awe of his dogged determination. That silly gadget he was rattling and bouncing against the end of his mattress looked more like an umbrella than a crib. It would have driven her to distraction ages ago. But Sean was a patient man, she was learning. She liked that about him. *Yes, he is not only patient, he has a good heart too,* she mused, feeling drowsy and content.

Slowly she continued rocking and humming the chorus of "Love Me Tender" that was boring a repetitive hole through her brain. The child was dead weight in her arms, and Julia doubted she'd be waking up anytime soon.

However, not wanting to test that theory, she resisted the urge to laugh out loud at Sean's frustrated gyrations with the baby's bed-to-be.

This evening had ended up being far more entertaining than she'd ever imagined. Usually her first days in a new town were fraught with terrible bouts of homesickness and loneliness. But not here at Hattie Hopkins's Boarding House in McLaughlin, Vermont. Funny, but she hadn't felt this contented and at home since she was a child.

Moonlight washed through the window, giving CarlyAnn's plump cheeks a porcelain quality that was impossible not to kiss. In wonder, Julia stroked the silky threads of gold that curled behind the shell of the tiny ear. Was there anything on earth more special than holding a sleeping child? Until this very day, she'd never known how deliciously sweet the feeling could be.

Glancing up, she watched as Sean pulled off a sneaker and began beating the stroller-crib, and had to bite down on her tongue to keep from laughing.

Voice low so as not to disturb the sleeping baby, Julia whispered, "*Psst!* Sean!"

"What?"

"I saw a movie once where the parents didn't have a bed for their baby, so they took a pillow and some blankets and made a bed out of a dresser drawer."

"Excellent idea," Sean grunted and, finally reaching the end of his rope, drop-kicked the stroller halfway across his room. Slamming into the far wall, the stroller suddenly ballooned into a small, boxy-looking crib. "Well, I'll be," Sean breathed, staring open-mouthed at CarlyAnn's new bed. "I should have thrown it at the wall an hour ago."

Julia shook with silent mirth. "I wonder what would happen if you threw her diaper bag at the wall?"

"I don't know. Wanna try?" Sean's grin was mischievous.

"Not tonight," Julia whispered, marveling at the fact that the ruckus hadn't caused CarlyAnn to stir. "I think we've had enough excitement for one night."

They looked at each other for a bashful moment across the room.

"True," Sean agreed, tugging the crib over next to his bed. Then he poked around in Kathleen's supply pile and finally came up with several baby blankets. Loading these things into the makeshift crib, he tucked and smoothed and plumped and folded until he was satisfied that CarlyAnn would be comfortable. "Okay," he whispered, moving over to where Julia sat rocking the baby. "All set."

"How should we do this?" Julia wondered, gesturing awkwardly at the sleeping baby.

"Hmmm." Sean pondered her question. "How about on the count of three, I help you to your feet, and then we'll put her in bed?"

"Sounds good."

"This is becoming a habit you know, me helping you get out of your seat."

Coloring, Julia made a face at him.

"Here we go then," Sean whispered with a grin and gripped Julia's forearms in his hands. Eyes twinkling, he winked at her, their noses mere inches apart. "Onnne," he whispered.

Onnne, Julia mouthed as her heart thundered in her ears. *Goodness.* Even in this dim light she could see the little flecks of gold dancing in the green of his eyes. Time was suspended as she stared up at him.

"Twooo," Sean whispered.

Twooo, Julia silently repeated. His hands flexed on her

arm, and she couldn't help but notice the way his muscles bulged beneath his shirt sleeves. *Heavens,* she thought defensively. No wonder Hattie had noticed his muscles. He had a lot of them. Big ones.

"Threeee," Sean continued.

Threeee, Julia thought, mesmerized. Three what? Muscles bulging dramatically, Sean was huffing and puffing and looking expectantly at her. *Oh! Three! Yes! Threeee!* Together, she and Sean managed to lift herself and the baby out of the chair.

The momentum they'd built worked against Julia, and before she knew it, she found herself propelled out of the chair and into Sean's strong arms.

Petrified, they both stood frozen and stared at the baby, now lolling halfway in Julia's arms and halfway in her uncle's.

Still sleeping.

Heaving a huge sigh of relief, they lifted their eyes and smiled at each other over the tiny fuzzy head. Slowly they shifted CarlyAnn into Sean's embrace then, with an incredible, albeit fumbling, team effort, managed to deposit the sleeping CarlyAnn into her own bed.

For a long moment they simply stood looking down into her crib and watched her sleep. The sweet poignancy of the moment took them both by surprise, and again their eyes connected, and they shared a smile born of the common bond this experience had brought.

"Well," Julia sighed, unable to think of another reason to stay and soak up Sean's compelling personality, "I should probably get going." Reaching over the edge of the crib, she stroked the baby's cheek one last time.

"I don't know how I can ever repay you." Exhaling raggedly, Sean plowed his fingers through his hair and shot her a grateful look. "If you hadn't come by with that rocker, I might have had a stroke or something. You're a real godsend."

Laughing, Julia shook her head. "In that case, I'm glad I could help."

"You're sure you're not a nurse, Beulah?" Sean asked. A set of deep dimples bracketed his finely sculpted lips.

"I'm sure, Don." Lifting her arms, Julia pushed her hair away from her face and smiled up at him. An unfathomable look flashed into his eyes as he watched her simple movement, but before she could analyze its meaning it was gone. Although, however brief as this expression was, it left her heart palpitating and her knees weak. "I, uh, should be going."

"Oh. Yeah," Sean's whispered words were disappointed, and the look on his face said he wished she could stay awhile longer and prolong this moment of easy camaraderie.

"Yeah," she repeated. Slippers slapping, she slowly began to move toward his door. Tightening the sash to her robe, she reached for the doorknob only to find Sean standing directly behind her. A tingling shiver traveled up her spine at his nearness. Reaching around her, he placed his hand on the doorknob and pulled the door open.

"I hope CarlyAnn is through crying for the night." He darted a quick glance back at his sleeping niece then smiled down at Julia.

She lifted and dropped her shoulders. "Even if she's not, no big deal. In fact, if you need me, just tap on the wall between our rooms—" lightly, she tapped three times on the door, "—like this, and I'll come a running." Her fingers trailed along the door casing as she stepped into the hallway.

Sean nodded. "Got it." He tapped on the door. "Three times." Leaning forward, he lightly gripped her hand, giving it a gentle squeeze. "Again, thanks. Nurse or not, you are a lifesaver."

"Oh, Don," she drawled, a playful tilt at the corner of her mouth, "the things you say."

For a long moment they just stood there, smiling at each other. Somewhere in the house, a clock chimed the midnight hour. The curtains at the end of the hallway danced lightly in the cool night air as summer gave way to fall and, outside in the distance, the cricket's soulful song echoed across the lake.

Slowly their smiles faded.

Julia didn't think her poor heart could take much more of the excitement that standing alone in the hallway with Sean was creating. Surely he could hear the wild thundering beneath her ribs. Pressing her hand to the hollow of her throat, she took an awkward step back toward her door.

"I'll s-see you," she stammered, unsure of when or how she would see him again but hoping—against her better judgment—it would be soon.

"Right." Sean shook his head as if to clear it then nodded and moved back into his room. "Good night," he whispered.

Reaching for her own door, she twisted the knob and pushed it open. "Good night," she said before disappearing into her room and gently clicking the door shut.

Suddenly feeling bereft on a sea of parental inexperience and lonely bachelorhood, Sean had to fight the absurd urge to run to their mutual wall and tap three times. After all, she'd said if he needed her all he had to do was knock.

Brother, he thought with nervous trepidation as he shut

his door and turned to face his first night as CarlyAnn's guardian. He'd only known Julia for a couple of days, and already he was beginning to get kind of dependent upon her. And though he'd lost out on the promotion of a lifetime that very afternoon, he not only hadn't thought about it all evening, he didn't even feel that bad anymore. He gave his head a clearing shake. He'd have to be careful with his feelings when it came to Julia. They were both busy career people. Too busy. Soon she would be transferred again, and eventually he'd get that promotion he wanted. Envisioning her as anything but an occasional date would surely lead to heartache.

Too bad. Julia Evans was a very special woman. Under different circumstances he might be tempted to toss off his "nothing serious" rule and get involved.

Slowly he moved across the room and watched CarlyAnn's lips puff softly as she slept. A love, so poignant it hurt, began to seep into the hollow spots of his heart.

What on earth was happening to him?

6

Hi! I got your message." Poking her head into Sean's doorway, Julia gestured to the wall that divided their rooms.

Morning sunshine streamed into his room that beautiful autumn Tuesday, giving the chaos therein a special, happy glow. Only minutes before, Sean had knocked three times on the wall. Having nothing penciled into her social calendar to fill the yawning chasm of the days that stretched before her, Julia had been—much to her chagrin—overjoyed to hear the muffled tapping that morning.

Of course, she rationalized, it was only because she had so much time to kill and not because Sean Flannigan had the most amazing dimples she'd ever seen on a man.

"Oh, excellent!" Looking harried and half awake but delighted nonetheless, Sean motioned for her to come in and have a seat. "I figured you were up by now. I heard the pipes howling when you took your shower."

"Do they always do that?" Julia asked, stepping around CarlyAnn as the baby rumbled across the shiny hardwood floor in her walker. Sean had cleared a path through the middle of Kathleen's pile for this purpose.

"Sometimes. It's an old house. Everything's pretty noisy."

"Yee-yee-yee!" CarlyAnn shrieked and, spinning in her walker, roared over to the other side of the room, where she smashed into the wall.

Smiling, Julia settled into the rocker. "Pretty noisy, indeed."

Sean grimaced. "We didn't wake you this morning, did we?" Moving across the room, he reached down and turned his frustrated niece around.

"No. Really. I'm always up at the crack of dawn for work. It's habit." She waved at CarlyAnn. "Hi, sweetie. Remember me?"

Setting her feet into motion, CarlyAnn paddled her way over to Julia and stopped directly in front of her. "Bap!" she cried and pounded her fists on the tray in front of her.

"I remember you too!" Julia leaned forward. "Wow. You have some teeth. Pretty neat."

CarlyAnn grinned. "Yee-yee-yee!"

"Looks like you managed to make it through the night." Angling her head, Julia studied Sean from the rocker. Obviously, he was dog-tired. His hair looked like it hadn't seen a comb yet that morning, and his sweatpants and soiled T-shirt looked familiar.

"Barely. She woke up a couple of times, but luckily I was able to persuade her to go back to sleep for a little while each time. I finally gave up about 4:30 this morning and got out of bed. I don't know how Kathleen does it."

"Maybe she sleeps better in her own crib at home with her folks."

"Hopefully. Oh well, she would have woken up by 5:00 anyway." He sighed. "That's when Kathleen started calling. The third time she called, I told her to hang up and leave us alone or get on a plane and come back. Five o'clock," he snorted. "Some vacation. Oh well. I had to get up and tell the boss I would be taking my two-week vacation starting immediately anyway."

"Wow! They'll let you do that with no notice?"

Sean shrugged. "Not normally, but I didn't get that promotion I was telling you about the other day and I—"

"Oh no. I'm sorry," Julia murmured.

"No, no. It's okay." He shrugged. "Anyway, for some strange reason, they gave me an extra two weeks of vacation. As a consolation prize, I guess. At any rate, they said I could use it whenever my little heart desired. So when I called in this morning and explained about CarlyAnn, they were really sympathetic. It was weird."

"Well, don't look a gift horse in the mouth, as they say."

"I hear that. Now," Sean said with a rueful grin, "if I could only get the hang of being Mr. Mom."

"I don't know," Julia mused with a shrug. "Looks to me like you're doing a great job. At least you got her dressed. Love the outfit."

Unable to suppress the grin that she knew crept across her face, she gestured to the multicolored, mismatched fashion combination Sean had selected for CarlyAnn. Purple socks, pink shoes, red corduroy bib overalls, a yellow-and-green shirt, and a pink sweater with yellow ducks. CarlyAnn's hair had been slicked back with water, and her chubby face sported a trace of mushy treat.

"Yeah, Kathleen would probably have a cow if she could see her."

"I don't know. I think she might be proud. I know I'd be pretty much in the dark about dressing a baby. All those wiggly fingers and feet . . ." Julia glanced up at him with admiration in her eyes and suddenly realized he was blushing. "Did you have a hard time getting her to sit still?"

"Two diaper changes, one tussle over shoes, and a cup

of spilt milk later, and I think we're finally beginning to establish a routine." Sean took a deep breath and held it. Slowly exhaling, his dimples appeared at the corners of his lips. "But that's not why we called you over."

"Oh?"

"No. We were thinking, if you weren't too busy, that you would let us take you out to breakfast this morning." He looked boyish and vulnerable standing there, looking so hopefully at her. "It was, uh, CarlyAnn's idea. You know, to thank you for saving our lives last night and everything."

A warm sensation spread from the tips of Julia's toes to the top of her head and finally settled in her heart. "I'd love to go out to breakfast."

"You would?" Sean said on a high note, then cleared his throat. "You would," he repeated manfully. "That's great. I'll just go get cleaned up, and we can go. I know a great little place just down the street."

"That would be lovely. Take your time," Julia said, tickled with how pleased he looked as she waved him toward the bathroom. "I'll watch Miss CarlyAnn."

"So," Julia asked as she blotted her lips with her napkin, "how exactly *did* you get the crib to fold back up into the stroller?"

Sean shrugged and arched a mischievous brow. "I threw it at the wall."

"Ohhh, don't make me laugh," Julia moaned. "I might explode. I'm stuffed."

"I'm just kidding. Kathleen told me where to find the button when she called the third time this morning."

Leaning back in his seat, he tossed his napkin on his plate and eyed Julia where she sat across the booth. CarlyAnn was playing contentedly in his lap, her fluffy curls resting against his shoulder. *What a wonderful breakfast, he thought. And it's not just the food.* The company had been excellent as well. For the last two hours, he and Julia had talked about everything under the sun and discovered that they had everything under the sun—and more—in common.

It was uncanny.

"I can't eat another bite," Julia signed, morosely eyeing some of the untouched food on her plate.

"Me neither," Sean said, giving his stomach a satisfied pat.

"You're sure Hattie won't mind us stepping out on her cooking?"

Tugging CarlyAnn's fists out of his hair, Sean smiled and shook his head. "She won't even miss us. With so many of us boarders coming and going at breakfast, she never knows who she's going to find at that giant dining table of hers."

Unaware of the odd, sticky arrangement CarlyAnn had massaged his hair into, he sent Julia a rakish smile, hoping she was enjoying the restaurant he'd chosen. *Man,* he thought, allowing his gaze to slide over her smile, *she sure is something.* Pretty, fun, loving, hard-working. All the girl scout virtues, all the same values and interests. As far as he was concerned, she was one in a million.

He was smiling at her, mesmerized, when Julia suddenly reared back in surprise as a tiny fistful of pancake came skipping across the tabletop, bounced off the front of her blouse, and landed in her lap. His jaw dropped, and for a moment Sean sat in shock and stared. Then, finally registering what had just happened, he grabbed his niece's small, flailing hand.

"*No,*" he barked. "No, CarlyAnn . . . we don't throw

our food. Leave Uncle Sean's pancake on the plate. Good girl." He shot Julia a contrite look as he appraised the damage.

Julia stared down at her soiled blouse, and Sean swallowed the laughter that welled in his throat. She probably wouldn't be able to appreciate the humor of the situation just yet.

"Ah, man! Sorry about that. She's so fast that I can't always . . ." Another chunk of pancake rocketed across the table. "*CarlyAnn! No, no!* Ahh, shoot, not again. Hey, I'm really sorry about that." Sean had to bite the inside of his cheek to keep from roaring with hilarity.

Julia blinked up at him in amazement.

Her wide-eyed look of surprise was his undoing. Wild laughter crowded unbidden into his throat and finally escaped past his lips, even as he fought it.

"Oh, man, that's rough," he commiserated even as he exploded with laughter. "You'd . . . better use a . . . napkin. Here, use mine. Ahhh, man. It's all over . . . your . . . cheek," he crowed, unable to contain his glee at the tolerant and vaguely amused expression on her face. She was being a pretty good sport, all things considered. "Yeah. Right there." He pinched his lips together in an attempt to stem some of his hilarity. "There's, uh, some in your hair. Looks like most of it got on your blouse though." Sean peered down at his niece, who sat staring at Julia, fascinated by the reaction her fast pitch had brought. He grabbed her hands and held them captive.

"My hair?" Julia fingered the sticky strands as a broad smile lifted her lips. Sean's mirth was infectious, and throwing back her head, Julia hooted with laughter.

"Bap!" CarlyAnn shrieked gleefully.

It only took one look at Sean's beet-red face for Julia to

dissolve into a fit of giggles again. Rapidly her laughter built, as did Sean's, and soon the other patrons in the restaurant were turning and smiling curiously at the yowling pair. Clutching their sides, they rocked back and forth, eyes streaming, gasping for air.

"It kinda looks like one of the Rorschach ink-spot tests," Sean crowed, pointing at her blouse.

"Oh," she squealed and wiped her eyes, "that'll come in handy. I can test people for personality disorders with my clothes. A real icebreaker."

"Hey, you never know." He angled his head and squinted in mock study of the dark and lumpy marks. "Looks like a couple of fighting lips, to me." Tossing his head back, he roared at the ceiling.

"That does it," she gasped as they collapsed with laughter again, "according to my blouse, you're certifiable."

"Ahhh!" Sean gasped, tears beginning to stream down his face.

For several more moments they shook with mirth, slapping their thighs and screaming with hilarity. Eventually, their laughter began to wane, and they sat, smiling at each other, wiping their eyes and breathing as raggedly as if they'd just run a mile.

"I really am sorry," Sean finally groaned.

"No problem," Julia sighed in resignation. "It's washable."

Sean sheepishly studied her face. "Are you sure? I'll be happy to pay the dry-cleaning bill."

"No, really. It's fine."

"You still have a little pancake on your cheek there," Sean chuckled and leaned forward to point the area out to Julia. "Oh well, I hear maple syrup is very good for the complexion."

"Do tell," she said drolly. "Had I but known, I'd have smeared some on my face at the beginning of the meal."

They laughed.

Mercifully, the waitress arrived and removed the items that most tempted CarlyAnn's busy hands. She loaned them a couple of damp paper towels to help with the mess.

As Julia wiped her fingers, she leaned back and, with a contented sigh, glanced around the room. The small café was every bit as quaint and delightful as Sean had promised. Red-and-white checkered tablecloths, lacy curtains, green foliage, and a host of antique kitchen paraphernalia gave the restaurant a homey feel. And the delicious aromas of cinnamon and maple syrup, onions and garlic that wafted from the kitchen . . . certainly they could tempt even the most discriminating palate.

"You know," Julia commented, bringing the conversation back to Hattie, "that's a lot of work, cooking for, and taking care of, all those boarders, even with Rahni's help. Hattie's an amazing woman."

"Yes, she is." Sean nodded and shifted the squirming CarlyAnn forward so that she could reach his spoon. "But you know," he said and paused reflectively, "as I mentioned last night, I think the most amazing thing about her is her unwavering faith in God. I've learned a lot from her."

Tilting her head, Julia propped her elbows on the table and cupped her cheeks in her hands. "I think," she mused aloud, "that was one of the first things that drew me to her. She sure exudes peace and happiness, doesn't she? My grandmother is a lot like that. For me, such a deep faith is a comfort to be around."

Sean nodded in agreement. "I know what you mean."

"Uh-oh!" CarlyAnn shouted. Hanging over her uncle's arm, she looked forlornly under the table.

Snorting noisily, Sean disappeared for a moment as he dove for the spoon CarlyAnn had tossed on the floor. "Here you go, squirt. Just don't throw it at anyone."

Leaning forward slightly so as to be heard above the clanking of CarlyAnn's spoon, he turned his attention back to Julia.

"When I first moved into the boarding house, I used to think that Hattie spent a lot of time talking to herself. I guess I thought that she was kind of dingee." His grin was penitent. "Then one day I walked in on her and realized she was praying. And I got this . . . feeling." Knitting his brow, Sean was thoughtful for a moment. "I can't describe it exactly, but an incredible sense of peace washed over me. And suddenly, I knew I'd really been dropping the ball with my own relationship with God, you know, not taking the time to pray and study the Bible."

Julia nodded in complete understanding.

"Sometimes I get so wrapped up in my career that I tend to forget the most important things in life. Like relationships. With God. With family. With friends. But Hattie's never too busy, you know what I mean? Unlike me," he said, a note of self-deprecation in his voice. "And, it's not like Hattie's not a busy person. She just always seems to remember that the Lord is right there with her. I really admire that."

"Just like my grandmother," Julia murmured, contemplating Sean's words.

"You were pretty close to your grandmother?"

"I still am. She raised me."

"Where were your folks?" Sean lifted his eyes to hers and grimaced. "I'm sorry. That's none of my business."

"Oh, no, really, it's fine. They were there too," she explained, her mouth twisting ruefully. "But, like me, they were—and still are—busy career people. Grammy was always the one who made sure I was turning out all right. She and I have a very close relationship, even across the miles."

Waxing nostalgic for a while, she told Sean about a childhood made happier because of her dedicated grandmother. She told him about her grandmother's faith and the impact it had had on her life and about the older woman's Victorian house, just a block away from her parents' house on Queen Anne Hill in Seattle. She told him about the sugar cookies, the Bible stories, the love.

She told him about being transferred so often and about the toll it had taken on her social life. She told him about the loneliness. The drive to succeed. The decision to put off having a family until she reached her goals.

The emptiness that came with the territory.

Sean listened so attentively that Julia had practically told him every minute detail of her life before she realized what she was doing. Embarrassed, she waved her hands and blinked at him.

"What about you?" she asked contritely. "I've been monopolizing the entire conversation."

"I don't feel that way," he said, shaking his head. However, before he knew it, Julia had drawn out more of his history than he'd ever volunteered to another living soul.

He told her of the untimely death of his father and, soon after that, the death of his mother. He told her of the faith that had held him and Kathleen together and had seen them through the pain of losing their folks. He told her of his decision to make his career number one in his life. He told her about the toll it had taken on his social life. He told her about the loneliness. The drive to succeed. The decision to put off having a family until he reached his goals.

The emptiness that came with the territory.

Having brought the conversation full circle, they stopped talking and simply stared at each other.

"When I look at you," Julia whispered, "I see a reflection of myself."

"Me too," he murmured, surprised.

"Looks like we really do need to get our priorities in order."

A wide grin stole across Sean's mouth. "I will if you will."

Julia returned his smile. "Deal."

Sean held his hand across the table to seal the deal, and as his strong, warm grip enfolded her hand, Julia could feel the heat steal into her cheeks. Something about the look on his face made her know that he was serious about their bargain. The idea of examining and making changes in her lifestyle was as scary as it was exciting.

"Deal," Sean murmured and, after a supercharged moment of awareness passed between them, released her hand.

The bell over the door jangled as customers came and went. In the background, silverware clanked, voices rose and fell, the radio played softly, and CarlyAnn babbled to herself.

But, lost in their own little world, neither Julia nor Sean were aware of anything but each other.

"Uh-oh!" CarlyAnn shouted, intruding upon their reverie.

"I'll get it," Julia volunteered and bent to pick up the tattered napkin, glad for the distraction from Sean's probing gaze. He was simply too wonderful for words. It was becoming increasingly clear that where he was concerned she would have to be careful with her heart. It wouldn't do to get too involved, what with both of them being such career-oriented people and all. It was obvious that it would be far too easy to fall head over heels for him. And then what? Short of a miracle, they would both go back to their busy lives. And after that?

Sooner or later she would be transferred again. Leaving a big chunk of her heart behind held little appeal. Perhaps after this breakfast this morning, she should make a concerted effort to stay away from Sean Flannigan and his engaging, playful grin.

Unfortunately the very idea had her feeling suddenly melancholy. Her sigh was heavy. Oh well, she knew it was for the best. That decision made, she tried to concentrate on what Sean was saying now.

Settling back in his seat, Sean regarded Julia thoughtfully.

"The day you moved in, Hattie mentioned that you might be looking for a church." He cocked his head to see better over CarlyAnn's curly top. "All of us from the boarding house attend McLaughlin Community Church. It's the little white chapel up on the hill. You can see the steeple peeking up through the trees."

"Oh!" Julia's eyes shined with recognition. "Yes! I love the way that looks, standing like a sentinel over the town. I saw that my first day here."

"If you want, you could join us this Sunday," Sean offered, trying to sound offhand. He didn't want to put any pressure on her. Just because he was dying to spend every spare second with her didn't mean she felt the same.

"I'd love that," Julia enthused, leaning forward, her gaze shyly flitting to his. "I have so much to be thankful for, I need to go give the Lord a big thank-you for all the blessings he's given me since I've moved here to McLaughlin."

Sean swallowed, and his heart hammered. *She wasn't*

referring to me, he thought, ducking his head and pretending interest in CarlyAnn's busy napkin shredding. *Was she? Nah. No way.* Nevertheless, he felt himself color slightly. What on earth had put that idea into his head? What a clown he was becoming. But he couldn't help it. Julia was just so . . . terrific. And though he feared what would happen to his poor heart if he let himself begin to care, he hoped she was beginning to feel the same about him.

"Great. This Sunday then." Sean's gut tightened with the ebullient feelings of a kid on Christmas morning. Where had this woman come from? It was almost as if she'd dropped out of the heavens, just for him.

"Sounds heavenly," she murmured, unable to tear her eyes away from the darling dimples that formed crevices in his whisker-shadowed cheeks. Where had this man come from? she wondered dizzily. It was almost as if he'd dropped out of the heavens, just for her.

She was the one who should be taking the ink-spot test, she thought with a clearing shake of her head, amazed at her insanity when it came to her new neighbor. Oh well. Maybe she could work on her steely resolve to steer clear of him after church. Yes. That was a good idea.

Beaming, Sean glanced at the waitress as she tossed their check on the table. "Well, we should probably get going." He grabbed the check and then scooted out of the booth, CarlyAnn dangling over his forearm. "If you're not too busy this morning, I could walk you past the church on our way home." He darted a quick and wishful glance at Julia.

Her heart skipped a beat. Yes. She was certifiable. But, who cared? "I'd like that."

"Good." He smiled. "I know just the way to go. From

the top of the hill, you can see the lake and Hattie's place. The fall colors are awesome."

Julia shrugged expectantly and clasped her hands together. "Lead the way."

Before they left the town proper, Sean ducked into an old-fashioned general store and bought some juice for CarlyAnn, a big bottle of soda pop for them to share, some fruit, cheese and crackers, pepperoni sticks, and other snackable odds and ends to tide them over during their little sightseeing venture. Tucking his bag into the stroller's diaper basket, he grinned at Julia, and they set off to explore the area.

The morning was already long gone by the time they left the café, and the afternoon literally flew by as they lingered together, hiking the winding streets in the foothills of McLaughlin. They pushed CarlyAnn ahead of them in her stroller and, tuckered out from her lively morning and full belly, the baby snoozed contentedly for several hours until they reached a picnic spot at the crest on one of the hills.

Sunshine heralded down from the cloudless, blue sky, and fortunately, the crisp fall air kept them cool as they climbed. Exercise, combined with a fantastic panoramic view, put them both in a happy-go-lucky mood. Sean felt marvelous. He couldn't remember feeling so alive, so completely happy and relaxed.

Sun-dappled leaves shimmered and danced in the light autumn breezes, casting mottled patterns on the ground. Sitting side by side on the ground with CarlyAnn playing between them, they feasted on Sean's impromptu lunch and pointed out landmarks as they spotted them in the distance.

"What's that?" Julia wondered over a mouthful of apple as she pointed into the valley below.

"What's what?"

"That old building. It looks like it's on stilts in the middle of the river."

"Oh," Sean said, retraining his gaze. "That's a covered bridge. Vermont has more than a hundred of them."

"Really?"

"Yeah. In the eighteen hundreds, they used to cover the bridges with roofs and walls to protect the trusses from rot."

"How did you know that?"

Sean shrugged and grinned. "I'm brilliant."

"You are," Julia agreed good-naturedly. "You're practically a walking brochure. I should know, I read about a dozen of them yesterday."

"Nah," he shook his head in mock modesty, "I had to learn a lot of this stuff in grade school. Vermont is really rich with history, not to mention," his eyes twinkled as he gave her the state sales pitch, "the most beautiful state in New England."

"I can't argue with that."

"You know," he began slowly, an idea beginning to form in his mind, "since there is so much to see around here and since you are unfamiliar with the area and," he sighed, glancing at the still-sleeping baby, "seeing that I have the next two weeks free and clear, I'd be happy to show you around the state."

"Oh," Julia demurred, coloring. "I couldn't impose on you that way."

"No imposition, really," he assured her. "In fact, you'd be doing me a favor."

"How's that?" she asked, giggling a skeptical giggle.

"Keeping me and CarlyAnn busy and out of trouble." He smiled engagingly and pressed his point before she had a chance to refuse. "There is so much to see and do." He held up his hand and began to enumerate. "Picnic spots, ski trails, country inns, historic landmarks and battlefields, orchards, museums, festivals, antique shopping, and concerts—"

Laughing, Julia reached out and pressed her palm over his mouth. "Enough already," she teased. "I guess if it will keep you and CarlyAnn out of trouble, I'm game. When do you want to start?"

"I-I . . . ," he stammered and plucked at a blade of grass. "Well, speaking of concerts, our church has one this Wednesday evening, and I was wondering if you'd like to go with me."

Julia studied his earnest expression and felt a smile creep into her lips. Again, that boyish, vulnerable spark lit his emerald eyes, and that, coupled with the lopsided, hopeful quirk at the corner of his mouth, made him utterly irresistible.

"I'd love to," Julia suddenly heard herself blurt out. *Good grief!* What about her recent steely resolve to stay uninvolved with the boy next door? What a goon she was.

"Super!" Sean enthused, looking exceedingly pleased. "It starts at eight, so maybe we could go out to dinner first?"

"I'd love that," she sighed. *Make that super-goon.*

Beaming, Sean glanced at his watch, and his jaw dropped in amazement. "It's already after five! We should be getting back. Kathleen has probably tried to call a half-dozen times since we've been gone. The cavalry is most likely waiting in my room as we speak."

Standing, he extended his hand to Julia and helped her to her feet.

"Are you sure your watch is right?" Julia asked, unable to believe that five hours had flown by since they left the café.

"Yep," he said holding his wrist up for her inspection. "Time flies when you're having fun."

"I guess," Julia breathed with a shake of her head. *And it must rocket when you're gooney as a loon over the boy next door.*

7

I had a really great time today," Julia told Sean.

"Me too," he responded with a sideways glance.

Together, pushing CarlyAnn in the stroller, they ambled up the sidewalk that led to the front porch of Hattie's old Victorian.

"Thanks again for breakfast," Julia continued. "And," her smile was playful, "for, you know, lunch and the history lesson and everything."

"Thanks for coming." Grinning affably, he gazed at Julia for a moment.

CarlyAnn's indignant squawk finally served to remind her uncle of her presence. Parking the stroller, he leaned forward and smoothly lifted the baby into his arms. Already he was becoming much more adept at carting her around and tending to her various needs, Julia noticed, feeling strangely pleased.

"I didn't expect breakfast to last until dinnertime, but I can't say that I'm sorry." He glanced at her, then away, then back again.

"Same here," Julia murmured, feeling suddenly bashful. They were home now, standing at the bottom of the front steps. Their breakfast date was over, and they had reached the awkward moment that signified the end of every first outing. "Well . . ." Self-consciously Julia looked away from him, around him, and anywhere but at him. She didn't know what else to say.

"Well . . . ," he repeated as if he didn't either. "Uh, I guess . . ." He glanced at his watch. "It's almost six-thirty. Are you going to dinner now?"

Tiny little butterflies took wing in her stomach. *That's right!* The day was not necessarily over. They still had the dinner hour together. She schooled her face into a pleasant mask of serenity. No need to jump up and down with glee. Not over a simple dinner anyway.

"Yeah, uh, sure. I could eat. How about you?" she asked casually, checking her own watch.

"I think so. Those crackers and stuff wore off about an hour or so ago, and well, I'm a growing boy."

"Me too." She went pink, then grinned. "*Girl.* I mean I'm a growing girl."

"So I've noticed," he responded, arching an appreciative brow.

Julia suddenly wished she had a mirror. No doubt she still had syrup in her hair and on her face. The last vestiges of her lipstick had most likely disappeared hours ago, and still, Sean had a way of making her feel lovely no matter how she looked on the outside. He was a genuinely nice person.

She glanced down at the syrup stains on her blouse. "Since we still have five minutes, I think I'll slip upstairs and change my blouse into something a little less—" she held out the ink-spot test, now dried, on her chest, "—Freudian."

Sean chuckled. "Sounds good. Well," he said, holding CarlyAnn securely in one arm and offering Julia the other, "shall we?"

Julia laughed as they headed up the front porch stairs together. "We shall."

"Surprise!"

The reverberating cacophony welcomed them as they closed the front door and stepped into the foyer. Julia and Sean paused just outside the giant archway that led to the parlor and exchanged bewildered glances.

Open-mouthed, CarlyAnn simply stared.

"Are you surprised, Beulah, dear?" Hattie wondered with a smile as, leaning heavily on her cane, she thump-hitched over to the foyer to greet them. The other members of the boarding house, their faces in various stages of animated excitement, stood in the parlor behind Hattie, wearing party hats and holding noisemakers.

"Well . . . yes . . . yes, uh . . . surprised. You could say that," Julia murmured, racking her brain for the reason behind this celebration.

Nonplussed, she slowly surveyed the congratulatory banners that hung in gay festoons from the ceiling and picture rails. Balloons and streamers, a curious assortment of presents wrapped in pink and blue, a cake in the shape of a baby bootie . . . Why, if Julia hadn't known any better, she would be tempted to think that this was a baby shower of some sort. And, if Don, Beulah, and little Caroline's names on the banners—hand-painted in dripping tempera watercolor—were any indication, the party was in *their* honor.

Allowing her eyes to slide back to Sean, she met his quizzical gaze with one of her own. *What on earth is going on?* she wondered, and could see the same questions running through his mind.

Each resident of the boarding house was decked out in his or her Sunday best: colorful skirts and dresses for the women and a sport coat for Ryan. And the Colonel was resplendent, despite the stains, missing buttons, and moth holes, in his military dress whites.

"We're having a special buffet supper here in the parlor tonight," Hattie trilled, clasping her hands beneath her bosom. "And after that . . . *your party!*" The breathless song in her voice revealed her excitement. "Come along now, you two. We've all been waiting and hoping you'd be back by six-thirty." Pausing, she winked. "I've had to battle the Colonel away from the cake more than once."

"Uh, ah, er, Hattie," Sean stammered, pressing his fingers to his temple, "*our* party?" He lifted his shoulders and smiled weakly. "I . . . we . . . I don't . . . What's the occasion?"

"You have eyes. Use 'em," Agnes groused. A mischievous spark in her faded eyes belied her sharp tone. "It's a baby shower for you and the baby's mother." Turning slowly, she shuffled into the parlor after Hattie, beckoning with a gnarled hand for them to follow.

"Me?" Sean asked dazedly, "and . . . the baby's mother?"

"Well, of course the baby's mother." Agnes turned and gestured in a grand manner at Julia.

Julia's heart lurched then plummeted to her tennis shoes. All these people were under the impression that CarlyAnn was Sean's and *her* daughter? *Oh, no,* she thought, mortified, then battled a burst of hysterical laughter. Why, they'd only just met two days ago. Producing an offspring was something she'd like to put off until after the wedding. Glancing at Sean, she blushed over her ludicrous thoughts. Wedding, indeed!

"Unless," Agnes pursed her lips, "you're planning on raising this child all alone?" The older woman pinned Sean with a suspicious look.

Sean gave his head a vigorous shake. "No! No! In fact, I don't expect to—" he attempted to explain.

"Good," Agnes crisply cut him off and gave her hands an irritated flapping. "Don't get me started on today's irresponsible parents."

"Please," Glynnis implored Sean.

"Anyway," Agnes continued, ignoring her sister, "we couldn't help but notice last night that you two don't have diddly-squat in the way of baby supplies for this poor child of yours."

Glynnis rolled her eyes and shook her head.

"Well," Agnes loftily informed them, "we couldn't do much about you not having a proper nursery, but we figured we could help out in some small way. So we decided to take matters into our own hands."

"You did?" Sean asked, flabbergasted.

As they moved into party central, Sean cast a stupefied look over his shoulder at Julia. *A baby shower?* he mouthed to her. Julia shrugged helplessly. She didn't have a clue.

CarlyAnn rode along over his arm, taking in the brightly colored scene with avid interest.

Julia glanced at the baby. This was simply awful. Where on earth had they come under the impression that CarlyAnn was her daughter? she wondered, feeling increasingly panicked and guilt ridden by the second. All the trouble they'd gone to was breaking her heart.

"Yes," Glynnis piped in, "good gracious, my knitting needles fairly caught fire today!"

"They *did?*"

Julia's eyes glazed over as she stepped with Sean into the parlor. *Oh, what were they going to do?* she wondered, lacing her fingers together and beginning to wring her hands in consternation. The balloons, the streamers, the presents, the cake . . . *Oh, merciful heavens!* Everyone had obviously gone to a herculean effort since breakfast to get this little party ready for them. Even Olivia and Ryan, who both had full-time jobs, seemed to be in on the secret.

The Colonel approached and patted the baby on the head. "And who might this be?" he cried, peering into her face.

"This is CarlyAnn." Sean hiked her a little higher in his arms.

Cocking his head, the Colonel glanced around. "Then where is little Caroline?" he wondered and scratched the wild fuzz at his crown.

Sean lifted and dropped a shoulder. "I don't know, sir."

Clearly puzzled, the Colonel's slack lips opened and closed rhythmically as he trained his watery gaze on Sean.

"You don't *know*? Good grief, man!" he cried then coughed like a roaring lion, his wispy mane fluttering with his exertion. "Go find her!" he gasped. "Call out the reserve unit and don't spare the mules."

"Uh . . . yes sir." Sean tossed a look at Julia and silently mouthed, *the mules?*

Covering her face with her hands, Julia bowed her head. This was too much, she thought, feeling suddenly frantic. Now they were supposed to have *two* children? When had *that* happened? Remembering Hattie's advice, she began to pray.

"Oh, Lord," she most earnestly began, murmuring under her breath, "please help all these sweet folks to understand. Please help them not to be too hurt or disappointed when we have to tell them the truth."

"Good man," the Colonel shouted. "They'll have the youngster back in no time." Then the Colonel cleared his mind of that topic as easily as he cleared his throat. Tugging on his watch fob, he checked the time. "It's nearly nineteen hundred hours," he croaked in his scratchy tenor. "Time's a-wastin'! Let's get this show on the road. Anyone care for a piece of cake?" he wondered, clicking and sucking at his dentures as he eyeballed the fuzzy coconut frosting.

Still calling upon the Lord for assistance, Julia surveyed the party scene with one open eye as she wondered what to do. Everyone was already having such a wonderful time. *How Lord,* she wondered dismally, *can we possibly ruin all their loving work with the cold, hard truth?* Especially the older folks. They were just so darling and sweet.

Agnes smacked the Colonel's hand as he went to pinch a bit of frosting from the toe of the baby-bootie cake.

Smiling invitingly, Olivia and Ryan were standing behind the extensive buffet table, poised to serve. "Come on, everyone," they beckoned, lifting the serving lids and allowing the aromatic steam to escape.

A cauldron of chili, a mountain of cornbread, a pile of shredded cheese and chopped onions, a tub of fluffy rice, and oodles of freshly cut fruit and veggies with various dips graced the filled-to-bursting table.

"Come and get it while it's still piping hot," Olivia encouraged.

Rahni patted the coffee urn. "Decaf," she proudly announced.

An ancient, toothless dog Julia had never seen before was sprawled under the buffet table. Limply lifting his head, the animal spotted the newcomers, gave a rusty woof, and—eyes rolling back in his skull—seemed to pass out. Julia's stomach twisted painfully. *Good grief!* It seemed that even breaking the news to the poor old dog would be wrenching.

"Don't mind Otis," Ryan advised. Noticing Julia's

expression, he gestured to the dog. "He's depressed. Sometimes older dogs are prone to that."

"Oh." Julia nodded but feared that depression was the least of Otis's problems.

The Colonel trained his bloodshot gaze on the animal and grunted. "I know just how you feel, old man."

"Well, come on, everyone. If God is your father, please call home!" Hattie instructed with a throbbing giggle and bowed her head.

Never wanting to interfere once Hattie began communicating with her heavenly Father, everyone else in the room followed suit. Otis began to snore lustily under the buffet table.

"Dear Lord," Hattie began, "we wanted to take a moment to simply bless you and to thank you for your bounty. Lord Jesus, we pray that you will grace our gathering today with your precious presence. Thank you so very much, Lord, for the opportunity to fellowship together as a family, of sorts, and to support and uphold Don and Beulah to you in their time of need. And, Lord, thank you for hearing our prayer for their little Caroline last night. She is such a blessing to us all. Lord, we ask that you take this food and bless it to our bodies. In your name we pray, amen."

A chorus of amens reverently filled the air.

Blinking as she opened her eyes, Hattie once again urged everyone to take a plate and fill up.

Sean grabbed Julia by the arm and drew her into a corner. Together they huddled, wide-eyed with worry.

Plowing a hand through his hair, Sean said, "I'm beginning to think that everyone is under the mistaken impression that we are CarlyAnn's parents."

"So I've gathered. But *why?*" she hissed. Casting a

furtive glance over her shoulder, she reached out and clutched at the placket of his shirt.

Caught between the two distraught adults, CarlyAnn's little face began to pucker.

With a heavy sigh, Sean shook his head. "Who knows? For whatever reason, we have to set them straight."

"Eeeeesshh." Julia exhaled like a leaking balloon.

"What eeeesshh?" Sean asked.

"I don't know. I just hate to do that to them, that's all." Julia looked pensively around the room. "They've gone to such trouble."

"I know." Sean's cheeks puffed in exasperation. "Look at the rocking stork over in the corner," he murmured. "Looks like it's made of something from the dumpster out back."

"Smells like it too," Julia said, wrinkling her nose.

"My guess is the Colonel."

"Yep." She grinned in spite of herself.

CarlyAnn began to fuss. Joggling her up and down, Sean attempted to keep her from rattling the rafters as she had last night. "Well—" Arching his brows, Sean took a deep breath. "What do you want to do?"

"I don't suppose it would be right to let them go on thinking we are, you know," she blushed, "CarlyAnn's parents." The idea of parenting a child with Sean made her heart shift into a higher gear.

"Nah." He shook his head.

"That would be a sin of omission, huh?"

"Uh, yep." Wrinkling his nose, he grimaced at her. "It sure is tempting though, isn't it?

"Uh-huh," she agreed.

"Well."

"Well."

CarlyAnn squealed fussily.

Sean joggled her some more, causing her reddening cheeks to bounce. "I suppose there is no time like the present."

"I guess not." Julia nodded.

"You want to tell them?"

"No, that's okay. You can."

"You're sure about that?"

"I'm sure. Unless," she hesitated, "you don't want to."

"I don't want to."

She grinned. "Neither do I."

He held up his hand. "Odds or evens?"

Julia thoughtfully pursed her lips. "Odds," she decided.

"One, two, three," he counted, and they each held up some fingers.

"Even," he murmured, tallying up. "You lose."

Julia winced. "Nuts."

"Tough break."

CarlyAnn slapped at their hands and screamed.

Julia *shh*ed and patted her back. "What should I say?"

"What do you want to say?

Julia closed one eye and squinted. "I vote that we only tell Hattie the truth right now and see how she wants to let everyone else know."

"You mean we should not tell everyone else right now?"

"Right." Julia's head bobbed. "I mean, why spoil their fun? They'll find out soon enough."

"Okay. Sounds good."

She looked balefully at the well-meaning group that crowded at the buffet table. "Ohhhh. Man, I hate to burst their bubble."

However, cheaters never prospered, she reminded herself. Besides, the Lord would surely disapprove. And since she'd moved into this house, she'd felt his presence in a most palpable, loving way. No, she couldn't disappoint the Lord like that. Not anymore.

Funny, worrying over a little white lie—especially one that would spare someone's feelings—wouldn't have figured into her decision before meeting Hattie.

Or before having made her pact with Sean over breakfast that morning.

"Yeah," Sean sighed. "I know. I don't particularly want to burst their little bubble either. But it has to be done."

Reaching out, Sean squeezed her shoulder, and Julia felt her mouth go dry. He was so sweet. So understanding.

"If you want, I'll tell her," he volunteered, resigning himself to the unpleasant task.

Julia waffled then shook her head. "No, you won fair and square. I'll tell her."

"Okay, but if you change your mind . . ."

Together they turned and, arms waving, flagged Hattie over to where they stood.

"You kids run along and fill your plates," Hattie chirped as she haltingly reached them. "After all, this party is in your honor!"

"Uh, Hattie?"

"Yes, Beulah, dear?"

Bored and impatient, CarlyAnn squirmed in Sean's arms.

Touching her tongue to her lips, Julia glanced at Sean. Seeing his reassuring expression, she forged ahead.

"Hattie, I'm really sorry to have to break this news to you, especially since you've worked so hard and everything."

Hattie nodded and smiled.

"Right," Sean chimed in. "Really hard. I mean, I can see by the hand-painted signs and the cake and everything . . ."

"Uh-huh, right, right, right," Julia said, an impatient note creeping into her voice. She waved a hand at Sean in a way that she hoped conveyed how badly he was messing up her concentration. This was not an easy task. She needed to think of the most tactful way to present this little bombshell.

"Anyway, this is really hard for us . . ."

"Really hard," Sean agreed, backing her up. "In fact we even thought about not telling you."

Hattie nodded and smiled some more.

"Sean," Julia muttered, "please."

"Sorry."

"Anyway, Hattie—" She paused to collect her thoughts.

"Go on, get to the point," Sean urged.

Julia turned and stared at him. "I'm trying."

"I know, I know. You're doing fine. Just, you know, spit it out."

CarlyAnn began to cry. Loudly.

"I will," Julia huffed. "I'm getting there. Just give me a second."

Sean sighed. "Okay."

Again she paused to marshal her concentration in the midst of CarlyAnn's histrionics.

Hattie nodded and smiled once again.

"Anyway, Hattie, as I was trying to say . . ."

"I should never have held up three fingers," Sean muttered. "I had a bad feeling about that."

"Would you rather do this?" Julia asked, growing frustrated with him.

"No, no. You go ahead."

"Are you sure?"

Hattie placidly watched their verbal sparring back and forth, waiting patiently for them to come to the point.

"Sorry. No. Really. You're doing fine," Sean called over CarlyAnn's caterwauling.

"Thank you." Exhaling heavily, Julia turned and smiled at Hattie.

"Yes, my dearies?" she encouraged.

CarlyAnn screamed and began to swing her feet.

Before Julia could formulate a sentence, Sean proceeded to bare his soul.

"Okay, Hattie, it's like this," he blurted out, shouting over CarlyAnn's outburst. *"I'm not CarlyAnn's father,"* he roared. "And Julia here . . . well . . . *she's* . . . *not* . . . *her mother!"*

"Oh dear," Hattie breathed, her eyes widening.

Everyone at the buffet table turned to stare in open-mouthed shock.

"Good job," Julia muttered drolly. Closing her eyes, she allowed her head to thump against his shoulder.

Well!" Agnes huffed as she helped Glynnis, Hattie, Olivia, and Rahni put away the last of the party dishes. The Colonel and Ryan were in the parlor taking down the decorations, and Julia and Sean had gathered their booty and carted it off to his room.

Adjusting her glasses, Agnes stopped in the middle of the floor and peered around the warm and cheerful kitchen at her fellow boarders. "What on earth do you suppose all that shouting about the baby not being theirs was about?"

The women all murmured under their breath and shrugged.

"I don't know, Aggie," Glynnis sighed, "but I don't believe we should gossip about them behind their backs."

"Gossip?" Agnes yodeled, her eyes snapping. "I don't *think* so. This is most certainly not gossip! Why, after all the time and trouble we went to, I believe we are entitled to an explanation. Whose child is she, if she is not theirs?" Agnes glared accusingly at Hattie. "Hattie, if you hadn't changed the subject so quickly and forced us all to gobble down our chili like a pack of famished vultures, perhaps they would have volunteered the details. As it was, you had them tearing through their gifts at such a frenzied pace my head was fairly whirling."

Hattie smiled benignly.

"Better than having you tear through their personal life," Glynnis muttered.

Rahni giggled then cast her eyes respectfully to the floor. It seemed her English was beginning to improve some.

"I would not have done that," Agnes harrumphed.

"Perhaps," Olivia offered, "the baby is adopted?"

Glynnis handed Rahni the last of the dry dishes, and she and Hattie hung up their dishtowels. The sunny, old kitchen fairly sparkled from the loving care the five women had put into sweeping, mopping, and polishing.

Agnes, having completed her tasks, considered Olivia's words and tapped her pointed chin speculatively with her fingertip. "No-o-o. He distinctly said that he was *not* the father and that she was *not* the mother."

"Maybe they are in some kind of complex custody battle," Glynnis said with a beleaguered sigh. "At any rate, what does it matter? The child needed some things, and just as the Lord would have us do, we provided for the need."

"Very good, Glynnis," Hattie said and nodded with approval. "The child will have to read eventually, yes."

Everyone was silent for a puzzled moment while Hattie reflected on the shower.

"You know," Hattie mused, "I've been meaning to bring up the little matter of Don and Beulah's claim that they are not little Caroline's parents."

"Hattie, that's what we've just been tal—"

"Save your breath, Agnes," Glynnis groused.

Hattie continued. "If they are embarrassed about the child's parentage, for whatever reason, it's none of our affair. So," she commanded, much to Agnes's annoyance, "I say we leave them be. Let it drop with no questions or remarks that might make them feel awkward. When they are ready to tell us what is on their hearts, they will. Until then . . ." Pausing, she motioned everyone out the door and snapped off the light, "remember: He who thinks by the inch and talks by the yard deserves to be kicked by the foot."

After having carried their shower gifts to Sean's room and depositing the now-sleeping CarlyAnn into her crib for the night, Sean and Julia flopped into the two easy chairs situated near his bay window and stared at each other.

Julia's eyes traveled over Sean's generally disheveled appearance, and she smiled. He looked as if he'd been through a war, what with his rumpled clothing and tousled hair. He was so cute, sitting there with the baby blanket that Glynnis had knitted draped over his shoulders.

"What," she giggled, amused at his shell-shocked expression, "on earth just happened to us down there?"

"I don't know," he murmured flatly. "But I think that at some point today, I became a husband and a father."

A little jolt of something tingling and unfamiliar zigzagged down her spine at his words. What would it be like to be married to someone like Sean? she wondered whimsically. To have a sweet little girl such as CarlyAnn to cuddle and call her own?

"I bet marriage and fatherhood came easier than you thought, huh, dear," she teased, propping her elbow on the chair's arm and cupping her chin in her palm. As she regarded him, she could see the little lines at the corners of his eyes fork and his dimples deepen.

"Like falling off a log backward, honey," he shot back and grinned, "a big, giant log, rolling down a big, giant hill, into the big, giant ocean."

"That easy, huh?" Julia laughed. "Did you get a load of the way Agnes kept staring in disapproval at the stains on my blouse? It was as if she thought I pulled this top out from under my bed this morning because I had nothing else to wear."

"You're such a slob," he deadpanned, a light of mischief in his eyes.

"Thank you," she murmured demurely. "I try."

Chuckling, Sean leaned forward and pushed the padded ottoman between their chairs so that they could share. Once their feet were cozily arranged, they both leaned back and began to relax. CarlyAnn's light breathing could be heard from across the room, her cute little snores and snorts occasionally reaching them from her crib.

"Would you like a cup of coffee?" Sean asked, his head lolling on the back of the chair as he looked at her.

"No thanks," she sighed. "I'm fine."

"Good, because I'm too pooped to make it."

"I suppose I was going to make it?"

"Yep." He grinned.

"Some husband you turned out to be."

"I never promised you a rose garden, sweetheart."

Julia shivered deliciously, more from his words than from the cool, autumn evening. The little endearment that she'd heard thousands of times rolling off her grandmother's lips took on a whole different quality coming from him.

"Sean?"

"Hmm?"

"What are we going to do with all of our shower gifts?"

"I vote we keep Agnes's gift."

Julia laughed. "Well, you can hardly return a pair of his and her earplugs, especially once they've been used."

"And Hattie's gift. Let's keep that one too," Sean mused.

"Baby-sitting? You're sure you'd want to leave CarlyAnn alone with Hattie?"

"Why not? She's had six kids of her own."

"The fact that she can't hear anything is one consideration."

"Yeah, but Rahni can. They'd be fine," he assured her, waving away her fears. "Besides, I have an ulterior motive."

"You do?"

"Yep. The church concert tomorrow night. Remember? You and I are going."

"Oh. Right."

"What?" Sean tucked his chin to his chest and studied her face. "You look like you don't want to go."

"Oh, no," she hastily assured him. "It's not that. It's just that I thought we'd bring CarlyAnn with us." They hadn't ever spent any time together without the baby in the room. Julia suddenly felt a little shy at the prospect.

"Trust me. We don't want to bring her to this. She'll just howl the entire time. I couldn't do that to the performers."

"You have a point." Julia slowly nodded in agreement. "So," she held up her fingers and began to count off. "We keep the receiving blanket from Glynnis. The earplugs from Agnes. The baby-sitting from Hattie. The shower cap and soap from Rahni for the," Julia paused and giggled, "baby shower. The stuffed puppy from Ryan. The darling swimsuit from Olivia. And, last but not least, the stinky rocking stork from the Colonel, no matter how ugly or dangerous or riddled with tetanus and salmonella, because he went to so much trouble making it out of—how did he phrase it again?—oh yes, recyclables."

"That about sums it up," Sean sighed.

"Do you want to write the thank-you notes, or shall I?"

Shrugging, Sean lifted a hand. "Odds or evens?"

"Oh, no. You're not catching me in that miserable trap again. Once burned, shame on you. Twice burned, shame on me. Besides," Julia giggled, "you'd just tear the thank-you notes out of my hands and scribble your own message because I wasn't writing fast enough."

Sean chuckled. "Are you ever going to let me live that down?"

"No."

"They still think we are married."

"I know." Julia rolled her eyes. "And for some odd reason, the Colonel is under the impression that we have *two* children. CarlyAnn and the mysterious Caroline."

Sean chuckled. "Good luck setting the Colonel straight on that. Once he gets something in his head, there is no reasoning with him. Believe me. I've tried on more than one occasion. He still thinks I was in the service."

"You weren't?"

"Does the fact that I was a boy scout count?"

Julia chuckled and, tenting her fingers, thoughtfully supported her chin.

"Hattie will set them all straight. Eventually."

"As straight as she can."

"Well, let's give her some time. If she can't make them

understand, we can broach the subject over dinner tomorrow."

"No. Let's do it over dinner on Thursday."

"Why?"

"I want to take you to dinner tomorrow night before the concert."

Julia smiled and tried to quell the sudden storm of excitement that filled her stomach at the prospect of a dinner with Sean. She shouldn't be looking forward to it with quite so much zeal. "That would be nice," she murmured blandly, even as her heart zoomed out of control.

Their eyes locked for a long, smiling moment.

A moment in which their relationship changed irrevocably.

A moment in which they both knew deep in their hearts that they had come together for a reason.

For part of a plan that was far greater than themselves.

The phone's sharp, incessant ring brought them out of their reverie and CarlyAnn out of her slumber. Squawking indignantly, CarlyAnn stirred and sat up in bed, her messy curls wild from sleep.

"That would be Kathleen," Sean sighed as the phone rang again. Lifting his feet off the ottoman, he propped his elbows on his knees and rolled his eyes.

"I should be going anyway," Julia said and stood. "Thanks again for the lovely day. Tell Kathleen that we all had a wonderful time."

"I will. I'm sure this will not be the last time she calls tonight."

"Aren't parents funny?" Julia wondered aloud, amused at the practice of calling repeatedly to check up on the baby. Reaching the door, she turned the handle and paused.

"Personally, I don't know why she doesn't just trust me," Sean grumbled, scooting out of his chair.

"Must be a parental thing." Julia waved one last time before he reached the phone.

"Must be," Sean sighed.

8

Do you think we should call?" Julia whispered, an urgent note creeping into her voice.

Leaning against Sean's arm, she looped her hand around his neck and tugged until he leaned toward her. "I think maybe we should."

Wednesday night had arrived, bringing with it the church concert and their first official "date." Although, considering they'd already been through the wringer together yesterday, the awkwardness of most first dates was now blessedly missing. How much more awkward could *anything* else be in comparison to that kooky baby shower? Sean wondered, a droll smile tugging at his mouth.

No, they'd spent too much time together to feel awkward anymore. And amazingly enough, he'd only known Julia since Sunday. It felt to Sean as if he'd known her a lifetime.

Today they'd spent the entire day together, playing with CarlyAnn and picnicking by the lake. The leaves were just now beginning to turn, putting on a glorious display that stole their breath. Sean would remember this day forever. Fried chicken, a squealing baby, Julia's brilliant smile. Even the ants were wonderful.

Only an hour ago they'd shared a most amazing dinner

at the House of McLaughlin, a little historical restaurant nestled in the trees near the church. Candlelight, fantastic fare, Julia's sky-blue eyes, and animated conversation. What more could a man want? he wondered, struck by his good fortune at an otherwise low point in his life and career. This was turning out to be one of the best—albeit wackiest—vacations in his entire life. And it was all thanks to the delightful woman seated at his side.

The delightful woman who was beginning to tug pretty viciously at his tie. "It would only take a second," she cajoled, her breath warm against his ear.

An involuntary wave of goose bumps traveled from his ear to his neck and down his spine. He leaned closer to hear better, although Sean didn't even have to ask what Julia was talking about. He knew. They'd only settled into the church pew moments ago, but his subconscious mind hadn't strayed far from CarlyAnn either.

Glancing around at the slowly growing crowd, Sean frowned. Was there time? The musicians were still tuning their instruments. He knew CarlyAnn was in safe hands with Hattie and Rahni, not to mention the other boarders who seemed to have taken a delighted interest in the baby. Olivia said she would look in on them all. Surely they would be fine.

But still, it wouldn't hurt to call and see, would it? He would certainly enjoy the concert a lot more, knowing everything was going well at home.

"Do you really think we should?" he asked, wondering if he was simply being silly.

"Yes!" she hissed. "I'll do it, if you want." Eyes round with typical parental worry, she looked beseechingly up at him. "Surely there must be a phone around here somewhere."

"There is," he sighed. "I'll be right back," he said, tossing his jacket over the back of the pew and getting ready to stand.

"I'll go with you," she said, her jaw firm with determination. Setting her purse next to his jacket, she waited for him to begin working his way past their neighbors on the pew.

He paused. "You don't have to do that."

She nudged. "I want to."

Sean could tell from the look on her face that there would be no reasoning with her. He'd seen that look on Kathleen's face more than once. A grin tipped his lips. As much as Julia might try to squelch them, her maternal instincts were beginning to bloom.

"Come on then."

"Oh. Uh-huh. Playing peekaboo." Nodding, Sean glanced at Julia. In the background, he could hear the music begin to play through the large double doors opening into the sanctuary. Oh, well. It had been worth it to miss the first number or two, just to touch base with Hattie. "Oh, sure. She loves that. LOVES THAT. Uh-huh.

"Yes, by all means. That was good thinking, Hattie. Good thinking. GOOD THINKING. Kathleen would kill me if she choked. Kill me. KILL ME. Yes. If she choked. Yes. YES!"

Julia grinned.

"So, she's being a good girl? GOOD GIRL? Fussy? Warm?" Sean swallowed and tugged at the neck of his shirt. "How warm?"

Arching a concerned brow, Julia took a step closer and hovered at his elbow, attempting to hear what Hattie was saying.

"Her forehead. Hot? Cheeks are flushed. Hmmm. Hattie, do me a favor. There's a thermometer in her diaper bag. THERMOMETER! IN HER DIAPER BAG! YES! OKAY, GOOD. YES, I'LL WAIT."

"What's going on?" Julia whispered anxiously.

Sean shifted the phone away from his mouth and, leaning against the vestibule wall, shook his head. "I don't know. Probably nothing. Hattie seems to think she's feeling a little warm. Rahni is looking for the thermometer."

"That's normal, isn't it?" Julia asked, more to herself than to Sean. "For the baby to be a little warm?" She frowned. "What does a little warm mean, exactly?"

"I don't know, Beulah. You're the nurse in this crowd."

Julia's grin was strained. "Maybe we should call the number Kathleen left and ask the pediatrician."

"That seems kind of rash for just being a little warm, don't you think?" He exhaled heavily. "Shucks, I don't know." Agitated, he ran his hands through his hair and turned his attention back to the phone. "Yes. That's it. Under her armpit. ARMPIT. YES! It will beep when it's finished. BEEP. Have Rahni listen for it. BONNIE, YES. Okay, I'll wait."

Unconsciously, Sean looped his arm around Julia's shoulders and drew her close. Planting a tiny kiss on her forehead, he closed his eyes. "Say a little prayer," he murmured.

"I already did," she sighed and snuggled closer into his embrace.

"They're on their way home," Hattie announced to the concerned group that had gathered in the parlor to offer advice and prayer. A flickering fire devoured logs in the fireplace as Rahni steeped the tea in Hattie's old rose-and-gilt porcelain teapot. Ryan's latest pupil, an anxiety-ridden toy poodle named Mimsie, sat shivering at Hattie's feet while Ryan ran upstairs for some baby Tylenol for CarlyAnn.

"Well, I should hope so," Agnes piped from her throne near the loveseat. "This child is fairly burning up!"

"She's warm, Agnes," Glynnis corrected, a worried furrow at her brow. "Let's not give in to undue worry, shall we?"

Mimsie whined, nearly vibrating with concern for CarlyAnn. Hiking her little body up on the couch cushion with one paw, she cried and nosed CarlyAnn's limp fingers.

"Even the dog can tell she's burning up," Agnes snapped.

"They don't seem like the worrying type, those two young folks don't," the Colonel mused, thoughtfully clicking his dentures as he lowered himself with slow and deliberate care into the middle of the rocking recliner. "Why, as far as I know, their other daughter, little Caroline, is still missing, and they don't seem the least concerned. More power to them, I say. Lay it at the feet of the Lord. What good does worry do anyway? *He's* in control." The Colonel stabbed a finger at the ceiling and coughed like a sputtering chainsaw.

"Dagnabbit," he muttered. He mopped his brow and watering eyes with an oversized handkerchief then trumpeted noisily into its folds. Next he fumbled among the periodicals lying on the small table at his side, eventually fished out the newspaper, and dragged the rumpled pile into his spindly lap.

"I'm not going to worry," he announced, shuffling through the pages. "I'm simply going to read the paper."

The phone rang so suddenly and shrilly even Hattie started. Mimsie ran to the extension and began to bark.

"Would you be a dear and get that, Colonel?" Hattie asked, waving an airy hand at the phone. "Push star three, then wait for the tone, and then push pound one, zero, zero. That will pick up the call from the main switchboard."

"Arkkk! Arkkk! Arkkk! Arkkk! Arkkk! Arkkk!" Mimsie chirped, running in frenzied circles near the phone. "Arkkk! Arkkk!"

Doing as he was bid, the Colonel reached to the table next to him and, pushing his glasses up higher on his nose, frowned at the phone. "Hmmm," he muttered. Lifting the receiver, he peered at the confusing selection on the push-button pad. "Come again, Hattie," he thundered. "I can't make heads or tails of this contraption."

The phone continued to ring shrilly.

"Arkkk! Arkkk! Arkkk!"

"At ease, animal!" the Colonel hollered.

Mimsie collapsed into a quivering, cowering pile of anxiety.

"Now, say again, Hattie?" Thoughtfully he rubbed his pendulous earlobes.

"Yes, dear. Simply push star, then three, then wait for the tone," Hattie instructed.

"Star? What the devil?"

"Star, Colonel," Olivia encouraged from the couch next to Hattie. CarlyAnn was nestled in her lap or she would have risen to assist him. "It's the one that resembles an asterisk."

"An ostrich?" Hattie queried and patted Olivia on the knee. "No, no, dear. That cannot be right." To the befuddled man, she instructed, "Simply push the star key, Colonel. The little star in the lower left corner."

"Hmm," the Colonel mumbled and began to push randomly at the buttons. "This one here could be a star, I guess. Hello?" he barked into the phone. "Hello? Hello? Hello?"

The phone continued to ring.

"Arkkk! Arkkk! Arkkk!" Mimsie began her frantic circular prancing and hopping once again.

Slamming the phone back into the cradle, the Colonel shrugged. "No one there."

The phone abruptly stopped ringing.

"Well," Hattie said with a philosophical smile, "if it was important, they will call back."

"I don't know why they have to make everything so complicated these days," Agnes groused. "All these buttons and gadgets. It takes a degree in rocket science to simply visit with a friend. Give me back the good old days of rotary dials and party lines."

"Yes," Glynnis said, a note of sarcasm in her tone, "the day the party line died in this town was a sad day for Agnes, indeed. Why, I think it was most definitely her main source of pleasure. She used to spend hours glued to the phone, learning the juicy tidbits about everyone here in McLaughlin."

Agnes was scandalized. "I most certainly did not!"

"Well, will you listen to this?" the Colonel sputtered, tapping at the front page of the paper with his arthritic finger. "It seems there has been a kidnapping right here in our little neck of the woods."

"A *kid*-napping?" Agnes trilled, glad to have the limelight off herself.

"Here in McLaughlin?" Olivia asked, alarmed.

"Close enough," the Colonel shouted, then coughed noisily for a moment. "Just up the road in Montpelier."

"Really?" Glynnis gasped. "What happened?"

Everyone leaned forward to better hear the details.

Even Rahni, who had just finished pouring and distributing the tea, moved to the edge of her seat and pushed her headdress away from her ears.

The Colonel flapped the paper and held it back at arm's length. "Says here that a little girl, just under a year old, was snatched from her backyard 'bout a month or so ago. Says she has blond hair and blue eyes and answers to the name of Caitlin."

"Oh, dear," Olivia murmured, stricken. Her face went white as her heart went out to the child's parents. "What must her poor mother be going through?" she wondered aloud. Obviously, by the tears that sprang unbidden to her eyes, memories of her own ordeal with her husband and daughter's tragic accident had resurfaced.

"Just under a year?" Agnes asked, her voice suddenly loaded with suspicion. "Answers to the name Caitlin?" Her rapier-sharp gaze suddenly riveted on CarlyAnn. "Just what do we know about this child, anyway?" she demanded, dramatically pointing at the child in Olivia's lap.

Everyone's eyes swung to the flushed and moaning child.

"Do you suppose," Glynnis pondered, then shook her head. "No. No. I don't . . ." She pursed her lips. "Hmmm. No."

"Why not?" Agnes demanded. "Just because that boy has a delightful smile and the charm of a United Nations dignitary does not exempt him from skullduggery."

Everyone knew she was referring to Sean.

"Oh, now," Olivia said, jumping to Sean's defense. "Let's not put the cart before the horse here. I'm sure there is a very reasonable explanation."

"He, himself, said that he is not the child's father,"

Agnes pointed out, hot on the trail of a mystery. Miss Marple had nothing on Agnes. "And that the girl is not the child's mother."

Once again, the phone rang, startling them all and causing them to jump.

"Arkkk! Arkkk! Arkkk!" Mimsie began to rotate.

"Colonel," Hattie instructed, "pick up the receiver."

"Receiver?" The Colonel wheezed as he pawed through the periodicals, looking for the jangling instrument. "Ah, yes. Here we go."

"Okay, dear," Hattie continued, contentedly waiting for him to adjust his glasses and cease coughing. Obviously by her placid demeanor, Hattie had obtained the peace that passed all understanding. "Now, simply press star and then three."

"Now then," the Colonel harrumphed, gaping at the phone. "Star?"

"Lower left." Hattie made wild hand signals that were supposed to uncomplicate the matter.

The phone continued to ring.

Mimsie continued to spin. "Arkkk! Arkkk! Arkkk!"

CarlyAnn began to wail.

"Yes, yes, I see that now," the Colonel mumbled, jabbing at the star key.

"Very good, dear," Hattie praised. "Now press the three."

"Three? Three what?"

"The three key," Olivia interpreted.

"The threekee?" the Colonel queried, confused.

"Number *three!*" Rahni finally stood and hollered; then, looking abashed, she took her seat again.

"Ah, yes, here we go." The Colonel found the three.

"Hello?" he shouted. "Hello?" Peering up at Hattie, he held out the buzzing phone. "Flat line," he announced. "No life here."

"Good, good," Hattie said and nodded happily. "Now, push pound, one, zero, zero, and you're all set."

The phone continued its incessant racket. So did Mimsie and CarlyAnn.

"Pound?" the Colonel wondered.

"Oh, for the love of—" Agnes huffed.

"Tic-tac-toe, Colonel," Olivia offered. "Push the one that looks like tic-tac-toe."

"Tic . . ." The Colonel scrutinized the instrument. ". . . tac . . . toe . . . hmm, ah, yes."

"Now, one, zero, zero," Hattie prodded.

"One . . . here we are, zero, zero," the Colonel said and cleared his throat. "Hello? Hello? Hello? Anyone there?"

Miraculously, a woman's voice buzzed across the miles and into the Colonel's ear.

"Thank you, Lord," Hattie murmured.

"Who?" the Colonel shouted into the phone then tapped it with his hand. "Say again? Kathleen? Kathleen who? The baby's mother? The baby's *mother?* The *baby's* mother?" Holding the phone to his chest, he mouthed for the benefit of the group that stared, intently watching: *The baby's mother.*

"Yes," he hummed and cleared his throat into the phone. "I'm here. Yes. *You* are the baby's mother. Yes. Hmmm. Yes. By any chance, was your baby kidnapped?"

The Colonel held the phone away from his ear as Kathleen's horrified cry reverberated around the room. "No, ma'am," the Colonel said, pressing the phone back to his head. "No, she's not here. No. Is the child's name Caroline, by any chance? No? Why? Well, because we've already lost one child here yesterday and were just wondering . . . Oh? CarlyAnn? Yes, now that one is here. Yes. Sick as a dog, that little one. Uh-huh. Your brother? Now, who would he be? Sean? Oh, yes. No. He's not here. No. He's out on a date. With whom? With the woman who lost her child. Little Caroline. We have no idea, ma'am. It made the front page up here in McLaughlin. Orlando? Florida? What are you doing down there, if your child is lost up here? I see. Keynote speaker. Yes, ma'am. Well, not to worry, we have it all under control up here. Yes, ma'am, I'll do that. Have him call you immediately. He has your number somewhere down there in Disney World? All right then. Over and out."

With that, the Colonel set the phone back into the cradle.

"Apparently," he informed his curious audience, "this CarlyAnn child has not been kidnapped. The mother is in Disney World, as we speak, and seems to realize that she left the child up here."

Agnes snorted and squared her shoulders as she mentally hauled herself up to her soapbox.

"Here we go," Glynnis groaned. "Again."

"Oh, Sean, dear, did I mention that your sister called while you were out?"

"No, Hattie," Sean murmured and shifted CarlyAnn to a more comfortable spot on his lap. "But I can't say that I'm surprised. What did she want?"

"Yes, yes."

"Yes?"

"Yes, she had a lovely conversation with the Colonel."

"Uh-oh," Sean groaned. Since he'd returned with Julia only moments ago, there had been a mass exodus of boarders. Rahni had chores, Olivia had an early morning, Glynnis and Agnes needed their sleep, and the Colonel muttered something about checking his mail for uncanceled stamps. Ryan had delivered the bottle of Tylenol and was now out with Mimsie for a stroll.

For reasons he didn't even want to contemplate, everyone except Ryan had looked rather strangely at him when he'd arrived and taken his niece into his lap.

"Here it is," Julia cried breathlessly, rushing back into Hattie's parlor. Waving the scrap of paper with the pediatrician's emergency number that Kathleen had given to Sean, Julia skidded to a stop and took in the scene before her.

Sean, eyes filled with grave concern, sat next to Hattie on the loveseat holding a cool cloth to CarlyAnn's head. The child's plump cheeks were flushed fiery red, and she looked as limp as a rag doll. Julia's heart lurched in fear. *Good heavens!* Something was terribly wrong. But what? She'd seemed just fine when they'd left her with Hattie a mere hour or two ago.

Oh, Lord Jesus, she prayed fervently, *please, please, let this little child be all right. In just such a short time, she's*—tears pricked the back of Julia's eyes—*she's come to mean so much to me.* She sniffed and rubbed at her nose with the back of her sleeve, amazed at the depth of her emotion. How could this have happened? How had she become so involved with these people in such a short time?

How had she begun to fall in love with them?

Swallowing, Julia forced her feet to move. "It, uh, was on your nightstand," she babbled as she began to quickly search the room for the phone, "under a pile of other stuff. I had to look everywhere. Sorry it took so long. I brought the whole . . . diaper bag down . . . with me. I . . . uh . . .

oh, dear," she nattered on, feeling the panic begin to rise. Stopping in her tracks, she looked helplessly at Sean. "Where's the phone? If you like, I'll call the doctor while you take care of CarlyAnn."

"Over on that little table near the rocker." Grim faced, Sean pointed at the antique, never once taking his gaze from his niece.

Striding rapidly to the paper-littered table, Julia located the phone and dialed, only to have the answering service inform her that the doctor on call would call right back.

Julia jumped when the phone rang almost immediately after she'd hung up. After punching in the proper code, Julia picked up the call from the main switchboard.

"Hello. Uh, yes. I'm, uh . . . I have a . . . my friend has a . . . Well, actually my neighbor has a . . ." Julia frowned. This was coming out all wrong. Taking a deep breath she willed herself to calm down. "I'm looking after a nine-month-old patient of yours, CarlyAnn Peterson, and she has a very high temperature. We were wondering what we should do."

Biting her lower lip between her teeth, Julia looked over at Sean. "It's 104. Almost 105." *Right?* she mouthed toward Sean.

He nodded.

"I'm not sure. Can you hold on a second?" Julia covered the mouthpiece with her hand. "Sean, do you know if CarlyAnn has recently had some immunization shots?"

Sean's face scrunched pensively. "You know, I think Kath said she had one of those baby checkups the day before she dropped her off. I'm not positive about the shots, but I think Kath said something about that too."

Julia relayed this to the pediatrician. "Uh-huh. Okay. Yes. We're pretty sure. We think so. We could call the mother, if you want. She's in Florida for a week or so on business. Oh, you'll check your records. Of course." Julia warbled a nervous laugh. "Yes, I'll wait. Peterson. CarlyAnn. Yes."

While she was on hold, Julia watched Sean tenderly holding his niece, pressing worried kisses to her fevered forehead and cheeks. Wasn't Kathleen a lucky woman to have a man like Sean in her family? she mused and fought a lump of some nebulous emotion that threatened to close off her throat. He was really very special. Suddenly, over the baby's head, Sean's eyes found hers and held. As her pulse roared in her ears, Julia knew then and there that keeping her resolve to stay away from him would be difficult, if not impossible.

Shifting her gaze away from Sean's, Julia focused on the notepad by the phone. Her voice was slightly breathless as she picked up her conversation with the doctor.

"The mother's brother, Sean Flannigan. Hattie Hopkins's Boarding House. Yes. Okay. Right. Let me see . . . You want us to give her baby Tylenol and take off her clothes? Call back when? Okay. We'll give it a try. Thank you," Julia breathed gratefully. "Bye." Pressing the phone into its cradle, she strode over to the loveseat and perched on the small settee opposite the little group that had permanently wormed their way into her heart. Quickly she relayed the doctor's instructions.

Sean was already searching for the Tylenol in the bag Ryan had brought down as she had spoken on the phone.

"You know," Hattie reminisced, seemingly oblivious to her young boarders' turmoil, "I went through this on more than one occasion with my own brood. One time, I remember, we had to fill the bathtub with ice and plunk my oldest boy in there. Gracious sakes, his fever was so high you could almost see the steam rise off his body when he hit the ice. Was delirious, he was. Kept saying there were hot bats in his pants." Hattie hooted. "Gracious. That had the whole gaggle of us down on our knees begging for the Lord's help."

Sean arched a fearful brow at Julia.

Hattie warbled on, oblivious to their fear. "If your knees are knocking, kneel on them!" she quoted wisely.

Julia smiled, patted Sean's knee reassuringly, and began to unbutton CarlyAnn's clothing.

Clasping her hands at her bosom, Hattie continued her trip down memory lane. "Of course, I didn't see the humor in the bat talk 'til his temperature came back down. From then on, though, don't you know, any time that child had a problem of any kind, we'd tease him and say 'What's the matter? Hot bats in your pants?' " Hattie's laughter filled the room. "Oh, my! What a night that was. Nearly gave poor Ernie—God rest his soul—a stroke. Ernie never was any good when the kids were sick. He liked to leave the hot bats and other childhood illnesses to me."

Shortly, CarlyAnn was stripped out of her T-shirt, and after several nervous and clumsy attempts, her uncle figured out the correct dosage of the liquid Tylenol.

"Come on, honey," Sean prattled in his best baby voice and poked the dropper between her lips. "Grape. Yum-yum. Deee-licious."

Listlessly, CarlyAnn downed the grape liquid.

Flopping her over on his knee, Sean helped Julia tug her overalls off while Hattie rinsed out the washcloth in a bowl of cool water and reapplied it to the baby's neck. Once she was wearing nothing but a diaper and the damp cloth, Sean turned her back over and cradled her in his lap.

"Her fussiness over the last two days is starting to make sense," Julia mused.

"Uh-huh." Sean nodded and patted CarlyAnn's plump thigh. "I'm sorry about the concert," he murmured, lifting his eyes to Julia's. Their knees bumped together as she leaned forward and touched her fingertips to the baby's brow. "But I'm sure glad you talked me into calling."

"There will be other concerts," she said, shrugging.

Sean's heart kicked his ribs an extra time. The concern in her eyes touched him immeasurably.

"Then you'll take a rain check?" He hoped he didn't sound as juvenile as he felt. For reasons foreign to himself, he really wanted another opportunity to take Julia out.

"Of course," Julia answered quickly then pulled her lower lip between her teeth. She glanced at CarlyAnn. "I mean, you know, if there's time."

"I'll make time." Sean's eyes dropped to his niece. Yes. From now on, he would be making time for lots of things he'd been too busy for in the past. Important things. Wonderful things. Things like concerts at the church and picnics by the lake and fried chicken and a baby's giggle and a special woman's smile and, yes, even ants.

"How you doing, squirt?" he murmured, fingering a silken strand of hair as it lay damply against the baby's brow.

"Bap," CarlyAnn sighed and, reaching up, grabbed his nose. Grinning, the child attempted to sit up.

Sean chuckled, suddenly weak with relief. "Ah. I think maybe you'll be okay after all."

9

Moonlight shivered into Sean's room through the filmy curtains at his window, sending shadows flitting across the sweet face of the sleeping baby. The sounds of fall filtered across the lake: a cricket's song, a light breeze skimming through the trees, dry leaves falling and crunching beneath the feet of the occasional passerby on the sidewalk beyond. CarlyAnn's fever had broken, and she slept easily in her makeshift bed, secure in the knowledge that Uncle Sean and Julia were both keeping watch.

All was peaceful now, as the day drew to a close.

Yes, all was peaceful with perhaps the one tiny exception of Sean's pounding pulse.

Steadying himself against the side of the crib, he took a deep breath, sure that Julia could hear the telltale thunder of his heartbeat. He couldn't be sure what exactly had his chest in such an uproar.

Certainly, CarlyAnn's fever, flirting with disaster that way, had taken its toll. However, truth be told, he suspected that it was the flirting with Julia that had him so tightly strung at the moment. Angling his head, he looked askance at his new neighbor—a small smile caressing her lips as she stood and watched his sleeping niece.

This special woman was an angel. At least she was to

him. So beautiful. So sweet. So giving and thoughtful. It was really too bad that she didn't have a family of her own, although secretly he was thrilled that, like himself, she'd put off that phase of her life.

Yes.

He could picture her with little ones of her own someday. Something told him she would be a natural at motherhood. Something else told him she would be a natural at marriage as well. A loving partner who understood his personal and family needs as well as his drive to succeed in business.

Good grief. *His* needs? He was picturing *himself* as her husband? All these years he'd managed to so skillfully avoid Cupid's arrow, and suddenly he was envisioning the new girl next door as his wife?

His gut tightened as his eyes swept over her profile, silhouetted in the soft white moonlight. With her alabaster skin and hair that fairly glowed, Sean had to tighten his grip on the edge of the crib to keep himself from reaching out to touch her.

What had come over him? Giving his head a slight shake to clear it, he groped for his sanity. He couldn't touch her. He'd only known her for a few days. Not even a full week. What would she think if he acted on the impulses he'd been feeling toward her since the moment they'd met? The impulse to stroke her hair and feel if it was as silky as it looked. The impulse to touch the high bones of her smooth cheeks, to trace them to her jaw line and then run the pad of his finger over her full lower lip. The impulse to take her in his arms and hold her and tell her how much all her help had meant to him.

How much *she* had come to mean to him.

No, he thought, his mind reeling as he willed his

runaway pulse to slow, he shouldn't do any of those things. It was crazy. She couldn't feel the same way.

The baby stirred in her sleep, and slowly pulling his gaze from Julia, Sean looked down into the crib. Her blankets had shifted, so he bent to straighten them, more to keep himself from doing something stupid and immature than any need to comfort the sleeping child.

As Julia watched Sean so lovingly tuck in his niece, she thought that surely her heart would burst with some tender emotion. She had to fight the impulse to move into the circle of warmth that radiated from his body. Had to fight the impulse to slip her arms around his waist and lift her mouth to smile at him then wait to see what would happen. Had to fight the impulse to tell him how she was beginning to feel.

Heavens! What had come over her? She had only known this man since last Sunday, and already she wished he would take her in his arms, hold her close, and fill the void her partnerless life had left in her heart. With each day that passed, this feeling of yearning, this ache to spend time with Sean, grew stronger. No matter how she resolved to steer clear and guard her heart, she felt drawn to him.

No amount of steely resolve had given her the strength to avoid her new neighbor and leave him to figure out his plight with his niece. Why? This question reverberated in her troubled mind. She was a career woman, not a family woman. Why, then, instead of feeling peaceful about the time when she would eventually move on with her career and into her future without Sean, did she simply feel panic?

How could that be?

Stranger still was the feeling that she'd known Sean Flannigan forever. That he'd been created just for her. That their meeting had been no accident. Uncanny how much sense it all made in her heart, even though her mind told her that any future together, with their careers taking so much of their time and attention, wouldn't work. Couldn't work. They were too much alike. Too driven to succeed.

Then why did it feel so deliciously wonderful simply being here with Sean? Staying home from work? Caring for a child?

Goodness!

She hadn't thought about her job for days. That was so unlike her. Before now, even so much as a day off work had her antsy to return. Normally she spent every off moment fearing that the whole business would fall apart without her capable, guiding hand. Especially during the transition periods when she moved from city to city.

But there was none of that now.

Had she lost her senses?

She stared at Sean in wonder. Being here with Sean felt right. It was the same kind of rightness—completeness—that she'd felt when she'd stepped into Hattie's parlor. With Sean, she had the feeling that she'd finally come home.

Confused, she took a deep breath and slowly exhaled. What on earth was she doing to herself, thinking along these lines? Soon CarlyAnn's mother would return, and her own life would go back to normal.

Julia lifted her eyes to Sean's profile as he watched over his niece, and she decided that, since her future seemed a little too bleak to contemplate here and now, she would shove her fears into the back of her mind and concentrate on the moment at hand.

A light breeze picked up outside and swirled through Sean's window, ruffling the curtains. Off in the distance a siren's plaintive wail split the silence.

Leveraging himself against the rim of the crib, Sean straightened and, as if he felt Julia's gaze, brought his eyes to hers in a collision so powerful it left him winded.

For there, mirrored in her eyes, were his own feelings of yearning for something he couldn't quite put a finger on. A relationship? A family? He couldn't say for sure but knew that here were the beginnings of something deeper than he'd ever felt before.

Slowly Sean reached out and touched Julia's hand as it rested on the top rail of CarlyAnn's crib. His fingers curled over hers and tightened. He swallowed, wanting to say everything, knowing suddenly that he need say nothing.

Catching her breath, Julia's eyes darted to his hand then back up to his face as she took a step toward him. Her eyes flashed with expectancy as they studied his. She leaned toward him, straining to see the expression on his face.

Exhaling raggedly, Sean groaned. Tired of fighting against the powerful urges he had to hold her, he drew her into his embrace, locked his arms firmly at her waist, and rocked her to and fro. He buried his face in her fragrant hair and knew that she could probably feel his wildly beating heart against the side of her cheek.

"Thank you," he finally whispered through the shadows.

"For what?" Julia murmured, nestling her cheek against the softness of his shirt.

"For being there. I don't think I've ever been so scared in my life."

"Me either," she admitted.

With his forefinger, Sean tilted Julia's chin up and gazed into her large, luminous eyes.

"I—" he began, but was unfortunately interrupted by the ringing of his phone. He shot a murderous look over his shoulder at the intruding instrument. *Rats*. Shifting his eyes, he scanned her sweet expression. *Double rats*.

"Just a second," he ordered and shook his forefinger playfully. "Don't go anywhere. Please. I want us to talk for a second."

"Okay." Julia agreed, her tone dubious, as Sean bounded across the room and snatched the phone out of its cradle.

It seemed to Julia that maybe it might be a good idea to leave now. Perhaps the phone had rung for a reason. Perhaps she needed some time to cool off. Perhaps she was beginning to get a little too caught up in her fantasies about husbands and children and a family of her own. Perhaps, she thought, as she stood anxiously wringing her hands, perhaps she needed to get back to work. To spend some time back on the job. In the real world. Her real world.

How had she gotten so caught up in this dilemma? she wondered, her stomach suddenly tightening with confusion. She was a career woman. What on earth was she thinking, daydreaming about a future with a husband and a baby? She didn't have time for that. Getting swept up in the idea wasn't realistic. It wouldn't be fair to anybody.

She glanced up at Sean as he sank to the edge of his bed and shoved the phone between his shoulder and cheek. It's just that it was so hard to think rationally when he looked into her eyes the way he did. Deciding to put a little more space between them, she moved to the other side of the crib and stood beside the fair-haired cherub who slept so serenely.

Sean glanced up at Julia and winked. "I'll only be a second," he vowed in a whispered voice. Turning his attention to the phone, he rolled his eyes. "Hi, Kath." His tone was impatient. "Yes, she's fine. She's not sick. No. Really. Just ducky. What do you need?"

"Say what? Kidnapped? Where did you get a crazy idea like that?"

He sent Julia a bewildered look.

"No. Who's Caroline? I don't know. Kidnapped? Really? Well, I guess I'll have to read the paper, then, won't I? Of course not. No. What do you mean, why? I've been busy, that's why. Watching your daughter, what do you think? Dating? Who me?" Sean winked at Julia. "Maybe. Why? A simple church concert. That's it. Well, okay, dinner too. No, I'm not neglecting her. She's right here. Asleep."

Sean sighed heavily.

"Exactly when are you coming back? The end of next week? Saturday? That's a long time to be gone. No, I'm not complaining. It's fine. Really. I've enjoyed having her. It's been fun. And enlightening."

He glanced across the room at Julia, his eyes locking with hers. He smiled that dazzling smile that had her heart thundering again.

"No diaper rash. No. I've been using that concrete white junk you sent along. You owe me a new comforter, by the way. That stuff is vicious. It won't come off. No. Bleach won't work either, Kath. Forget it."

Sean held up his hand and rapidly opened and closed it, signaling Julia that his sister was jabbering her head off. He rolled his eyes and grinned.

"No. She hates them. Come on, Kath. No, I'm not going

to make the poor kid eat any more mushy treats. Gross. Sounds like something you'd give the dog. No. *No.* She's learning to like pizza. Pizza. Yes. No, she hasn't choked yet."

He sighed and looked forlornly across the room at Julia.

"No, I don't put those bows in her hair. Because they're stupid. I don't care if everyone thinks she's a boy. No way. Because she hates them. Yes, she does."

Julia had to suppress a giggle. What a wonderful relationship he had with his sister. Was there anything about this man that she didn't like?

Therein, she thought with a sigh, lay the problem.

"—just a little fever. I handled it. She's fine. The doctor said she's fine. I had to call the doctor."

Sean winced.

"Kath, listen! I said she's fine. Will you listen? *Fine!* Yes! The fever is gone. The highest was 104, maybe 105; I don't know the final number." Grimacing, he held the phone away from his ear. "Criminy, Kath, I'm going deaf here.

"From the beginning? Oh, for the love of . . . Kath, can't this wait? Because I'm tired."

Sean sank to the edge of his bed.

"Because I have other things to do."

He looked meaningfully at Julia.

"More important things."

He snorted. "Did I say CarlyAnn was not important? When did I say that?"

Cradling his head in his hands, Sean exhaled heavily and sent a beseeching look at Julia. Kathleen's voice—now a yammering buzz—filled the room as he covered the mouthpiece with his hand. A doleful expression crossed his face.

"She's going to be a while."

"That's okay." Julia was relieved. She had some serious thinking to do, and try as she might, she couldn't seem to unscramble her jumbled thoughts with Sean so near. Moving quickly across the room, she squeezed his shoulder, gave a little parting wave, and started to move away.

However, Sean had other ideas. Drawing himself to his feet, he tossed the phone on his bed, and Kathleen—oblivious to her lack of audience—didn't miss a beat in her lengthy diatribe. Without a word, he pulled Julia into his arms and angled her mouth beneath his for a quick kiss that left them both breathless.

"Sweet dreams," he murmured, nudging her away.

"Uh . . . yeah," she sighed, feeling woozy and completely confused all over again. Rushing to the door, she made good her escape.

"Don't cry, Kath," came Sean's harried voice as Julia shut his door. "Ahhh, come on. You're making me feel rotten."

Gleeful bubbles of joy surged into Julia's throat as she slipped into her room and closed her door behind her. Leaning against the door, she sighed and touched her lips with the tips of her fingers.

That did it. She was definitely developing a split personality. One minute she was convinced that they were meant for each other, and the next she was certain that prolonging this temporary arrangement was a heartache just waiting to happen. Oh well. She was too giddy at the moment to care.

What an amazing evening. What an amazing man. As she finally moved in a dreamlike state toward her bed, she heard three soft taps on the wall that divided their rooms.

He was thinking of her.

A riot of goose bumps coiled up her spine as she answered his code with three taps of her own.

Later that night as Julia lay in her bed and tried to catch the elusive train to dreamland, she watched autumn clouds scuttle across the sky through her window, occasionally obliterating the light of the full moon.

That was how she felt each time she left Sean's presence, as if a cloud separated her from the light of the moon. It was a sad feeling, filled with more gloomy foreboding than any "new-town homesickness" she'd ever felt before.

What was the matter with her? she wondered restlessly, trying to shake the disturbing feeling.

As she tossed and turned and beat her poor, innocent pillow to a fine pulp, it suddenly occurred to her that she needed some advice. Sitting up straight in bed, she stared out the window and wondered if it was too late to call her grandmother.

Peering at the illuminated numbers on her clock, Julia did some mental calculations. Just after ten-thirty here. In Seattle it would only be seven-thirty. Surely Gram would still be up.

Tucking her pillows beneath her back, she reached for the phone and automatically dialed the familiar number. A golden glow suffused her little room as she turned on her bedside lamp. She could still hear the low tones of Sean's chocolaty voice filtering to her through the wall as he spoke with his sister. It was as comforting as it was confusing.

Her grandmother picked up on the second ring.

"It's me. Have you got a minute?"

Julia sighed with relief at her grandmother's soothing voice. Thank God Gram always had time for her.

"What were you up to? *Wheel of Fortune?* Oh, I like that one too. Before and after? I can never figure those out. You did? Why don't you get yourself on that show and win us some money? Yes, us. You wouldn't? Well, there goes your Christmas present. It just so happens that I picked out a nice Cadillac for you. Was too. Uh-huh. Well, now you'll never know." Julia giggled.

"Me? Oh, nothing. I just wanted to hear your voice. Really. No, really. You really are as tenacious as a pit bull; you know that, don't you?" Julia snorted. "You *would* take that as a compliment.

"Okay, I'll spill, but you have to promise to be objective. Objective. Yes. Because I know how you feel about career-driven women. Well, of course I know you love me and Mom. I also know you wish we were both a little more . . . I don't know . . . settled."

Julia absently twisted a loose thread on her sheet.

She took a deep breath. "Okay, here's the deal. I've been helping my neighbor with his niece. Sean. Yes, the one you think I have a crush on."

Julia laughed. "Grammy, cut it out. You're not helping. No. Because, if you had a boyfriend, I wouldn't make smooching sounds on the phone to you." Cheeks flaming, Julia remembered the kiss Sean had given her right before she'd left. Her lips still tingled.

"Did I say he was my boyfriend? No! When did I say that? Okay, listen. His sister had to go to Florida on business, and she left her nine-month-old baby with Sean. The father? Martin. He's in Alaska on business. Yeah, they do sound a little like Mom and Dad, don't they?"

Julia pursed her lips reflectively as she listened to her grandmother reminisce about the times her parents had left her with Grammy when she was just a baby. Vaguely Julia remembered feeling abandoned and vowing that she would never do such a thing to her own child.

And, so far, she hadn't.

"Well anyway, I've been helping him take care of her. Not much. We've sort of been figuring it out as we go."

She paused and considered her grandmother's question.

"Fun. Lots of fun. A ton of fun actually. In fact, that's the reason I called. I'm having too much fun."

Groaning, she flopped miserably back against her pillows.

"Well, I mean that I'm enjoying myself so much I'm beginning to wonder who I am anymore. Yes, that's it exactly. I never knew how wonderful taking care of a child could be. Well, okay, yes. Spending time with Sean is cool too. Too cool."

Julia passed a hand over her brow.

"Because I'm going to have to go back to work in another week. So will he. We won't have time for a relationship. Because I put in too much time at the office. So does he. It wouldn't be fair to anyone to pursue this . . . this . . . thing that seems to be happening.

"Uh-huh," Julia sighed. "Yes. Right. No. I haven't done that." She exhaled heavily again as she finally allowed herself to be honest. With her grandmother. With herself.

"Because, along with everything else that matters in my life, I've put God on the back burner. I don't know. I guess I figure I'll get to him when I have more time. No, I never have more time.

"No. I haven't prayed about it.

"Nope. I haven't turned it over.

"Uh, no-o-o. I haven't asked anyone to pray for me.

"No," she sighed. "I haven't done that either. But I will. This Sunday morning. Yep." She laughed. "With Sean, yes. I did manage to do some thinking about changing my priorities. That's a start, isn't it?

"No, I don't know how he feels."

Julia lifted and dropped her shoulders as she allowed her gaze to focus on the harvest moon.

"I think maybe he's beginning to feel a little something." She bit her lower lip. "But, like me, he's a busy guy. I think both of us need some serious counseling or prayer or," Julia laughed, "a hammer to the head or something.

"You will?" Julia closed her eyes and felt the tears well in her eyes. Rapidly, she blinked them back. "Oh, Grammy, you're such a love." Knowing that her grandmother would be praying for her made all the difference. "I will. I promise. I'll do it tonight. As soon as I hang up. I promise. Uh-huh."

Julia frowned. "The bonus round? Oh, no, you don't want to miss that." She smiled a melancholy smile. "You will? Tonight? Thanks. I'll be asleep, but it's nice to know that someone is on duty even then.

"I love you too, Grammy. Okay. Good night."

Slowly replacing the phone into the cradle, Julia flipped back the covers and swung her legs to dangle over the edge of the mattress. It was time to get down and have a serious conversation with her maker.

She'd meant to do it a long time ago. Entertained the idea. But just never seemed to actually get around to it. Perhaps she was afraid to let God call the shots on something so important to her.

After all, she thought, fearfully clutching the blankets

into a wad, what if he thought it best that she stop seeing Sean? Forever. Her heart surged into her throat.

What if he thought she was one of those people who wasn't really cut out for family life? After all, she never really had much of an example with her own folks. What if God knew that this particular talent wasn't up her alley?

Stop it, she told herself, and hopping out of bed, she ran to the window, threw up the old-fashioned sash, and took a deep breath of cool air. Peering up into the heavens, she suddenly knew why she was feeling so afraid.

It was easy to trust God for things that didn't matter.

But it was hard, she was finding, to place the future of her heart in her Lord's hands. She felt a lump growing in her throat and suddenly wished for Hattie's unwavering faith.

"I'm so sorry, Lord," she murmured, trying to swallow past the tightness there. No wonder she was feeling so up in the air. So confused. So fearful. She wasn't trusting the Lord to take care of her. To provide for her and ultimately give her what was best for her life.

Just like so many times in her climb up the corporate ladder, she was acting like one of the disciples, standing in the boat with Jesus, panicking because she didn't know what was going to happen next as the wind began to howl and forgetting to trust in God. Well, in her career, the Lord had bailed her out of more Seas of Galilee than she cared to admit. Certainly her personal life would be no different.

She simply had to ask. A sudden sense of peace washed over her at the realization.

Where is your faith?

The question Jesus asked his disciples after he commanded the storm to subside echoed in her mind.

Ever since she'd become involved with Sean and his niece, Julia had been in an emotional turmoil. Like a storm swirling over the sea, she felt torn between the comfort zone of the career life she was accustomed to and the taste of family life for which she was beginning to yearn.

And she knew she would continue in this miserable vein until she turned the whole thing over to God. Stepping over to her bed, she dropped to her knees and clasped her hands beneath her chin.

"Oh, Lord," she whispered. Tears stung the backs of her eyes as they always did when she felt his presence. "Lord, you tell us that you won't step in and handle a situation in our lives until we ask you to. So, Lord, it is with great relief and a little fear that I turn this problem over to you." Julia swallowed hard. A tear squeezed its way passed her lashes and splashed on her hands.

"I'm only sorry that I didn't do it sooner than this. Then maybe I could have avoided worrying so much about the future. Lord, like my parents before me, I've always seen myself as a career person. Aside from my grandmother, I don't really know anything about real family life. So," Julia sighed, "the idea is kind of scary to me. I mean, I didn't really have that great of a parental role model. Not that my parents were bad," she quickly amended. "It's just that they were . . . well," Julia shrugged, "you know, busy, I guess is the word.

"So, Lord," she continued reverently, "I don't know if I'm cut out for family life. I don't know anything other than the business world. But I'm sure you probably figured that out when I put CarlyAnn's diaper on backward." She sighed heavily.

"Anyway, Lord, I don't know what I want anymore, but the idea of a future without Sean is incredibly depressing.

So, if it's not meant to be, please give me the strength to endure, because—" Julia sniffed as another tear rolled down her cheek and wet her hands. Her voice was broken as she continued, "—I can scarcely believe it, but I think I've gone and fallen in love."

10

Lazily, one day of fall slid into the other, and in what seemed like a blink of an eye to Sean and Julia, a week had passed, and it was once again Sunday afternoon. And in that whirlwind passage of time, only their nights had been spent apart.

Since deciding to reexamine their priorities, both of them had made good on their promises to turn the future of their relationship over to God. For now, they would spend what little time they had together and sort out what might happen later, after Kathleen returned and Sean and Julia went back to their respective careers. Surely God would see them through, no matter what. No use worrying about the future, they each figured. Tomorrow would take care of itself.

Julia, especially, enjoyed a newfound peace in this attitude of faith. So the past few days had been filled with wonder, the powerful wonder of blossoming love and the precious wonder of baby love. With each passing day, Julia tried to envision her future without these things and couldn't. And with each passing day, Julia watched Hattie and learned, from an expert, the art of faith.

The fact that CarlyAnn slept through the numerous trips to the petting zoo, the children's museum, the maple syrup festival and pancake feed, not to mention the story hour at the library, did not daunt Julia and Sean. A whole new world of experiences opened itself up to them, and doing these things together only served to enhance their pleasure. Julia would never forget the surge of happiness that swelled in her heart when she overheard a woman at the country market exclaiming over what a lovely little family they made. Never had she felt as if she belonged quite so well.

Not even with her grandmother.

And the closer she grew to Sean, the more at home she began to feel in his tiny room and in the process of sharing the care of his niece. Sometimes, much to her mutual chagrin and delight, Julia couldn't be sure with whom she'd managed to fall more deeply in love: the chubby bundle of shrieking joy or the baby's wonderful uncle.

It was for precisely that reason that Julia felt so unusually bereft when Sean announced that he and CarlyAnn were going to lie down for an hour or so after lunch that lazy Sunday afternoon and catch some z's. Suddenly finding herself at loose ends, Julia wandered down the hall toward the front porch, an afghan, a novel, and an apple in tow. She wasn't sleepy enough for a nap, but relaxing in a wicker chair and watching the leaves fall sounded vaguely appealing. Though not nearly as appealing as spending time with Sean, she thought ruefully.

Perhaps this would be good for her. Perhaps she needed to remind herself that she could still enjoy life without using his charismatic personality as a crutch for her loneliness. Perhaps she would even go sightseeing all by herself tomorrow, she thought in a sudden fit of independence.

Nah.

Julia shook her head. Where Sean was concerned, she was hopeless. She didn't have one ounce of will power when it came to him, she mused with a sigh. And worse yet, she didn't even have the decency to be disgusted with herself.

Opening the front door, the brisk, clean-smelling autumn air greeted her along with the sound of Agnes and Glynnis arguing from the sitting area on the porch. Spying her as she stepped into the sunshine, Agnes beckoned her over with a fluttery hand.

"Come here, dear," she commanded, "and settle an argument for us, will you?"

At some point during the last week, everyone who lived in the boarding house had finally come to the realization that CarlyAnn was Sean's niece and that Julia was simply their friend and neighbor. Blessedly, from that time on it was business as usual, much to their mutual relief.

"I'll do my best," Julia murmured, a light smile touching her lips.

Moving across the porch, she joined the Ross sisters in the wicker grouping that faced the rose-covered gazebo and shimmering blue lake. The view was incredible: oranges and golds and, as a backdrop, shades of green from forest to emerald. Here and there a few cottony clouds floated lazily by in the sky but did not interfere with the dazzling sunlight.

"What's the . . . discussion about?" Julia asked as tactfully as she could. Settling in the wicker chair between the two elderly women, she curled her legs beneath her and, draping the afghan over her knees, made herself at home.

"Dropping in," Agnes sniffed.

"Dropping in?" Julia repeated. A tiny frown marred her brow as she glanced back and forth between the pair.

"As in . . . *un*announced," Glynnis bristled.

Feeling like the moderator on *Point, Counterpoint,* Julia mentally took off her shoes and tested the waters with a tentative toe. "Golly, now, that's a tricky subject. Who is pro, and who is con?"

"Pro," Agnes snapped. "I don't see a thing in the world wrong with us going over to visit Bea this afternoon. She lives right around the block, and I don't mean to boast, but I think she enjoys the company."

"That's simply because she's too polite to say otherwise, Agnes," Glynnis informed her. Grasping Julia's hand in hers, Glynnis captured her attention. "Agnes knows that since Sunday is the day of rest, Hattie fixes sandwiches. Bea, on the other hand, puts on the feed bag for her husband and family. Every Sunday, Agnes just 'happens' to be in the neighborhood about the time everyone is washing up."

Agnes's head reared back, and her eyes blazed. "I most certainly do not!" Grasping Julia's other hand in hers, Agnes battled for her attention. "In my day, we didn't have telephones and other contraptions that keep people apart. In my day, we would drop in now and then to visit. To share a cup of tea. To enjoy each other's fellowship."

"Well, this is not your day anymore, Agnes!" Glynnis cried. "That's why Al Bell invented the phone—to keep people like you from showing up, unannounced."

"Well, I never!"

As if watching a tennis match, Julia looked first to her right, then to her left, then back to her right, then back to her left once again.

"Agnes, admit it, sometimes you don't even knock." To

Julia, Glynnis confided, "She just *yoo-hoo*s her way into the house until she finds some poor, unsuspecting soul. I'll never forget the time she found Mr. Miller across the way busily at work on his crossword while doing his . . . er . . . daily business in the bathro—"

Agnes's head suddenly looked as if it was engulfed in flames of mortification. "That was not my fault! The man said, 'Come in'!"

"Come into the *house*, Agnes, not come into the *bathroom!*" Glynnis rolled her eyes. "And then there was the time she couldn't find Bea, so she made herself at home in Bea's kitchen to wait. While she waited, she not only answered their phone, she read all of their personal mail and then, finding a rough draft of a letter Bea's granddaughter was in the process of writing, proceeded to redline it!"

"I'm a former English teacher," Agnes defended herself, pulling on Julia's arm. "I was only trying to help."

"Help? Agnes, you told that poor child she should give up her dreams of becoming a nurse. You said that with her simple personality, she would make a lovely waitress."

"She *would* have made a fine waitress!"

"No thanks to you, she's a doctor now. Agnes," Glynnis continued, "the point I'm trying to make is, not everyone enjoys the surprise of your unsolicited advice and unexpected company. Perhaps if you could give proper warning, you might be better received."

"Give me one good reason why I should go all the way to the phone and call, when I'm right there in the neighborhood?"

"So people will have a chance to hide their mail, for one thing. And, for another, you might walk in on someone in the . . . the . . . *altogether!* Have you ever thought of that?"

Tugging on Julia's hand, Glynnis snorted, "I bet she's

never thought of *that!* And what about people who are sick or asleep or exhausted or have work to do or company or—"

"What kind of a dodo would walk around the house in the middle of the day in their birthday suit, I ask you?" came Agnes's shrill query as she pulled Julia closer to her seat.

"Someone who wanted to take a shower!" Glynnis snapped and pulled Julia back.

"Ladies, ladies!" Julia cried, artfully extracting her arms from their clutches.

"Well," Agnes demanded. "Who is right?"

Julia shook her head. "I'm no King Solomon, but I think you both are, in your own way."

"Both?" Glynnis asked, lifting her brows in amazement.

"Yes," Julia nodded. "On the one hand," reaching out, she patted Glynnis's hand, "you are right about the etiquette issue. I think everyone from Dear Abby to Miss Manners advises people to let the party you wish to visit know of your intentions to do so. That way, they don't have to rearrange what could be an important schedule to drop everything and cater to your needs."

Glynnis shot Agnes an I-told-you-so look.

Suitably miffed, Agnes blinked down at her hands.

"On the other hand," Julia continued and patted Agnes's hand, "I think it's wonderful that you enjoy visiting people and socializing. In the Bible, didn't Jesus chastise Martha for working so hard and not simply enjoying a good visit? Her sister, Mary, was very much enjoying their fellowship, but poor Martha was too stuck in the rules to just go with the flow."

Agnes's slow smile was tremulous.

Julia continued. "And wasn't it Barbra Streisand whose song said, 'People who need people are the luckiest'? And I'm sure, Miss Agnes, that when you visit, you bring lively conversation and good, sound advice with you."

Agnes's eyes grew suspiciously bright, and her expression softened. "I only drop in because I'm afraid Bea will be too busy to make time for me. She has such a full life, with her husband—" she continued haltingly, sniffing into her handkerchief and dabbing a bit under her glasses at her watering eyes, "—and children and grandchildren. Those," she smiled a wobbly smile, "are things I never had, you know." Her pointed chin quivered.

Julia snuggled under her afghan and turned to study Agnes's face, curiosity making her bold. "Do you mind," she asked gently, "if I ask why you never married?"

"Oh, no, no-o-o. I was very career minded back then." Her prunish face twisted sorrowfully at the memories. "A real 'woman before my time' and all that rot." Her mind drifted for a moment as she tucked several gray tendrils back into her tidy bun. "But I tell you right now, young lady, if I had it to do all over again, I'd marry that fella who asked me, have a few children I could call my own, and leave the schoolteaching to someone else."

Glynnis stared at her sister as if she didn't recognize her. "You would have?"

"If I had it to do all over again, I most certainly would. Life speeds by far too quickly to throw it all away on a career that won't love you back in your old age."

Unbeknownst to Agnes, her words hit their mark in Julia. Is that what she'd been doing? she wondered as she stared, unseeing, out over the lake. Throwing her personal life away for the sake of a career?

"I had no idea that's how you felt, Aggie," Glynnis murmured.

"Why do you think I was always dropping in on you when Edward was alive?"

"I thought you were trying to drive me batty."

Agnes rolled her eyes. "I wanted to be around you and Ed. And you never seemed to get around to inviting me."

It was Glynnis's turn to be in the hot seat. Taking a deep breath, she shook her head, a smile of regret tipping her lips. "We did have some good times, back then, didn't we, Aggie?"

"Yes, Glynnie, we did."

The sisters took no notice of Julia's silence as they chattered down memory lane together, reminiscing fondly, bickering occasionally, but all with a little better understanding of each other now.

Julia found her mind wandering back to the church service that morning. The message, oddly enough, had been on the importance of family. It was uncanny how, no matter where she went to church or when she went to church, it seemed that the pastor was speaking directly to her. A brief passage from the sermon that morning had stayed with her, and as she sat, unhearing and unseeing, she mulled the psalm over in her mind.

Unless the Lord builds the house, those who build it labor in vain. Unless the Lord guards the city, the guard keeps watch in vain. It is in vain that you rise up early and go late to rest, eating the bread of anxious toil; for he gives sleep to his beloved. Sons are indeed a heritage from the Lord, the fruit of the womb a reward.

Was she toiling in vain? She glanced at Agnes, alone in her dotage with Glynnis. Did their friend, Bea, with her large, loving family, know something she didn't know? She was beginning to think so.

This new way of looking at life excited Julia. Nearly as much as it terrified her.

Later that afternoon, after the Ross sisters had taken themselves off to Bea's house for a prearranged visit, Julia sat staring at the lake and thinking. And praying and thinking and praying some more.

She was becoming acutely aware that she was arriving at a crossroads in her personal life. God was pulling her close and urging her to make some changes. She could feel it. She simply didn't know why.

"I don't understand what you expect of me, Lord," she murmured into her tightly closed fists. A giant lump began to form at the back of her throat, and cleansing tears sprang to her eyes.

"But I know you must have some kind of plan for my life, a plan that doesn't necessarily have anything to do with Gerico Industries. That's so hard to believe, Lord." Her voice faltered with emotion. "I don't even know if I want to believe it. I mean, after all, I've worked so hard to get where I am. I can't believe that you would want to take that all away from me." She paused and sniffed and wiped her eyes on her sleeve. "Oh, Lord," she sighed raggedly, "I still don't understand how Sean fits into this murky picture.

"Grammy says that you came so that we could live life more abundantly. She says that you never simply tear things away from us but that you are more of a delicate surgeon, removing stumbling blocks in our relationship with you as you prepare our hearts. So, Lord," Julia hiccuped, "please, please, prepare my heart. For whatever you have in mind to . . . ," she sighed, ". . . remove."

After a much-needed nap, in which he slept the dreamless sleep of a rock, Sean finally roused and sat up in bed. Peering at the clock on his nightstand, he started.

Good grief! Doing a quick double take, he ground his fists into his fuzzy eyes and looked again: *4 P.M.?*

4 P.M.!

What?

Bolting upright in bed, he suddenly realized he'd been sleeping for more than four hours. What about CarlyAnn? Who'd been taking care of her? For pity's sake, how could he have let this happen? he wondered, frantically tearing back his covers and stumbling to CarlyAnn's crib.

Oh, merciful heavens! The scenario was worse than he expected, he thought dazedly, raking a hand through his sleep-tousled hair as he stared down at the lifeless form of his niece. *CarlyAnn wasn't moving!* Not even a little bit. It didn't even look as if she were breathing anymore. And her skin had taken on a pale, sickly pallor in the late autumn light.

Something was wrong. Very wrong. This child, in his experience anyway, never slept more than an hour or two at a time. A sick feeling filled his belly, and his head began to spin. Why hadn't he woken up? What kind of a monster was he, he wondered—his belly twisting into a tangle of dread—falling asleep when his niece needed him the most?

And what about Kathleen?

Had Kathleen called? If she had, he had slept right through it. *Man!* He must have been dog-tired to sleep so long in the middle of the day. Suddenly he had an image of himself as a little boy, groggily waking up from a nap and not knowing where he was and panicking and calling for his mother. Then there was the time he fell asleep on the bus. Good heavens, now his stupid life was flashing before his eyes! He had to get a grip. No.

No, he had to get a doctor.

"Oh, Lord," he prayed under his breath, "please! Help me!"

Frantically he bent down, reached into the crib, and snatched CarlyAnn out, holding her tightly to his chest as he strode on autopilot to the phone.

"Nine, one, one," he muttered, "nine, one, one."

As he advanced toward the phone, CarlyAnn, indignant at being so summarily yanked out of her own deep sleep, yowled angrily in his ear.

Startled but awash with a sudden wave of relief, Sean sank to the edge of his mattress, turned on his nightstand lamp, and looked down into the face of the squalling child. In this light, her skin was its usual healthy pink.

"Thank you, Lord," he breathed in thanksgiving as she took a swing at his jaw.

"Shhh," he murmured, "don't cry, sweetheart. Uncle Sean was just being an idiot. I was asleep, you see, and when I woke up, I was, well, out of it. You'd been asleep for so long I thought maybe something was wrong, and I, well, I freaked." He grinned sheepishly at CarlyAnn as she began to calm. Together they came out of their exhausted stupor and smiled at each other.

"Boy, oh boy! You were really zonked. Me too." Sean wrinkled his nose and winked at her. "We must have been plumb tuckered out."

"Baaaa-baaa," CarlyAnn crowed.

"I don't know what I'd do if anything ever happened to you," he crooned, clutching her soft, pudgy body to his chest and rocking her to and fro. Planting tender kisses over her cheeks and forehead, he stroked her curls and hummed gently. "You have no idea how much I love you, little one," he whispered. "No idea."

CarlyAnn, her smile revealing gums adorned with four tiny teeth, burrowed against her uncle's body and, reaching up, patted his nose and cheeks. "Daaa."

Sean's heart melted right then and there. Was there anything on this earth more touching and sweet than a baby's love? The only thing he could think of was a woman's smile. A certain woman, with sparkling eyes and hair like silk, who just happened to live next door.

"Wonder what Julia is doing," he mused, more to himself than to the baby.

"Zzzggggzzzz-laa!" CarlyAnn squealed and kicked her feet.

"Yeah, I miss her too," Sean said. He set his chin thoughtfully on top of his niece's head. Taking one of her tiny feet in his hand, he studied her delicate toes with wonder. "We should probably go scare up something to eat, huh? I bet you're pretty hungry. I know I am."

"Yee-yee-yee," CarlyAnn burbled.

"Okay, lamb chop, let's go get all gussied up and then try to find Aunt Julia. Maybe if we're lucky, she hasn't eaten yet either."

"And then, I was just about to call 911 and demand the jaws of life . . . when she woke up."

Wiping a dollop of mayonnaise from her lips with her napkin, Julia giggled. Sean had made wonderful, thick, roast-beef sandwiches in Hattie's kitchen for them to eat out on the porch in the last hours of the afternoon. Besides the sandwiches, he'd brought a bag of chips, some bananas, and a couple of bottles of juice. Off in the distance, vivid colors lined the sky as the sun began its glorious descent over the western hillside. It was an evening made in heaven. "The *jaws of life?*"

"Hey, I didn't know what was wrong with her. I would have performed surgery on her with my toothbrush if I'd thought it would have helped."

Julia leaned back in her seat—the same chair she'd been parked in all afternoon—and laughed. CarlyAnn was seated in her lap, wrapped in the afghan, contentedly sucking on her bottle. "Remind me never to doze off around you. You might try to remove my lungs with a butter knife or a teaspoon or some such thing."

"Oh, now, with you I'd probably try mouth-to-mouth first. Then," he said with a playful shrug, "I'd remove your lungs."

Julia blushed crimson at his teasing. She remembered vividly his lips on hers. She could tell by the look on his face that he did too. Luckily for them, the Colonel burst out on the porch just then, redirecting their attention before the moment became stilted.

Reaching for the porch's light switch, the Colonel batted off the lights and muttered something under his breath about how there was still more than adequate light from the sun. Feeling his way along the wall, the elderly man squinted into the dusk. "I can hear ya'," he chortled, "so I know you must be there." The wild gray hair he was too miserly to have professionally cut was backlit by the setting sun, giving him a crazily exotic look as he hobbled forward, his twiggish arms extended to the front, fingers fluttering.

"Over here," Sean called. Rising, he strode over to the Colonel and, after they'd performed their ritual salute, led the old man to the wicker grouping where Julia sat with the baby in her lap.

"Ah, yes. There you are, ma'am." He doffed an imaginary hat then wiggled his fingers at the baby. "Caroline." With great care, he eased himself into the seat that Agnes had vacated several hours before and then wheezed like a pair of leaky fireplace bellows. "I'd like a word with you two, if you can spare a moment," he finally got out.

Sean glanced at Julia, then nodded affably at the Colonel. "Sure, sir, what's on your mind?"

"Well, now," he gasped and, fishing around in his breast pocket, finally extracted three unmatched envelopes. "I'm here to invite you two to Hattie's annual boarding-house harvest party. It will be this Friday night beginning at nineteen hundred hours in the parlor. The particulars are all in the invitation."

Lurching forward in his chair, he distributed the envelopes, hesitating a moment before deciding not to waste one on CarlyAnn. "She doesn't read yet, does she?"

"Not yet, sir," Julia murmured. "She can say ba-ba, maaa, daaa, bap, and yee-yee-yee."

As if on cue, CarlyAnn happily screeched. "Yee-yee-yee."

The Colonel cleared his throat. "Now, that's really something, but still, it's not reading in my book. I'll just keep hers and use it again next year," he told them, stuffing the child's invitation back into his pocket.

CarlyAnn grabbed Julia's makeshift invitation and began to chew on it. Wresting it away from the curious little hands, Julia held the invitation up to the waning light of the sunset and looked it over. It appeared as if the Colonel had taken the Christmas cards he'd received last year, crossed out the correspondence with a black marker, and laboriously printed the party information in the remaining space.

"As you can see, young lady," the Colonel told Julia as he watched her scan the information in her card, "it is a costume party with a theme. This year's theme will be 'Great Characters of the Bible.' So," he slapped his bandy legs with enthusiasm, "come dressed as your favorite Bible character. It's a contest, and Hattie is awarding a prize for the most creative costume. So put on your thinkin' caps."

Turning his head, the Colonel squinted at Sean. "I've already planned to come as Moses, young man, so set your plans accordingly."

Sean grinned. "Yes sir."

"Hattie has requested that you two be in charge of parlor games. Will that be amenable to you?"

Julia shrugged as she exchanged glances with Sean. "It's okay with me," she said. She loved any excuse to spend more time with him and CarlyAnn.

"Me too," Sean agreed.

"Good! We shall count on you then." Pulling a tattered notebook and pencil stub from his pocket, the Colonel touched the lead to his tongue and then proceeded to make some energetic chicken scratchings on his paper. "Olivia and Ryan will be in charge of entertainment, and the Ross girls will be in charge of the food. You know, I have to admit that Agnes can bake a mean pumpkin pie when she sets her mind to it." His droopy lips lifted at the thought. Winking at them, he confided, "Don't ever tell her this, because I'd deny it, but that woman has the key to my heart, what with her baking skills." He gave his dentures an enthusiastic sucking and clicking.

Sean chuckled. "Your secret is safe with us, sir."

"Good, good," he muttered, popping his teeth back into place. "Well, I'll be on my way then. I've got some more invitations to deliver before the day is through. I will see you all at breakfast?"

"We'll be there, sir," Sean said, unconsciously answering for Julia.

"Very well," he grunted, bringing himself to a stand. "Good night to you all then."

"'Night," they called as he retreated into the shadows.

"Baaaa, baaeee," CarlyAnn murmured drowsily.

"Well," Julia said with a little chuckle, "it looks like we'd better start thinking up some good party games."

"My guess is that Twister would be out for this crowd," Sean deadpanned.

"I guess," Julia's nod was droll. "Probably don't want to go too far in the sack race direction either."

"Nah." He frowned.

"Musical chairs might be fun," Julia suggested.

"Yeah. If we played really slowly."

Julia giggled. "I know of another fun game where you don't have to do anything physical."

"Sounds right up our alley," Sean said. Leaning forward, he eyed Julia with keen interest. "What is it?"

"I don't know the name of it. Actually, it's very easy. All you need is a dictionary, some paper, and some pencils."

"So far, so good," Sean said around a mouthful of roast beef. "How do you play?"

"Well, everyone sits in a circle. Then the leader holds the dictionary and finds an obscure word that he or she thinks no one else in the group will know. Then he reads the word aloud and tells how it's pronounced. All the others write down a definition. It can be a definition they think is right or one that they make up if they don't know what the word means. Then you put all the definitions in a hat. The leader pulls them out one at a time and reads them out loud, along with the *real* definition that the leader jots down. Everyone else is supposed to vote for the definition they believe is the real one."

"How do you tell who wins?" Sean wanted to know.

"Scoring is pretty tricky. You get a point for every person who picks your definition. And you have to try to pick the real definition, because you don't get a point if you pick the wrong one. You play until everyone has had a chance to be the leader."

"Sounds like something that will start World War III with this group." Sean tented his fingers under his chin, a thoughtful look on his face. "I vote we keep things spicy and play that game."

"Sean Flannigan, you're my kinda guy."

Sean grinned. "I was wondering when you'd get around to noticing."

Ducking her head, Julia's heart picked up speed. He was such a tease. She decided to change the subject before she got all flustered and couldn't put a coherent sentence together.

"We're, uh, going to have to think about picking our costumes for the party. The Colonel said it was a theme party: great characters of the Bible," she murmured. Julia's brow knit as she pondered the possibilities. "Do you have any brilliant ideas?" she wondered, casting a sidelong glance at Sean over the top of CarlyAnn's head. The baby was beginning to doze.

"How about Adam and Eve?" he suggested.

Julia snorted. "I vote we try to pick characters that actually wore clothes."

"Hey, they wore some foliage," Sean said, defending his

idea. "I bet we'd win the prize for the most creative costumes."

"Yeah, right. Can you imagine the look on Agnes's face if we showed up wearing nothing but smiles and fig leaves?" Julia rolled her eyes and laughed.

Sean wiggled his brows. "Oh, she'd act scandalized, but secretly I think she would think it was funny. Underneath it all, I think she's an old softy."

"I think you're right," Julia agreed, thinking back to her discussion with the Ross sisters earlier that day. She'd seen a warmth in Agnes, a vulnerability that she'd never dreamed she'd see in the stern woman. A long time ago Agnes had probably been a delightful woman, filled with the hopes and dreams of youth. It was amazing how time could turn people into curmudgeons, if they let it.

Is that what would happen to her someday? Julia wondered. Would she wake up one day and realize that her life had passed her by and all she had to show for it was a gold watch from Gerico Industries? There had to be more to life than that. Even if she never had a marriage and family of her own, there had to be more time for relationships. With her parents. With friends.

She cuddled CarlyAnn a little tighter. With children. She glanced at Sean.

With a man.

Thoughtfully, Sean chewed the inside of his cheek as he stared with glazed eyes out at the horizon. A look of inspiration suddenly lit his face.

Noticing, Julia studied him. "What?"

"What what?" he wondered, turning to look at her.

Eyes narrowed, Julia scolded him. "You're up to something, so 'fess up."

Sean's grin was mischievous. "I'll tell you later, after I

work out all the logistics, but I think, my dear, that we have the best-costume prize all sewn up." He wiggled his brow. "Pardon the pun."

"We?"

"It's a two-part deal."

"So we will be wearing this character . . . together?" Julia asked dubiously, her heart kicking her in the ribs.

"Yep. Sort of."

"Sort of? Give me a hint," she demanded, a smile tugging at the corners of her mouth. Sharing a costume with Sean all evening sounded like more fun than she should admit. Even to herself.

"Nope."

"Just a teensy-weensy one."

"Nope."

"Ah, come on. I'm gonna find out sooner or later."

"I'll tell you tomorrow night."

"Why tomorrow night?"

"Because I have to gather a few tools and supplies."

Julia groaned. "Tools? Supplies?"

"A few. And a book from the library."

"You're not planning on building an ark, are you?"

"No, but I'll keep that in mind for us for next year."

The way he took for granted that he and Julia would still be here next year, planning their harvest costumes, warmed her heart. If only it were possible. A tiny voice in the back of her head whispered, *With God, all things are possible.*

"I don't have to be the back end of the donkey, do I?"

Sean laughed. "Now, Beulah, would I do that to you? I promise, this is a great idea."

"Well, Don, you do seem to have it all worked out," Julia said with a suspicious smile.

"You're gonna love it."

"Okay." She exhaled the word on a long, slow breath and shrugged. "As long as I'm fully dressed and don't have to be the back end of a donkey, I'll leave the costume designing to you."

"You won't regret it," he promised solemnly.

"Somehow," she sighed, "I doubt that."

11

Can I open 'em?"

"Not yet," Sean murmured, his voice low in her ear as he guided her. "Just a second. All right, take two steps to your left. Okay, good girl." He held the backs of her arms in his hands as he gently guided her toward their costume. "Good. Now turn around, but don't look until I tell you, okay?"

"Ohhh-kaaay." Julia exhaled the word on a beleaguered sigh.

She hoped she sounded calmer and more adult than she felt. His strong hands had the butterflies in her stomach on parade, and the warm breath at the side of her neck sent waves of goose bumps up one side of her body and down the other.

All that Monday long, from dawn until dusk, she'd been waiting in breathless anticipation to see the final outcome of their harvest party costume.

Bored and lonely in her room with the sporadically napping CarlyAnn, she would listen to the myriad noises Sean made as they filtered through the wall that divided their rooms. Every now and again, unable to tolerate the sheer boredom any longer, Julia would grab the baby, prop her on her hip, and look for entertainment among the others at the boarding house.

Unfortunately, nobody was really in the mood to be very social. It seemed that they, too, had caught Sean's costume fever and were busily vying for the grand prize.

At Julia's knock, Agnes had cracked open the door, demanded to know what she wanted, then told her unless it was a matter of life and death to remove herself from the immediate vicinity. There was a sparkle of enthusiasm in her eye that softened her outrageous words—just before she giddily slammed her door in Julia's face.

And even though Glynnis had been much more receptive, Julia got the feeling from the way the older woman guzzled the scalding tea she'd prepared for Julia and herself that she was dying to get back to her own project.

The Colonel had been out in the recycling bins all day and prowling the attic for decorating treasures and pieces for his costume, and Hattie and Rahni could be heard laughing and giggling and up to heaven only knew what from behind Rahni's closed door.

Everyone, it seemed, was deep in secret preparations for the upcoming party, with the exception of course of Ryan and Olivia, who both had day jobs. Ryan was working on a special show-dog project, and Olivia was extra busy this season with her work at the Vermont Department of Travel and Tourism. But even Ryan and Olivia, when they arrived home that afternoon carrying various packages wrapped for secrecy, had little time for more than a cursory hello. Then it was off to their respective rooms to conjure up the entertainment and a couple of prize-winning costumes.

Six-thirty came and went, completely unnoticed by

everyone but Julia, who was bored and hungry. Evidently prodded by an overweight bulldog named Petunia, Ryan had called the pizza parlor and ordered dinner for everyone. After letting the delivery boy in, paying for their dinner, and giving him a generous tip, Ryan had grabbed a slice for the salivating Petunia and one for himself and then, with a mysterious smile, trotted back to his costume plans. Julia and CarlyAnn stared after him, left to sit alone at the massive dining table, nibbling on a slice with Canadian bacon and pineapple.

Julia had had no idea that this party would end up being such a huge deal to everyone. Apparently Hattie was big on parties. According to Glynnis, there were four seasonal parties a year, not to mention the various birthdays, anniversaries, and religious and state holidays. Julia sighed. Friday night was still five days away, and already all the boarders were losing their minds in breathless anticipation.

For Julia, however, the day had been anything but exciting. Without the pleasure of Sean's distracting company, the hours had seemed to ooze along at a slug's pace. Julia could hardly wait to see what on earth he'd been up to all day long. After another slice of pizza and a fizzy can of soda pop that delighted CarlyAnn's spirit of adventure in dining, Julia returned to her room to do some more waiting. As CarlyAnn dozed on Julia's bed, Julia was left with nothing better to do than climb the walls.

Gracious! Who was she these days? She used to love having an entire day to herself. Blessed solitude was a luxury she would look forward to all week. And now? Now she loved every second spent with CarlyAnn and could hardly stand a minute away from Sean. She simply couldn't wait to see his smiling face.

Exhaling heavily, she shrugged. Unwilling to delve into this particular glitch in her sanity, she decided to spy on Sean instead.

What in thunder could be going on in there? she wondered, rabid with curiosity as she pressed her ear to the wall in hopes of discovering a clue. It sounded like the World Wrestling Federation had built a practice ring in his room. Various crashings and thumpings, coupled with his mutterings and occasional yelps of pain, had Julia glued to the wall with interest.

Then, she jumped and screamed when, just beneath the spot where she so intently listened, Sean rapped loudly three times. This signaled that he was finally ready for the unveiling.

Willing her pounding heart to slow, Julia took a deep breath and headed toward her bathroom. On her way, a quick glance at CarlyAnn told her that the baby was down for the count, so Julia slipped to her sink, dragged a quick comb through her hair, freshened her lipstick, checked her teeth for remnants of pizza, popped a breath mint, and then after another peek at CarlyAnn, dashed to Sean's room.

When he greeted her at the door, he demanded that she cover her eyes as he led her into the room. Following his directions, she came to a stop in the middle of the floor and turned around. Her pulse was pounding in her throat. This was so thrilling! She could feel the warmth of his hands on her shoulders as he guided her, and her breathing became shallow.

"Okay," he whispered, unmistakable pride and excitement in his voice, "now you can open your eyes."

Slowly and with great anticipation, Julia uncovered her eyes and focused on the object that had taken every waking moment of Sean's time and attention that day.

"Oh . . . my . . . ," she managed to say, then swallowed.

What in heaven's name is it supposed to be? she wondered frantically, blinking and trying to find the focal point on the mishmash of chicken wire and other metal moving parts tied together by what looked like baling wire and chewing gum. Her mind groped for the proper response. Surely it couldn't be anything that came out of the Bible. It didn't even resemble anything that came out of the bombing of Pearl Harbor. Truth be told, it didn't resemble *anything*. "Oh . . . my . . ."

"Can you tell what it is?" Sean asked, sounding like a high school student showing off his first art class assignment. Releasing her shoulders, he rushed forward and fondly patted his metallic *thing*.

Julia simply couldn't let him down. It was obvious that he'd worked so hard all day long. "Oh, well, yes!" she burbled, forcing enthusiasm into her voice. "I can see exactly what it is!" *It's a giant chicken coop.* She had to bite her tongue to keep from blurting out this idea.

This was the prize-winning costume she was to wear with Sean? *Good grief!* Surely it would tear them both to pieces before the evening was over. Visions of them scratched and bleeding flitted through her mind.

Was it supposed to be a lion's den?

"This is just the rough frame," Sean eagerly explained.

"Aha! Of course. The rough frame." She was still clueless.

"When I get it all covered with papier-mâché, it will really be cool."

"Cool," Julia murmured, squinting at the wires and trying to discern some recognizable shape. "Oh, yes. You certainly have worked hard; that's obvious," she praised for lack of another opinion.

"I figure if I work on it a little bit tomorrow and Wednesday, we can paint it on Thursday. It should be all dry and ready to go by Friday night."

"Wow," Julia murmured. "That soon?" She didn't mean to burst his bubble, but if he could get this chicken coop of his whipped into any kind of shape at all by Friday, it would be because the Lord performed a miracle. She would make sure to add this request to her list of evening prayers.

"Yep," Sean said, taking a deep breath that puffed his chest with pride. "I think we have the grand prize all sewn up." He stretched and yawned, then smiled at her in a lop-sided, endearing way that melted her heart.

"Well," Julia said, her stomach sinking as she nodded her head in agreement, "I can guarantee you that no one else will show up with the same outfit."

Laughing, Sean gazed at her, the warm light of love in his eyes, and suddenly, it didn't matter one whit to Julia that she would be going to the party dressed as a chicken coop. If Sean made it and thought it was a winner, then by golly, she did too.

The next two days whipped by in a tornado of activity for all the boarders as they scurried around, getting ready for Friday night's party.

As Sean continued to work on their mystery costume, Julia dug Hattie's old sewing machine out of the laundry room and began to work on CarlyAnn's costume. A quick trip to the craft store for some sparkly pipe cleaners, a bag of feathers, a bottle of glitter, and a couple of yards of white netting and bleached muslin, and CarlyAnn would look like the angel she was.

Julia had always loved to sew, but she simply never seemed to have the time anymore. Sewing CarlyAnn's costume brought back wonderful memories of her Grammy's arms over her shoulders as she guided Julia's young hands in her first attempts at cross-stitch.

She'd made her first dress at the age of ten and proudly worn it to school. It was a lumpy little affair with crooked seams and crazy top stitching, but she'd adored it. More because she'd made it herself and spent precious time with her grandmother who loved her so well than anything else.

Maybe, she mused, as she ran the fabric of CarlyAnn's costume under the pressure foot with expert fingers, maybe she would buy a sewing machine of her own while she was here in McLaughlin. She could sew herself some clothes. Perhaps even some for Sean, she thought, feeling suddenly cozy and wifely. The Colonel had a few things that needed some mending as well. And making a real dress for CarlyAnn, maybe as a Christmas present, well, that would be a blast. Yes. As soon as she had a spare moment, she would go and get that machine.

Finally, after much secrecy and furtive activity by each and every member of the boarding house, Thursday arrived.

Sean was still laboring away in his room, plastering and painting the giant sculpture that Julia had begun to suspect was a submarine. She hadn't been aware that the submarine had been invented as far back as the Old—or even the New—Testament, but who was she to quibble? She knew next to nothing about nautical history.

Through the kitchen door, Agnes could be heard screeching and flapping about as she noisily fussed over the elaborate hors d'oeuvres she was preparing. And Glynnis clucked and tsked and shouted back, loudly advising her sister to back off. In spite of the bedlam kicked up by the

Ross sisters, the smells that wafted into the rest of the house were tantalizing, causing the Colonel to visit far more often than was appreciated. More than once Agnes had smacked his hand and tossed him, wheezing and laughing raucously as he went, out of the kitchen.

When the Colonel wasn't busy trying to pilfer a bit of this and a bite of that from Agnes's mouth-watering buffet, he was in the parlor, putting up his "decorations."

Having put the finishing touches on the baby's angel costume, Julia poked her head into the parlor for a quick preview of the Colonel's labors. Not noticing his audience, the Colonel—his dentures smiling at her from his back pocket—balanced precariously on a ladder and tied up the banner made from a tattered sheet.

"HAPPY HARVEST!" read the crooked letters. The banner on the other side of the room announced, "GREAT CHARACTERS OF THE BIBLE!"

Colorful balloons hung sparingly from the chandelier and alternately said "HAPPY BIRTHDAY, ROGER" and "OVER THE HILL." The buffet table was covered with funny pages from the Sunday paper. On top of that, a yellowed stack of matching paper plates and napkins from someone's wedding reception decades ago read, "ROBERT AND SUZANNE—1978."

The streamers made of newsprint hung gaily from the ceiling and picture rail, reminding Julia of the endearing baby shower that had been thrown in her honor. A number of Hattie's vases and pitchers held faded and wilting flowers, obviously raided from the dumpster behind the flower shop.

Odds and ends from the Christmas trunk—dragged down for the occasion from the attic—adorned a nook here and a cranny there. Tinsel and autumn leaves had been tossed higgledy-piggledy everywhere and the pièce de résistence was the pair of haphazardly carved jack-o'-lanterns nestled in a bed of moss that leered at her from the buffet table.

Yes, Julia thought with a satisfied smile as Agnes's shouts of dismay over a soufflé gone south suddenly burst from the bowels of the kitchen. The shrieks and screeches interrupted her reverie, not to mention nearly sending the Colonel off the top of the ladder in the process. *Yes, indeed,* she thought and nodded happily, *it was perfect.*

"Man," Sean groaned and flopped into the overstuffed chair that rested near the window in Julia's room, "I'm beat." Kicking off his shoes, he pulled her afghan up under his chin and made himself at home.

It was after dinner on Thursday night. Rahni had washed and dried their laundry, but in her haste to help Hattie prepare for the party had neglected to sort and fold. So Julia, Sean, and CarlyAnn's clothes all sat in a tangled lump on top of Julia's bed, waiting to be put into some semblance of order.

Thinking this was all some kind of giant playground designed especially for her enjoyment, CarlyAnn frolicked in the laundry pile. She rolled hither and thither with gleeful abandon, tossing socks and underwear to the four corners of the room as the mood struck.

"I'll bet," Julia said, tugging CarlyAnn away from the stack of neatly folded towels she'd finally managed to complete, "you've worked hard this week." Grabbing the stack of towels, she disappeared into her bathroom for a moment to put them away before they were tossed overboard.

He snorted. "I would have gotten a lot further a lot faster if Kathleen hadn't felt the need to call every five minutes and give me some more instructions."

Julia chuckled as she came out of the bathroom then paused in the doorway and watched him, appreciating the attraction of this man she was beginning to feel so deeply for.

Sean stretched, his powerful chest expanding as he raised his arms up over his head, the afghan puddling in his lap. He yawned and lightly rubbed his pectorals. Leaning back into the comfy chair, he folded his arms over his stomach and watched Julia work with lazily hooded eyes.

"She also has this nutty idea that there is a kidnapper on the loose up here in McLaughlin who preys on little girls whose uncles aren't keeping an eye on them."

Julia's laughter was slightly breathless. "Can you blame her?" she asked, rescuing a stack of folded T-shirts before CarlyAnn could get hold of them. Moving over to the bureau to put them away, she continued. "I mean, it must be tough to trust your baby's welfare to someone else. Even someone as trustworthy as you."

A slow smile caused creases to appear at the corners of his lips at her words. "Nah," he sighed, "I can't really blame her for calling to check."

"Me either," Julia said, darting a fond look at the delightful child. "You know, I had no idea that in such a short amount of time a person could grow so attached to a baby." The words "and a man" hovered at the tip of her tongue, but she would never have the courage to say them out loud. At least not yet. "I guess I always thought that, in my life anyway, children would be more of a nuisance than a joy."

Sean's eyes strayed fondly to his frolicking niece. "I

know exactly what you mean. I always thought that way too. But that's not the way it is at all, is it?"

"No. In fact, I think I've managed to fall a little bit in love with this little gal for sure."

Not to mention her uncle. Julia bit her lips to keep from giving voice to these wild thoughts. Saying something like that to Sean this early in their relationship would seem far too premature, she was sure.

Moving back to the bed, she rolled CarlyAnn off the pile of jeans the child was currently scaling. She patted the baby's diaper-clad bottom with affection before setting back to work.

"Yee-yee!" CarlyAnn screamed happily, her wispy hair full of static electricity and standing on end. Beaming, her broad smile revealed her tiny teeth. She sat up and extended her arms to Julia, wanting to be held.

"Come here, squirt," Sean said and pounded his lap. "Come sit with Uncle Sean."

"That sounds like a fine idea." Scooping CarlyAnn off the bed, Julia expertly carried her over to her uncle and deposited her into his waiting arms. "Maybe now I can get something done around here."

The brush of Sean's warm hands against Julia's arms as she handed him his niece sent tingles of awareness skittering down her spine. Her eyes darted to his for a millisecond, and she could see a brief reflection of her feelings mirrored in his eyes. Glancing away, she swallowed, then beat a hasty retreat back to her pile of clothes. Her heart beat an erratic timpani beneath her breast, and she struggled to regain her calm demeanor.

CarlyAnn sat on her uncle's knee and looked around, slightly perplexed. It was clear she wanted to get back to her laundry climbing.

"Oh, now, don't be a sad Sally," Sean chided, and tickled her neck and chin until she began to giggle.

"I'll bet Martin can hardly wait to get back to his daughter too. He may not call as often as Kathleen, but I bet he misses her just as much," Julia mused as she spread out Sean's white T-shirt and began to expertly fold it into a tidy square. It was amazing how much she was enjoying folding his clothes. She detested doing her own. Somehow, it just seemed so *personal,* drawing them together in some intangible manner.

"Yeah. He cracks me up. Yesterday he asked me if I sang to her at bedtime. When I said no, he proceeded to teach me this little ditty he'd made up, called, 'Cinderella, I Love You.' "

"Really?" Julia giggled. "How does it go?"

"Well, you sing 'Cinderella,' three times then sing, 'I love you.' Then for the second verse, you sing 'Cinderella,' three more times and wrap it all up with a big, 'it's true'! I guess he just sings it over and over again until she goes into some kind of Cinderella-induced trance."

Julia laughed. "Does it work?" she wondered.

"Seems to."

"How about that?" she said with an incredulous shake of her head. "I'll bet he's dying to see her."

Sean nodded. "I know if it were me, I'd sure be champing at the bit," he admitted.

"When is he due back?"

"Not until Sunday."

"Oh. Must be rough."

"Yep. Kathleen will be here sometime tomorrow though."

"Tomorrow?" Julia asked, feeling suddenly blue. She would miss CarlyAnn something fierce.

"Yeah. I'm not sure the exact time her flight arrives, and she has her car, so I don't need to worry about picking her up," he explained. Then, propping his fidgeting niece on his knee, he began to bounce her up and down, holding her hands in his. "Trottie, horsy, up and down," he chanted as CarlyAnn drooled and giggled in delight. "Trottie, horse, down to town. Careful, horse, don't . . . fall . . . DOWN!"

"Eeeeee!" CarlyAnn screamed, loving this new game, as she dangled backward over her uncle's knee.

Sean grinned. "I know it must be rough on both Martin and Kathleen to be away from each other for so long too. They have a really cool marriage," he murmured, bringing CarlyAnn to his chest and raining kisses all over her chubby cheeks.

"I'm glad," Julia said, melancholy but relieved that the precious CarlyAnn had a secure home life.

"You know, until last week, I didn't think anything of their busy schedule and how it takes them away from each other every so often. But now, after spending a little time with this bundle of joy, I don't know how they do it." He nuzzled CarlyAnn's neck with his nose. "Because if it were me, I'd have come home days ago." He glanced anxiously at Julia. "In fact, I'm beginning to worry that once Kathleen comes to get her, I'm going to go through some kind of horrible baby withdrawal."

Julia nodded sympathetically. "Me too."

"Really?" Sean wondered and looked at her with keen interest.

"Really. I think I've enjoyed having her here every bit as much as you have." Lifting her shoulders, she tossed him a sheepish smile.

"Who'd have thought?" Sean mused thoughtfully as

CarlyAnn occupied herself by chewing on the zipper to his jacket.

"Are you surprised?" Julia looked askance at him as she paired his socks.

"That we up-and-coming, workaholic, career-driven types would enjoy having a nine-month-old bundle of energy under our feet for two weeks? Yep. I'm surprised."

"Maybe we are getting our priorities straight after all," Julia murmured as she deposited a stack of his socks and T-shirts into his laundry basket.

"Do you think?"

"I'm trying. And praying about it."

"Me too."

They smiled at each other for a long moment. Sean leaned down to deposit CarlyAnn on the bed and picked up one of Julia's T-shirts to fold. It was as if he had touched her instead.

Turning, Julia fussed with a sweater she was folding. Wool crackled with static electricity as she pried her light blue knit away from Sean's heavy black ski sweater. She peeled them apart, and as the two sweaters strained toward each other she felt a smile tug at her lips. That was how she felt about Sean all the time. All filled with electricity and drawn toward him. Odd, she thought as she folded the sweaters and put them in separate piles. In the past that was how she had felt about a job promotion. But even a promotion and a healthy raise could not compare to the ways she was beginning to feel about Sean Flannigan.

Glad that he couldn't read her mind, Julia began to fold the never-ending stack of CarlyAnn's cloth diapers.

"So," Sean began conversationally, steering the topic to new territory, "are you ready for tomorrow night?"

"Ready as I'll ever be," she sang, suddenly filled with excitement at the thought of the party. "I hope you aren't totally bummed out when CarlyAnn wins the prize for best costume," she taunted teasingly.

"Not a chance," Sean bragged, ruffling his niece's hair. "She might win for cutest costume, but the prize for originality will definitely go to us."

"That's for sure," Julia agreed.

She still hadn't figured out what that gray blob in Sean's room was, and she was too concerned about hurting his feelings to ask. So, she'd steered clear of the fledgling chicken coop, telling Sean she wanted to be surprised all over again on Friday night. That way, she would have no chance to blurt out anything that might give herself away. He'd seemed pleased with her spirit of adventure and her trust in his abilities.

"So," she asked, tucking the now-tidy stack of diapers into CarlyAnn's laundry basket, "how's it going in there? Are we going to be ready for tomorrow night?"

"Just great," Sean enthused, wrapping his niece in a bear hug that had her squirming for freedom. "You won't believe it when you see it."

"I'll bet you're right about that," Julia muttered.

"I still have a little work to do on your part of the costume, but I think I found most everything I need at the thrift store."

"My part of the costume?"

"Yes." Sean ran a hand through his thick, auburn hair. "I still have to fashion you some kind of beard, but that should be no big deal."

"Beard?" she squeaked. This just kept getting stranger and stranger.

"Sure. They didn't have electric razors in those days, you know."

"Oh." Well, she hadn't thought they had submarines in those days either. "You live," she murmured with a shrug, "and learn."

12

"Okay," Sean said, and pasted the last of Julia's beard to her chin with spirit gum. "That ought to hold just fine."

"I doubt that it will ever come off, with as much glue as you have slathered on me," Julia moaned, holding her jaw perfectly still so she didn't ruin all of Sean's hard work.

They were standing in his room, preparing for the party, late on Friday afternoon. The sun's dying rays slanted through the window, signaling the end of another spectacular fall day. The smells of freshly mowed grass and burning leaves wafted in through the screen and mingled with the mouth-watering aromas of Agnes's party appetizers. Somewhere outside, a dog barked.

"Don't worry," he teased. "If we can't get it all off, you can borrow my razor."

"How comforting," she said dryly, her lips twitching with a tiny grin.

There was only a half-hour left before the party began, and the air at the boarding house fairly crackled with anticipation. The only one oblivious to the excitement was CarlyAnn, who was now at the tail end of her afternoon nap. As soon as they were finished with the final touches on their own costumes, they would wake her and pop her into her angel getup. Sean made a mental note to take a picture to show Kathleen.

Leaning slightly back away from Julia's face, Sean scanned his handiwork with critical eyes. The beard, he thought as he checked for loose spots, did nothing to hide her feminine charms. Beneath the fuzzy whiskers he had pasted to her delicate chin and cheeks, her unmistakably girlish lips curved into a tempting bow. He longed to touch her lips with his own, but something about even a quick peck with a bearded person gave him the willies.

Although, for a bearded guy, she was cute as a button, he mused as a grin spread across his face.

"Speaking strictly as a whale with a voracious appetite, you're looking pretty delicious," he murmured. As he worked, his knuckles brushed her rosy cheeks, which were now flaming at his flirtatious words.

"Oh, sure," she groused, pretending to pout. "I bet you whales say that to all the humans who fall off the boat."

"No, only the cute ones."

Reaching up, Julia fingered her whiskers and snorted. "I don't see why I have to be Jonah. You could have grown your own beard." Extending her arm, she traced the stubble of his jaw.

Sean cleared his throat and tried to rein in his galloping heart. "Yes, but you make a far more fetching Jonah than I would," he said, pleased at his placid demeanor, considering how near Julia stood. "Besides, the whale costume is a bit much for a little gal like you."

"I don't see why I can't go as Joan and just skip the beard." She groaned and scratched at a spot just beneath her nose.

Because then I wouldn't have an excuse to spend twenty

minutes touching your face, he restrained himself from saying.

"Come on, now," he cajoled, putting on the finishing touches, "it's great characters of the Bible. I don't recall anyone named Joan in the Bible."

"Wasn't there a Joan on the ark?"

"Ha!" Grasping her wrist, he led her to the mirror over his bureau. "Take a look and tell me if you don't look just like Jonah."

Peering into the mirror, Julia's eyes widened in surprise, and then her head dropped back, and she crowed at the ceiling with laughter.

CarlyAnn began to stir.

"What is this?" she wondered, fingering the rubbery green tube Sean had pinned to her tangled hair. It suspiciously resembled an old leek from Hattie's garden.

"Seaweed, of course."

Julia laughed. "Of course." Eyes crinkled with delight, she looked down at herself and perused the rest of her costume.

The tunic she wore looked like it had been soaking in battery acid, and a row of teeth marks left little holes across her midriff. A starfish and some clamshells dangled strategically here and there about the neckline. The legs of the trousers she wore must have been hacked off with a saw, the edges were so ragged. Sean reasoned she needed no shoes to complete the ensemble, as she most likely would have lost them at sea.

"I love it," she announced, sending Sean's pulse singing in his ears.

"You do?" he wondered, needing reassurance. Needing her approval. Wanting to hear her talk about love some more.

"Yes. It's perfect. And I think you're right. I think we have a chance at the grand prize." Turning, she inspected his costume as it lay on the floor, waiting for him to bring it to life. "The whale is really wonderful too. I have to admit when I first saw it, I had my doubts, but it really looks authentic."

Sean ducked his head bashfully. "I got a book on whales at the library."

"You were able to build this guy, with a movable mouth and a blowhole and everything, just by looking at a book in the library?" she asked, an incredulous expression on her face.

"Yep." He shrugged, his eyes darting around from sudden embarrassment.

"You are something else, Sean Flannigan."

"Ah, shucks," he said, pretending to kick at some pebbles on the floor with his foot.

"No, I really mean it," she said, tilting his chin with her fingertips and looking into his eyes. "You are really talented."

For some reason, hearing those words from her meant more to Sean than she would ever know. He knew that going to a party dressed as Jonah and the whale was a kooky idea, one that most women would probably hate. But here she was, caught up in the spirit of the occasion, loving his hard work and eager to be off. He couldn't imagine special ordering a woman who would turn out any more wonderful than the woman who stood gazing up at him.

"We should probably finish getting ready," he was finally able to say when he'd come to his senses. A quick glance at the clock on his nightstand told him they had less than twenty minutes before they had to be down in the parlor.

"Do you need a hand getting into your costume?" Julia wondered as he lifted the head of his unwieldy contraption and stepped into its mouth.

"No," came his muffled answer as he wrestled the whale on over his head. His Levi's and tennis shoes stuck conspicuously out from beneath the whale's belly, giving the mammal a certain twenty-first-century charm. "I designed it so that it would be really light and easy to steer." Squirming around, he winked at her through the wide-mouthed opening at the front of his costume.

"Okay, then," Julia nodded. "I guess I'll wake the baby, and we'll get her dressed and go."

"Sounds good."

Unfortunately, CarlyAnn took one look at Julia and started to cry. And the next look at Uncle Sean had her screaming with terror.

"All right, everyone!" Hattie warbled, excitedly clapping her hands together. "Now that everyone is finally here, I want us to all gather in a circle in the middle of the floor," she motioned grandly with her cane, "and make introductions. In character, of course."

Nineteen hundred hours had finally arrived, and the great characters of the Bible were assembled in the parlor for fellowship and good eats. CarlyAnn sat in her walker, gazing up at the nutty gathering of adults, her pipe-cleaner halo wobbling back and forth with each movement of her little head. It seemed she was getting used to the idea that everyone, herself included, was dressed rather strangely tonight. And though she wasn't eager to be held by anyone, she didn't seem quite so bothered anymore by the gaggle of ugly mugs that smiled down at her.

"Come on, everyone. To the middle of the floor now." Hattie's eyes darted around the room. "Has anyone seen the Colonel . . . rather, Moses?" she queried, a tiny frown adorning her brow.

"He's still over at the buffet table, pilfering my sweet-and-sour meatballs and trying to part the red punch with that ridiculous thing he calls a staff," Agnes sniffed, pointing into the corner as she blew the whistle on Moses.

"Oh, yoo-hoo, Colonel!" Glynnis called. "Come on now. We'll be eating in a little while. You can perform your miracles after we've eaten."

Chortling, the Colonel snagged another pâté-coated cracker and shuffled into the circle of great characters of the Bible, smacking his lips and clicking his dentures as he went.

Julia turned her back on the main group and hid her face in the privacy of the whale's mouth.

"Trying not to laugh?" Sean asked with a grin.

"I was just hoping that he doesn't try to reenact the burning-bush scene here in the parlor," she whispered.

"I could do without the frog plague, myself," Sean quipped. "Man," he muttered, squirming, "I wish I had made my blowhole bigger. It's getting hot in here."

Julia giggled and pulled her head out of the whale's mouth. "I'll give you some air."

He thrust out his lower lip. "Come back. It's not that hot . . ."

"All right now, everyone," Hattie sang out. "Circle around and let's begin. Brian? Darling, why don't you stand in the center, tell us who you are, and then we will go around the circle clockwise and let everyone take a turn."

Ryan, dressed in his bathrobe and a pair of flip-flops, grabbed his staff—made of an upside-down umbrella bound to a broom handle—and stepped forward. A bath towel was draped over his head with a shoelace wrapped around his forehead and knotted at his temples to hold it securely in place.

"I am one of the shepherds who saw the star and went to visit Jesus in the manger," he explained, then gestured to his flock. "And these are my sheep." Behind him, sitting in an obedient group in the corner, were Moondoggie, Sweetpea, Otis, Petunia, and Mimsie. "Stay!" he roared and brandished his staff as they began to fidget under everyone's scrutiny. "Good sheep," he praised.

Everyone applauded with enthusiasm.

"Lovely!" Hattie trilled. "Glynnis, tell us about yourself, dear."

Glynnis sashayed to the middle of the floor and twirled, model style. "I am Noah's wife." She was wearing her infamous two-piece swimsuit, a gaudy, polka-dotted affair with a blousy skirt. A colorful inner tube graced her midriff, and she sported a bright orange pair of fins on her feet. A plastic dove with an olive branch glued to its beak bobbed from her swim cap.

Laughing, the crowd cheered and whistled.

Agnes snorted.

The dogs barked.

"Excellent!" Hattie turned to Agnes. "Aggie, dear, who are you?"

Shuffling with smaller than usual steps, Agnes made her way to the middle of the circle. On her head she wore a cap fashioned from tinfoil with holes punctured in the top. Her body was clad in a large white tube with slots for her arms. The Morton Salt logo was artfully painted on the front.

"I am Lot's wife," she announced with a mischievous grin pushing through her sour expression, "*after* the peek."

Much applause and laughter turned her cheeks bright pink.

Otis threw back his head and gave a few hollow woofs.

Olivia introduced herself as David and Goliath amid much hilarity. She was David, dressed in a toga and sandals, and Goliath was a giant dummy she'd fashioned from stuffing some extra-large men's long underwear and attaching a fierce-looking rubber mask to the neck to serve as his head. Goliath, too, wore a toga and sandals. Olivia entertained the troops by shooting him with rubber bands and cuffing him upside the head.

The Colonel made a wonderful Moses, with his eccentric hair and the Santa beard he had found in the attic. Twin tablets under his arm and a cane he used to perform his miracles had everyone in stitches. Hattie and Rahni came as Naomi and her daughter-in-law, Ruth, and were draped in yards of fabric and clad in Birkenstock sandals purchased just for the occasion. "I always wanted a pair of these," Hattie explained, lifting her gown and showing off her footwear.

As the littlest angel, CarlyAnn was the darling of the event, but Sean and Julia stole the show when Jonah was chased around the circle and eventually caught and eaten by the whale. The dogs barked and lunged at the mysterious sight, giving their shepherd a run for his money.

When the costume judging was complete and the award of a gift certificate for dinner for two at the House of

McLaughlin had been bestowed upon Jonah and her whale, Agnes and Glynnis announced that the buffet was open and all should "Come and get it."

Olivia picked up CarlyAnn and took her to the table to pick out some munchies.

"You were right," Julia whispered, excitedly brandishing the gift certificate into the whale's mouth. "We won!"

"Of course I was right," Sean teased. "When do you want to go?"

"I don't know." Shrugging excitedly, Julia scratched her beard and studied the certificate. "There is no expiration date, so I guess we could go whenever."

"Great. Don't lose that puppy," Sean warned as Julia folded the certificate and stuffed it into her pants pocket. "I worked hard for that."

"You sure did." She patted the giant whale. "And you were right all along about winning first prize. Thanks for including me." Julia planted a kiss on the whale's lower lip.

"I wouldn't have it any other way." His tone was filled with a special warmth, meant just for her.

"Come on, Free Willy," she teased. "I'm starved. Let's go to the buffet table, and I'll see if I can round up a raw fish or two for you." She laughed and tugged on his fin.

"Just a second," Sean said, reaching through the whale's mouth and pressing the fuzz on her chin. "You're losing your beard."

"Good," Julia said and heaved a beleaguered sigh. "I don't know how you men stand all this fur on your face."

"Well, hang on, and I'll put you out of your misery." He placed his hands at the sides of her face and, with a quick jerk, removed her beard.

"Ouch!" she yelped and rubbed her stinging cheeks. "I thought you said you'd put me *out* of my misery."

"Sorry," he murmured and, pulling her into the whale's mouth, kissed her chin. "Is that better?"

She offered her cheeks. "Almost," she conceded, "but you need to keep trying."

A crash came from somewhere behind them.

They ignored it.

"Sean!" Agnes called, "look out with that tail of yours!"

"Oops," Sean muttered, releasing Julia and turning around. "Sorry."

Another crash.

"Sean!" Glynnis cried. "Hold still!"

"Oh, man, I'm sorry." Again he whipped around and knocked one of Hattie's antique lamps off the end table.

"Hit the deck!" the Colonel screeched. "Friendly fire!"

The dogs began to bark.

"Sean!" Olivia cried, shielding CarlyAnn from a blow. "Perhaps you should let us bring you a plate."

"Good idea," he agreed and cast a sheepish glance around the room. Kissing Julia's rosy cheeks had certainly thrown him into a dither. "I'll . . . uh, just, uh . . . wait here."

"The word," Agnes brayed, adjusting her glasses and peering at the dictionary, "was *obovate.*" She reached into the basket Hattie had provided and pulled the first of the nine definitions that had been scribbled on slips of paper. "Prepare to vote, because I am only going to read these once," she instructed sternly, squinting at the handwriting on the slip she held.

Taking a deep breath, she began to read, dramatically pronouncing each syllable.

"Obovate: to rototill with an oboe." Agnes rolled her eyes, and everyone snickered. She fumbled for a new slip.

"Obovate: to thrust oneself upon another without request or warrant."

Agnes continued as everyone chuckled at the different definitions.

"Obovate: to dance wildly to the beat of a drum."

"Obovate: the feeling one gets from too much of Agnes's pumpkin pie."

Agnes frowned.

"Obovate: broad end upward."

"Obovate: a pregnant oboe."

"Obovate: a rite of passage."

"Obovate: a collision in the wind section of an orchestra."

"Obovate: surgical removal of the oboe."

Finished reading, Agnes pursed her lips into a tidy knot and waited while everyone voted.

Sean, who had to stand because of his costume, leaned over Julia and whispered rakishly, "Care to obovate?"

Julia giggled and batted at him. "I don't date outside my species," she quipped.

"No talking," Agnes barked from long habit of overseeing English exams.

Blessedly, this was the last round, and so far Agnes, with her superb mastery of the English language, was in the lead. However, her championship did not come easily. A shouting match between her and her sister had to be broken up by David and Goliath, and at one point, Sean's prediction of World War III seemed eminent when everyone rioted over the true definition of Rahni's word, *zend*.

When everyone had finally finished and the votes had been tallied, Agnes revealed the correct meaning of *obovate*.

"Broad end up!" she cried and laughed until her glasses

fogged. "Inversely ovate, with the broad end upward, as in a leaf," she read aloud from the dictionary. "My goodness, it appears that I won!"

The Colonel wheezed his mirth. "Agnes, old girl, you wield the English language like a double-edged sword. Good job, soldier."

Agnes beamed, and her eyes grew suspiciously bright as Hattie presented her with a gift certificate for two to the House of McLaughlin.

"I believe I shall give this to Bea and her husband as a thank you for the many lovely Sunday dinners I have enjoyed with her family," Agnes announced and smiled at Glynnis.

"How lovely, Aggie, dear," Glynnis murmured and nodded with approval.

After the game was over and the furniture had been pushed against the walls, the folding chairs were arranged into an audience formation. The sun had long since set, and the air had a chill that required a fire to be set in the fireplace. Once the sparks were swirling up the chimney and the room began to warm, it was time for the entertainment.

Olivia took her seat at Hattie's old upright piano and began to play some lively carnival-type music at Ryan's introduction. Leaping to the middle of the stage area, Ryan performed a hilarious routine as the ringleader of a doggy circus. He involved each of his befuddled animals in events that had them clearly stymied.

"Jump, Otis!" he commanded the ancient dog as he held a Hula-Hoop high over his head.

Otis groaned and limply flopped his tail.

Looking with astounded pride over the audience, Ryan

shouted, "Did you see that? No?" he asked when they all laughingly shook their heads. "He's simply too fast for the human eye. Jump again, Otis! A little slower now," he shouted, holding the hoop up near the ceiling. Otis moaned and sank to the floor. "Not *that* slow," Ryan commanded. "We'll be here all night."

Once the dogs had been put through their dysfunctional paces, the show came to a grinding halt when Moondoggie discovered Agnes's sweet-and-sour meatballs and covered them with enthusiastic kisses.

"Get that beast out of my meatballs!" Agnes roared.

"Arkkk! Arkkk! Arkkk!" Mimsie rotated in fear at the woman's stern command.

And thus ended the circus. After the dogs had been sent to the corner to lie down, Ryan and Olivia played the piano together and sang some corny duets. Occasionally, Moondoggie would join in.

Julia was touched by the look of happiness that transformed Olivia's usually melancholy face. She was such a lovely, caring, and gentle woman. It was so sad the way tragedy had transformed her life. But it seemed she was learning to cope and to accept the fact that life went on whether or not she wanted it to. Hattie's unwavering faith in God and her special zest for life had done the young, grieving wife a world of good. That was clear.

Together, Julia and Sean orchestrated several more parlor games, and when they were finished, more prizes, both grand and booby, were awarded amid much good-natured teasing and laughter.

Rahni had concocted a special culinary treat for dessert, a recipe from her country that had been handed down to her from her mother. When the dishes were cleared and stacked on the kitchen counter, the folding chairs were packed away to make room for a makeshift dance floor.

Hattie wound up her old Victrola, dug out her favorite 78s, and soon the crowd was tripping the light fantastic—*tripping* being the operative word. Tails wagging, the dogs took the music as an invitation to mingle. They nosed fingers, rubbed against knees, and vied for attention. Even Sweetpea seemed sociable.

Olivia grabbed Goliath and proceeded to fox-trot over the gleaming parlor floor. Breathless and giddy as a schoolgirl, Agnes wobbled across the dance floor on the arm of the less-than-steady Moses, and CarlyAnn, squealing with delight, clung tightly to Ryan's neck as he jogged her around the room. The dove whipping wildly on her bathing cap, Glynnis tapped her orange flipper to the beat of the music and shouted words of encouragement to the crowd on the dance floor.

Sean, still wearing his whale costume, wiggled his brows at Julia. "Come to papa," he chortled, moving toward her, his fins outstretched and beckoning.

"Not by the hair of my chinny-chin-chin," she cried and ran around the buffet table, laughing all the way.

Finally, after catching her and wrestling her into—and out of—the belly of the whale, Sean held the giggling and shrieking Julia as close as his costume would allow. After a lot of teasing and tickling and scuffling behind the buffet table, they eventually headed upstream to the middle of the dance area and began to slow dance to the mellow strains of an era gone by. Though they were unaware of it, they made an amusing picture. It appeared to all who watched that the whale had consumed all but the lower half of Jonah's body as they swayed to the music.

As Julia rested her head lightly against Sean's shoulder, she could feel his heart beating beneath her cheek. It was such a wonderful feeling—to be so safe and secure and, at the same time, so alive and filled with excitement.

"Having a good time?" Sean murmured.

"Mmmm," she hummed and nodded against the firm wall of his chest. "The best."

"Me too." He paused for a moment. "In the three years that I've been living here, this is the best harvest party yet. And," he whispered, nudging her head up with his chin, "I think it's all because of you."

"Me?" she squeaked, her pulse suddenly thundering in her ears as she gazed up into his face. In the darkness of the whale's mouth she strained to read the meaning behind his words. The look in Sean's eyes was filled with a tender, poignant emotion as well as something else she couldn't quite pinpoint. A fire. A yearning. A longing for something that she had come to know recently herself.

"Yes, you."

"Oh," she breathed, wishing she had something more witty and clever to say.

After a quick peek to make sure CarlyAnn was still in Ryan's care, he danced her through the human and canine throng, beyond the beautifully fashioned archway, and into the foyer. Though the music was harder to hear, they had more room to move and more privacy. Lifting his costume over his head, Sean stored it in the foyer under the stairs in order to keep from knocking anything over. Once he'd straightened out his clothing and run a hand through his hair, he turned to look at Julia.

Slowly he advanced and entwined her fingers in his.

"You feel it, too, don't you?" he asked, his voice loaded with meaning as he came to a standstill in the shadows.

Pulling her into his embrace, he cupped her face in the palms of his hands and looked deeply into her eyes.

Julia swallowed. "Yes," she whispered.

"Something is happening to me." Sean took a deep breath and exhaled slowly. "Something that has never happened to me before."

"Me too."

The grandfather clock that stood in the foyer ticked away moments that to Julia would remain suspended in time for the rest of her life. Laughter and the sounds of party hilarity wafted to them unnoticed from the parlor.

"I don't know if I'm ready for this," he murmured.

"Me neither."

Sean nodded. "It's kind of scary, huh?"

"Terrifying."

A lazy smile tipped his lips just before he brought them to Julia's. As they stood in the shadows, it seemed to Julia that bells went off in her head. Wedding bells, alarm bells, celestial bells, the bells . . . of . . . heaven. Sighing, she melted against him, even as the bells continued to ring.

Ding-dong! Ding-dong!

Ding . . . sigh . . . dong.

Ryan, with CarlyAnn riding along on his shoulders, her pudgy fingers gripping his ears for balance, finally intruded upon their stolen moment.

"Hey, I think someone is at the door ringing the be—" Coming to an abrupt stop, Ryan cleared his throat and blushed. "Oh, sorry. I didn't mean to uh, you know . . . intrude."

The doorbell rang impatiently once more.

Ding-dong! Ding-dong!

Sean and Julia stepped apart, their gazes darting around in embarrassed confusion.

"No need to apologize, Ryan," Sean told him. "We didn't hear the doorbell." Shrugging sheepishly, Sean reached up to pull CarlyAnn from Ryan's shoulders and into his arms.

"Okay," Ryan shrugged and patted Sean on his shoulder. "I'll just go let Hattie know that she has some company."

"Thanks," Sean called, watching him weave his way back into the party.

"ZZZgggjjjaa-la!" CarlyAnn squealed and held her arms out to Julia.

Pushing her seaweed-strewn hair out of her eyes, she scooped the baby out of Sean's arms and propped her on her hip as naturally as if she'd been the child's own mother. Sean snapped on the foyer light, and Julia blinked against the brightness. With regret that their private moment was over, she smiled wistfully at Sean.

"I'll get it," she murmured.

Ding-dong! Ding-dong! Ding-dong!

CarlyAnn dangled over her arm as Julia headed toward the massive front door and the incessantly ringing bell.

"Just a minute," she groused at the intruder, disgruntled that this thoughtless person would have the nerve to interrupt what was promising to be one of the biggest moments in her life. "I'm coming, I'm coming," she called. Rushing with the baby to the door, she twisted the intricately fashioned brass knob and, with a flamboyant sweep, yanked it open.

"Hi," she said, staring uncertainly at the sophisticated woman who stood in the doorway. The woman looked eerily familiar. Julia's throat closed, and her heart lurched in her chest. Julia blinked and attempted to swallow her foolish shock and dismay.

"CarlyAnn!" Kathleen screamed and reached for her baby daughter. "I got an early flight! Mommy's home!"

13

Hattie, do you mind if I ask you a question?" Julia leaned forward on the settee and patted Hattie's knee to get the older woman's attention. "HATTIE!"

"Hmmm?" Hattie set down her teapot and looked expectantly at Julia.

"I wanted to ask you a question!"

It was Monday evening after her first day on the new job. Julia hadn't seen Sean since Kathleen had arrived to pick up CarlyAnn Friday night.

Without so much as a backward glance, Kathleen had swept Sean into his room for an interrogation that had outlasted the party. Julia took solace in the fact that, with Sean all to herself the next day, they could pick up the threads of the conversation that had been so rudely interrupted.

But it was not to be.

Mysteriously, there had been no answer to her knock on Sean's door Saturday morning, let alone Saturday afternoon and evening. Julia was desperate to ask the other boarders if anyone had seen him go or if he'd told anyone when to expect him home. But she simply couldn't get the words past her lips. Her relationship with Sean was so new and fragile at this point, it almost seemed that bringing it out in the open could somehow damage it. So she suffered in silence.

Now he'd been gone the entire weekend, as well as today. For him to simply disappear for several days without telling her was certainly his prerogative, but it was definitely out of character. Especially considering the words that had passed between them just before Kathleen's arrival.

Nervously, she wondered if he'd regretted broaching the subject of their relationship at the party. Was that why he'd disappeared? Her heart thudded painfully against her ribs at the thought.

Never before had she felt so completely and utterly lonely. And never before had a weekend taken such an unbearably long time to pass. Even today, her first day at work in the Vermont division of Gerico Industries, where she was surrounded by a bevy of smiling and friendly new faces, Julia had felt bereft.

A large part of her heart longed for CarlyAnn.

But an even larger part longed for Sean. She wanted to tell him all about her day. She wanted to ask his opinion about several things she'd noticed on the job. She wanted to see his smiling face, to laugh with him, to share her fears, to resume the conversation they'd left dangling.

However, more than anything, she simply wanted Sean to come home.

That being the case, Julia had decided to leave the self-imposed solitude of her room after dinner that evening and venture down for a visit with her kindly old landlady. An hour spent shouting at Hattie was better than wondering what would happen between her and Sean, now that she was back at work and CarlyAnn was gone.

"Yes, Beulah, darlin'. What's on your mind?" Hands trembling with a slight palsy, Hattie held out a rattling and sloshing cup of tea perched precariously on a fine china saucer.

Julia had finally succumbed to her rabid curiosity. Deciding to bite the bullet, she grasped the tea, settled it into her lap, and bravely inquired as to Sean's whereabouts.

"Well, I was just wondering—" she raised her voice in order to be heard, "IF YOU KNEW WHERE SEAN HAD BEEN ALL WEEKEND." She smiled brightly and hoped she appeared blasé. As if she were asking in a fashion that could be construed as nothing more than neighborly.

"Don?" Hattie cried.

"Yes!" Julia shouted back.

"Oh, my yes."

Julia sighed. "Yes what?"

"He is a hard worker." She pondered the tea in her cup before speaking her mind. "He works too hard, if you want my opinion, but that's none of my business."

"Is that where he is?" Julia shouted. "Has he been at work all weekend?"

"He has?" Hattie's brow furrowed. "That's odd."

"What's odd?"

"Why, he told me that he was going to go to his sister's home early Saturday morning to visit his sister and the baby. Didn't you read his note?"

Julia's pulse quickened. "What note?"

"Why the note he wrote to you on the back of that napkin . . ." Hattie frowned. "Uh-oh."

"What uh-oh?" Julia demanded anxiously.

"Well, I had a leaky teacup, don't you know. I just hate when that happens. Old china. Cracked. A little like me." She hooted, her laughter gaily ricocheting off the walls. "Old things do tha—"

Julia hated to interrupt, but she was desperate. "What note, Hattie?" she shouted.

"Why, the one on the napkin I used to scrub the tea off

the floor. Claimed he missed the child. But I suspect it had more to do with the phone call he got that morning than anything else."

"Phone call?" Immediately Julia was concerned. Was something wrong with CarlyAnn? *Oh dear!* Unfortunately, she would simply have to wait to find out. "Did he say when he was coming home?" Julia hollered and used hand signals, hoping to make herself heard, but it was no use.

"Didn't say what it was about, but Don had the strangest look on his face. I know. I saw it. He took the phone call right here in the parlor, don't you know. I suppose whoever it was had tried to reach him in his room but couldn't. That's understandable, because he was down here with me. Well, we got it all straightened out after a bit. That happens with phone calls, especially in a boarding house, don't you know. Picking a call from the switchboard can be a tricky thing. It took that poor phone man a month of Sundays to teach me the art, I tell you. But, as I always say, learn from the mistakes of others. You won't live long enough to make all of them yourself! Hee-hoo-hee-haa!"

Hattie rattled on about this and that for the better part of an hour, but try as she might, Julia couldn't concentrate on a single thing the woman said. Glancing at the clock, she decided she might as well call it an evening and head to bed. Just because her heart was no longer at the office was no reason not to keep up professional appearances.

After bidding Hattie a fond good night, Julia shuffled listlessly up the stairs to her room.

Once in the upper hallway, Julia hesitated between her room and Sean's.

He wouldn't be trying to give her the brush-off, would he? she wondered fearfully. Uncertainty filled her mind.

No. He wouldn't do that. He was much too good of a man to resort to such cowardice.

On impulse, she tiptoed over to Sean's door and knocked. She could use the fact that he still had her rocker as an excuse if he wondered why she was there. However, just as she suspected—and gathered from Hattie—there was no answer. Unbidden, worry crowded into her throat, closing it off and making it next to impossible to swallow.

What had the mysterious phone call been about? Surely he wasn't going to be transferred, was he? She caught her breath. What would she do if he *was* being transferred? People in the hotel business surely moved around as often as they did in her business.

Almost of its own accord, her hand strayed to the brass knob. The metal was cool to the touch and, surprisingly, with gentle pressure, the door clicked open.

How odd. Why hadn't Sean locked his door? Unable to resist the temptation, Julia slipped into his darkened room and was suddenly bowled over by a fit of melancholy. In the shadowed light of the moon, everything looked exactly the same as it had—with the exception of CarlyAnn's belongings, which were quite noticeably missing.

Stepping quietly over to her rocker, Julia settled into its seat for one last nostalgic rock. Oh, how she missed Sean.

"Dear, Lord," she whispered simply, closing her eyes and settling her head against the backrest of the chair, "please send him home to me." Sighing, she set the chair into a slow, rhythmic motion that seemed to soothe her weary soul. She missed the warm weight of a baby in her arms.

"Oh, my darling, I love you," she hummed the Elvis lyrics quietly, the way she and Sean did every evening to CarlyAnn just before bed. "And I always will," she

whispered, suddenly wishing for a baby of her own. Blinking back the silly tears, she stared unseeing out the window.

"Hattie?" Sean called into the parlor. The lights were still on, so he figured she must still be up. *"Hattie?"*

"Don?" a tiny voice sputtered from the other side of the couch. Hattie struggled to consciousness, blinking and patting her hair into place as she sat up. "Is that you, Don?" she sang.

"Yes, Hattie," Sean yelled, grinning. It was great to be home . . . for so many reasons. "It's me."

"Oh, wonderful, dear. We were beginning to grow worried about you."

"We?"

"Myself and Beulah."

Sean's heart skipped a beat. So Julia had been worried. The thought bothered him as much as it pleased him. Hadn't he explained his absence well enough on the note? He hadn't wanted her to worry. He had just needed some time to get his head together. To straighten out his priorities. To make some decisions.

Saturday morning, just as he'd been about to bid Hattie good-bye down here in her parlor and go for a head-clearing run, his boss had called. It seemed that the new guy wouldn't be taking the job after all. Would Sean still be interested in taking the prestigious promotion?

Well, that was an excellent question and one Sean did not have the answer to. Not, that is, until he'd spent an entire weekend hashing out his muddled thoughts with Kathleen and her husband, Martin. He'd hopped into his car and taken off without so much as a toothbrush.

Without so much as taking the time to lock his door or hand-deliver the note to Julia.

He had needed some time to get his head together before he set eyes on the beguiling Julia Evans again. He knew Kathleen and Martin would have the answers he sought. After all, in his opinion, they had everything he wanted. A loving marriage, careers that—for the most part anyway—seemed to work for them, the sweetest little girl in the world and, most importantly, an unshakable faith in God.

Plus, Sean had been glad for an extra few days with his niece. Having Kathleen show up early and whisk her away had been a little too abrupt for his taste. Surprisingly, he'd even heard himself offer to take her again next time Kath had a business trip. But Kathleen had declined. Said it had been too hard on her to be away from her child and she didn't expect to be leaving her again anytime soon.

After two weeks with CarlyAnn, Sean understood.

After two weeks with CarlyAnn, Sean understood a lot of things he never used to understand.

"Don, darling," Hattie warbled, bringing him back to the present, "is everything all right? Beulah suggested that you might be working this weekend."

Sean smiled at the curious, birdlike eyes that shone from the depths of the old woman's wrinkled face. Taking a deep breath, he shook his head and shouted for her benefit,

"I've been trying to sort out my life and get to the truth."

"Ah," Hattie nodded. "The truth will set you free," she said sagely. "But first, it will make you mad."

Sean laughed. "Yep. You got that right. Well, anyway, this weekend I figured a few things out. Got some priorities straight," he stated loudly.

"And are you happy with what you found, my dear?" Hattie clasped her gnarled hands in her lap and looked at him with interest.

"I don't know, exactly," he shouted. "But I did learn that I," he lifted his voice, "need to get a life outside of my career."

Pursing her lips, Hattie nodded. "Mmm," she agreed. "You do need a wife, it's true. Uh-huh." *Hmmm, and one without an outside career? What an odd request,* she mused to herself. She frowned slightly, but her shrug was agreeable.

Raking a hand through his hair, Sean—now on a roll—continued hollering. "I know I need to slow down or I'll end up dead and buried before I'm thirty!"

"*Hmmm,* four-thirty." Hattie clucked and tsked, making mental notes.

Sean pressed on. "Just like my dad. He died far before his time because he was so busy trying to do right by us. But the thing all of us wanted more than anything was *him*. Just him."

"Ah, yes," Hattie whispered.

"You know, Hattie, I think the Lord has a plan for my life, and I'm beginning to think," again he shouted to make himself understood, "it has nothing to do with a high-powered career or lots of money."

"Oh? Light showers? Hmm . . ." Hattie's lips moved as she watched him speak. "Sunny. Yes. Good, good."

Stretching, Sean stood and yawned broadly. Leaning forward, he pecked the elderly woman on her lightly rouged cheek.

"It's late, Hattie. We need to get our beauty sleep."

"Straight away, my darling. Just as soon as I've had a word with the Lord. Remember, feed your faith, and your doubts will starve to death."

Sean couldn't suppress the smile that tugged the corners of his mouth. Hattie never ceased to encourage him. "Good night, Hattie," he called and, turning, headed into the hallway.

"Good night, Don, darling."

Bowing her head, Hattie began to converse once again with her Lord. "Dear heavenly Father," she whispered, clutching her fists under her chin, "please bring Don a wife who has no outside career. For some odd reason, he does not seem to want a woman who works outside, although I think gardening is a wonderful way to relax, but . . . well, never mind . . ."

She sniffed. "His idea, of course, so I'll just keep my nose out of it. So, if you could see fit to bring him a woman who enjoys working indoors, well, that would be just fine. And, Lord, while I'm bending your ear, if you could see your way clear, he'd like to be married at four-thirty. Although what day, Lord, he did not specify, but perhaps he's leaving that up to you. He did mention any day with light showers would be all right; however, he prefers it to be sunny.

"Lord, you are so mighty. So loving. So good. I know that these simple requests will be no problem for you." Hattie clapped her hands in finality then paused. "Oh, and Lord, if perhaps I've neglected to mention it today . . . I love you."

"Julia?" Snapping on the lights, Sean stared in surprise at the woman who sat in the rocking chair by the window.

Julia jumped and rubbed her eyes in astonishment. *How mortifying!* She must have fallen asleep. Leaping to her feet, she attempted to explain her odd behavior.

"Oh, ah, hello there, Sean. I'm so sorry. I . . . I uh, didn't mean to bother you. It's just that you . . . you . . . had the rocker here, and I was surprised to find your room open and, well . . ." She smiled sheepishly as her ridiculous explanation petered out. "I must have fallen asleep."

"That's okay," Sean said, grinning at the pinkish print of her hand on her cheek, where she'd obviously been cradling her face as she slept. She had never looked more beautiful to him than she did at that moment.

"No, Sean, I—I," she stammered. "It's not okay." Blinking rapidly, she tried to quell the trembling of her chin and lower lip. "The real reason I came in here was because I was lonely. Lonely for CarlyAnn . . ." She looked plaintively up at him. "And lonely for . . . you." Embarrassed beyond words, she turned and faced the window.

Sean's heart caught in his throat at her words, and crossing the room, he came to stand directly behind her and circled her waist with his arms. "Me too," he sighed and pulled her into the curve of his body.

Tucking her chin into her shoulder, Julia peeked up at Sean. "Really?"

"Really."

She turned in his arms. "Well, then, as long as I'm admitting things, I may as well tell you," she shrugged, a look of consternation crossing her face, "that I'm not as thrilled with my new job as I thought I would be."

Sean gaped at her, surprised. "Really? Why?"

Shyly she lifted her eyes to his. "Because I suddenly realized that working isn't the most satisfying thing life has to offer me anymore."

"You too?" Grinning broadly, Sean stared at the woman in his arms in awe. "So," he murmured, tightening his arms at her waist, "what are you going to do?"

"I think I'm going to continue working on getting my

priorities straight." Wriggling back so that she could look at him, her eyes sparkled with excitement as she shrugged lightly. "The way we promised we would that morning at breakfast. I think I'm going to try working part-time for a while. I've been so buried in my work for so many years, I've forgotten how to simply live."

"Will they let you do that?"

Julia smiled up at Sean, a look of satisfied happiness on her face. "Yes. Believe it or not, they said thanks to some of my—and I'm quoting here—innovative ideas, the company can support two people at my level, right here in Vermont. One part-time. One full-time. Can you believe that? All my hard work is actually paying off in a way I never expected."

Sean inhaled deeply, suddenly filled with a deep sense that something much bigger than the two of them was happening here. He hugged her close and, leaning his chin on the top of her head, stared out the window in wonder.

"That's so amazing."

"Why?" Julia murmured against the firm wall of his chest. He smelled so good. Like Hattie's laundry soap mixed with spicy aftershave.

"Because every day I'm more convinced that God has a special plan for our lives. Just thinking about it gives me chills."

"Sean, what are you talking about?"

Shifting her in his arms, he looked into her face and, searching her eyes, attempted to explain. "Saturday morning, as I was down in the parlor getting ready to go for a run, the phone rang. It was my boss at the New England Inn. It seems that the new guy didn't take the job after all." He took a deep breath and tipped her chin with a forefinger. "They offered it to me."

Julia's eyes widened, and she smiled happily up at him. "Really? What did you say?"

"That I needed a few days to get my priorities straight."

Her jaw dropped. "No way."

"Yep. I told him I needed to mull it over, and I'd be in bright and early Tuesday morning with my answer."

"What's your answer?"

"Well, that depends on you."

"Me?"

"Yes. I know it's a little early in our relationship to discuss long-term commitments." He arched a playful brow. "But we did make a deal that morning at breakfast."

Dumbfounded, Julia stared up at him. "To get our priorities straight?"

"Uh-huh."

"I think that's a wonderful idea," she breathed, then laughed joyfully.

Pulling her back against his chest, Sean nuzzled her neck. "Julia Evans, it has come to my attention that I might, just maybe, be falling madly in love with you."

"No!" Julia cried in mock horror.

"Oh yes." Rearing back, he peered down at her. "It was not my idea, but there you go. Can't fight city hall, can't fight God's will, can't fight love."

"No," she murmured. "Can't fight that."

"So, that being the case, Beulah, do you think I should take the job?"

"Well, Don," Julia sighed, filled with a glorious happiness that left her heart leaping with joy. "I think maybe we should spend a few minutes prioritizing before we make a decision."

"Beulah," Sean said, his nose hovering just a hair's breadth from hers, "I think that's a wonderful idea."

Thank you, Jesus! Julia thought, sending the silent thanksgiving for answered prayer heavenward as, looping her arms around Sean's neck, she pulled him close for a kiss.

Epilogue

Six months later

June was a beautiful month in Vermont but most especially in McLaughlin, at the edge of the crystal-clear lake in Hattie Hopkins's backyard. The Victorian gazebo was festooned with white streamers and flowers, and luckily for the wedding party, not a cloud was in sight on this perfectly sunny day.

The guests numbered about 180, as near as Hattie could figure. The elderly woman glanced at her watch as the old clock at city hall chimed half past four. Yes, she thought happily, everything was going off exactly as requested. God was so good.

The weather was sunny.

The bride, radiant with love for her groom as she walked slowly down the aisle, for the last six months had been enjoying her new part-time status with Gerico Industries, a job that, Hattie was relieved to discover, kept her indoors.

This had worked out perfectly, as Don had been promoted recently to a new full-time job. Luckily, he'd been able to negotiate better hours than he'd originally expected yet keep a salary that would allow the young couple to live quite nicely on their combined incomes.

It was such a beautiful occasion.

Olympia was especially bright-eyed as Beulah's maid of honor, and Brian looked fetching in his tuxedo as he took his place as Don's best man. Don's lovely sister was thrilled to act as matron of honor, and little Caroline, the official flower girl, stumbled down the aisle beside her mother, tossing rose pedals hither and yon as she went.

Beulah's father, who marveled, dewy-eyed, at how grown up his daughter had become, immediately took to Don, sensing in him a fellow businessman. Her mother also was thrilled to be gaining such a wonderful, good-hearted, and handsome son-in-law. Beulah's parents had flown in from South Africa just for the occasion, beaming with pride and bearing exotic gifts for the bride and groom.

The young couple had been inundated with a mountain of gifts. Agnes and Glynnis had been busily crocheting and embroidering fine linens for months. The Colonel, per usual, preferred to make his own gift and had taken a vow of silence on the contents of the eccentrically wrapped box. However, the most amazing thing of all happened when Beulah's grandmother arrived and presented the young couple with a cruise as a wedding present.

Not one single prayer had remained unanswered. Just as Hattie had expected.

The older woman smiled as she watched the loving couple join hands and take their solemn vows. There would be a baby in the house within a year, she felt sure.

Thank you, Lord, she whispered. *Bless this union. And, just in case I've been too busy with the wedding preparations to mention it, I love you.*

Look for the next book in Suzy Pizzuti's
Halo Hattie's Boarding House Series!

An Excerpt from:

RAISING CAIN . . . AND HIS SISTERS

Available June 1999

1

Zach Springer cast a dismal glance at his surroundings. It had been raining like Niagara Falls for the better part of the month now, which was not exactly typical for October in McLaughlin, Vermont. Usually there were plenty of crisp, sunny fall days with a brilliant blue sky as a dazzling backdrop for the glorious colors of autumn. But, alas, not this October. This October was one foggy, soggy dishrag from beginning to end.

Made Zach's job a living nightmare, it did.

Slowly his gaze traveled over the landscape of the project he'd been hired to do. As a building contractor specializing in the renovation of old houses, Zach was looking for a way to beef up the eroding property around one of Vermont's many historic landmarks, the McLaughlin House. Sitting up so high on the hill, the old place was in desperate need of a retaining wall around much of the perimeter.

As he surveyed the situation, water rushed in tiny rivers over his yellow rain hat, and from there, the rivulets drizzled down over his slicker and puddled at his feet. Zach cupped an icy cold hand over his eyes in order to better see the dismal situation.

Just how they were going to pour concrete in this weather was beyond him. *What am I doing out here?* he wondered, longing for the thermos of hot coffee that lay in his rig down the hill a piece. The weather was definitely turning unfriendly.

As if the threatening sky could read his thoughts, lightning, like so many fiery fingers, reached out of the clouds toward him, causing the little hairs at his nape to come to attention. Then, mere seconds later, a great clap of thunder roared across the sky, sounding like a stampeding herd of buffalo.

"Yep," Zach muttered to himself, "time to head for shelter." He stood for a moment, peering through the sheets of rain at the old house on the hill and then at the ground beneath it.

Bad situation.

"Hmm," a suspicious note rumbled in his chest as he leaned forward to get a closer look at the backyard. *The wind must be blowing something fierce, because it almost looks as if . . . as if . . . well, as if that little tree behind the house is . . . moving.*

Zach blinked.

Yes, he was certain now. The soil around that area had begun to crack. Funny. Even the old McLaughlin House looked as if it were suddenly tilting. He stood there processing this information for a moment before the warning bells went off in his head.

Uh-oh! Landslide!

"Uhh . . . uhh . . . uhh . . . ohhh!" Zach shouted and ran

backward toward his truck. He had to get out of there. He had to get out of there fast!

"O, Jesus! O, Lord! *O, Lord Jesus, help me!*" he cried as the earth beneath his feet began to ooze down the hill. Stumbling, bumbling, fumbling, he dragged through the sucking, waterlogged mud and headed as if in slow motion toward his truck.

"Yoo-hoo! Olympia! Where are you, dearie?" Hattie—elderly owner and proprietor of Hattie Hopkins's boarding house—yodeled as she wobbled toward the back of her old Victorian home.

Behind the large country kitchen, Olivia Harmon had been sitting in the sunroom, enjoying a good novel and listening to the incessant rain drum on the roof above. She loved to read there, enjoying the view through the large expanse of windows. From her favorite seat she could see Hattie's rose garden, the hillside beyond the house, and the lake beyond that.

A smile tugged at Olivia's lips. "I'm in the sunroom, Hattie," she called to her darling old landlady. Closing her book, she stood and folded her afghan.

"No," Hattie warbled, her voice reverberating off the mahogany paneling in the giant hallway. "No, no. She's not in the front room; I looked there."

Olivia's smile blossomed. Everyone knew that Hattie had a hearing problem, with the unfortunate exception of Hattie herself.

"Olympia? Dearie? Where have you run off to?"

"I'm *in here*, Hattie!" Olivia shouted.

"Oh! My stars! *There* you are!" Hattie huffed as she made her way with her cane into the large, glass-walled sunroom. "Why didn't you say so?" Wreathed in a mass of smile lines, Hattie's beaming face appeared around the corner. Her gray hair was falling loose from the clip that held it in a bun at the crown of her head. The flyaway wisps, coupled with her bright pink cheeks and sparkling, raisinlike eyes, gave an oddly youthful look to her eighty-plus years. "Olympia, darling girl, you have company."

"I do?" Olivia looked around, puzzled. No one was with Hattie.

"Well now, that's funny." Turning in a circle, Hattie pursed her lips. "She was right here behind me moments ago."

"Here I am," Nell sang. Her nervous giggle floated into the room before her. "I took a detour to the powder room, to get a cup of water. Hope you don't mind." More self-conscious giggling bubbled forth from the depths of Nell's generous body. She held up a small paper cup filled with water.

"No, of course not, Nell," Olivia responded, stepping forward and giving her friend a light hug. "Come in! Come in and sit down. I was just sitting here, wishing I had someone to visit with." She motioned to a longer couch, away from the window, that could better accommodate two.

"Oh?" Nell twittered. "Well, good." She smiled, her birdlike gaze darting here and there and settling nowhere in particular.

Turning, Hattie slowly worked her way to the door. There she paused and smiled at the two young women as they took their seats near the glass wall. "It is lovely to see you again, Belle."

Nell colored. "Thank you, Mrs. Hopkins."

To Olivia, Hattie said, "Olympia dear, I'll have Bonnie bring you ladies a bit of tea and some cookies. We can do better than paper cups of water around here."

"Thank you, Hattie," Olivia called after her, sure there was no way the woman had heard.

"Who is Bonnie?" Nell asked, smoothing her wiry auburn hair away from her face. Arching a brow at Olivia, she shrugged out of her coat and made herself at home.

"Rahni," Olivia said and grinned. "You remember her?

She's Hattie's assistant from the Middle East. She goes to school at night to learn English."

Bubbly laughter danced past Nell's lips. "Oh yes, of course."

"So, Nell, what brings you here on this dreary Saturday afternoon?" She studied her friend's face with curiosity. Her friend was strung as tightly as Scarlett O'Hara's corset.

"Oh, nothing really." Her words rang hollow.

Olivia was skeptical but remained silent, waiting.

"Actually," Nell confessed, "I had to stop at the pharmacy to pick up a prescription for myself, and since I was in the neighborhood, I thought I'd drop by so we could chat for a few minutes."

"A prescription? Are you all right?" Olivia leaned forward and peered at her friend. *Come to think of it, she did look a little green around the gills.*

"I guess," Nell said as she rummaged in her purse with her left hand. The water in her right hand sloshed about, dampening her skirt until she finally set the cup down and concentrated on locating her new bottle of pills. Once she found them, she busied herself extracting a letter opener from the mysteries of her voluminous leather bag.

"What are those?" Olivia wondered aloud, leaning across the white wicker settee to watch in amazement as her friend and coworker began viciously attacking the childproof lid with the letter opener.

"These?" Nell asked as she stabbed and clawed at the top of the stubborn vile of medicine. "These are my nerve pills." Her rounded shoulders bobbed to and fro as she giggled again nervously.

"Nerve pills?"

"Yep, for my anxiety," Nell grunted. She slipped off a shoe and hammered at the stubborn lid with the heel when the letter opener proved useless.

Jaw dropping, Olivia watched Nell's futile, energetic attempts to open the bottle. After a moment she could hold back no longer. "Nell, honey, that's a good way to break a tooth," she warned.

In spite of Nell's best efforts, the cap wouldn't move, and eventually she threw up her hands in exasperation. "Oh, for pity's sake, if I didn't have a problem before, this . . . this . . . lid will land me in the nut house for sure."

Olivia bit back a smile. Taking the bottle from her flustered friend, she pushed on the top with the palm of her hand, easily opened it, then handed it back. Nell gave her a grateful smile.

Olivia and Nell had worked together at the Vermont Department of Tourism for at least half a dozen years now, and they were as close as sisters. Still, Olivia had no idea that someone as grounded in faith as Nell could ever suffer from an anxiety problem. While it was true that Nell continually lapsed into fits of nervous, twittering laughter, for the most part she was as stable as the Rock of Gibraltar. *Salt of the earth; good old Nell.*

In fact, Olivia mused as she thoughtfully reviewed her friend's life, it seemed that Nell had very little to be anxious about. Unlike herself, Nell had a loving husband and two wonderful children to greet her every night. Not to mention a very close relationship with the Lord, a beautiful house—complete with the latest décor—three newish cars, and a charming little dog.

Now I, on the other hand—Olivia thought with irony—*should be the one on nerve pills, considering what I've lived with for the past five years.*

"Anxiety?" Olivia probed, adjusting the pillows between them on the settee and leaning toward her friend as Nell studied the directions on the label.

"Mm hmm," Nell mumbled, her warbling giggle braying through her nose as twin spots of crimson stained her plump cheeks. "And panic."

"Panic?"

"Oh, lately, yes. All the time. That's me! Worry, worry, worry. Panic, panic, panic. It seems . . . well . . . ," thoroughly embarrassed, Nell glanced up at Olivia, ". . . that I have somehow or another developed something called 'panic-anxiety syndrome.' Ever heard of it?"

Now Olivia was worried. "No . . ."

"Me neither." Snorting, Nell slapped her thigh. "Not until last month anyway."

Outside, a clap of thunder rattled the windows.

"*Yiikkkessss!*" Nell shrieked. Pills spilled into her lap, and gripping Olivia's arm, Nell clutched her in a hold that would do the World Wrestling Federation proud. When the sound had rumbled by, she slowly opened her eyes and shot a sheepish glance at Olivia. "Sorry." She giggled, released Olivia, and sitting up, retrieved a pill from her skirt. Quickly tossing it into her mouth, she chased it down with what was left in her cup.

"Oh, Nell," Olivia murmured. Reaching out, she gave her friend a gentle squeeze. "I didn't know you had an anxiety problem! Why didn't you tell me?"

"Ha, oh well, I guess because I didn't really have a problem until about a month or so ago. Plus, it's more than a little embarrassing, being terrified of everything this way. I kept hoping it would go away. Silly me!"

"You should have told me."

"And said what?" Nell wondered with a self-deprecating grin. "Hey, Olivia, guess what? The phone rang and I think I'm going to faint? A customer came in and my heart is pounding a mile a minute and I can't catch my breath!" Rolling her eyes, she slapped her forehead with her open palm. "Hello? Basket case!"

"You know, I kind of thought you hadn't been yourself lately."

"I know. That's why I thought I'd better stop by and come clean. It's a relief, really, to confide in you."

"I'm so glad you did. What can I do to help?"

Nell clasped her hands together and lifted her shoulders in a light shrug. "Nothing really. Just pray for me."

"I . . . I will." Olivia's promise was tentative. She hadn't exactly been on the easiest of terms with God since the accident, but for Nell she would try to humble herself. Besides, there were one or two other items she'd been meaning to bring to God's attention. *May as well break the ice with a request for Nell.*

"Oh, bless you, Livie, hon. I know I'll get a handle on this dumb thing. Eventually." Nell waved an airy hand. "I hope."

Olivia smiled tenderly at her dear friend. "I don't think it sounds dumb at all. It sounds kind of scary actually. How did this thing start?"

"Well, that's the weird part," Nell twittered. "It just hit me out of the blue! One minute I was up there singing away in the soprano section of the church choir, and the next minute I was being carried offstage by the bass and baritone sections." Nell patted her well-rounded hips. "A few tenors pitched in for good measure. It was the single most mortifying moment of my life."

Olivia winced. "I can imagine. I wish I'd been there for you." In the last five years, Olivia's church attendance had been sporadic at best.

"Oh, it's okay, hon. The doctor thinks it's something I have to work through. He says it's a chemical imbalance in the brain and it can happen to anyone. Usually stress brings it on. But not always."

Olivia nodded. "It has been pretty stressful at work since the management changes. Wow. I hope it isn't contagious," she teased, then sobered. "I guess you simply have to keep telling yourself you have nothing to be afraid of and try to believe it."

"That's what I've been chanting over and over in my head. 'Nellie, old girl,' I say, 'get a grip! God is with you! You have nothing to fear.'"

"That's the spirit," Olivia praised and patted Nell on the back.

Still, she wondered. God hadn't exactly jumped in and fixed anything for her lately.

It looked as if the earth beneath his truck was ready to give any second. *Too late to reach the driver's side door,* Zach determined grimly. Luckily he had left his tailgate down because he surmised that his only chance was to reach *anything* solid. Immediately.

As the mud swirled and slid past his heavy feet, Zach slogged toward his pickup, closed his eyes, and taking a deep breath, leaped into the bed of his truck, praying through gritted teeth. "Lord . . . help me! Get me . . . through this . . . alive! I'm . . . too young . . . to die," he grunted as he rolled into his toolbox, banging his head and bruising his shoulder. Rattled as he was, Zach had the presence of mind to reach behind him and yank his tailgate closed. Just in time.

For he'd no sooner heard the lock click than his truck began to move. Zach blinked with disbelief as he watched the scenery go by. At first the rumbling movement was slow. Then as the earth—and his truck—built momentum, raw terror gripped his throat, making it impossible to scream for help. Before he knew it, his trusty pickup was turning in lazy circles, then faster and faster, until it was spinning and careening out of control down the hill. In back, Zach was tossed about like a marble in an empty coffee can.

"Ohhhh, Looorrrddd!" he cried when he could finally

catch his breath. "Thave me, God!" he lisped over the tongue he'd bitten until it was numb and bleeding. Madly he prayed the truck wouldn't roll. He moved across the bed of his truck and tried to grab his bouncing toolbox before it rendered him unconscious.

A quick glance over the edge told Zach that he was now sliding down the hill at a pretty good clip, heading directly toward an old boarding house at the bottom. *Ohh, man*, he thought, staring with morbid fascination, *maybe jumping into the back wasn't such a bright idea after all.*

"You know," Nell continued as she sipped on the tea that Rahni had brought only moments before, "that verse in the Bible about the faith of a mustard seed keeps running through my brain."

"Oh really?" Olivia asked and reached for one of Hattie's homemade cookies. "Why is that?"

"I guess I find it comforting that if I have the faith of a mustard seed, which is the least of all the seeds, maybe I can beat this thing. After all, God promises that with that much faith it's possible to move mountains."

"Then I must not have much faith," Olivia mused dryly. "I'm sure if I ever told a mountain to move, it would just sit there and mock me."

"Have you ever tried?" Nell queried and peered with her ever perky smile at her friend.

It was amazing to Olivia how Nell could be so chipper, considering what she was going through. "Well, no," she confessed.

"You should try sometime," Nell advised and patted her friend's knee. "All you have to do is point at your 'mountain,' whatever that may be for you, and in faith order it to—" Nell pointed dramatically out the window and commanded "*—move!*"

"Somehow I doubt it's that simple, Nell," Olivia sighed. "For years now I've been wondering why my prayers went unheard when it came to . . . John and Lillah and. . . . uh, Nell?" Leaning forward, Olivia stared at her friend's suddenly ashen face. "What is it, honey? You look as if you've seen a ghost."

Mouth gaping, eyes bulging, Nell pointed shakily out the window behind Olivia.

"*Ahhbbaa . . . Ugghhh . . .*," Nell gasped, her lips opening and closing like a dying carp.

"What is it, honey? Are you having a reaction to your pill?" The fearsome look on Nell's face sent great waves of goose flesh rippling down Olivia's spine. Something awful was happening. Nell couldn't control her speech . . . or her arm! This was simply terrible. Olivia always felt so useless in an emergency. Reaching out, she grasped Nell's hand as the woman pointed out the window and appeared to be going into shock.

"*Leesshhh . . . Gaaaa . . . Ohhh!!*"

"Nell, do I need to call 911?" Rattled, Olivia groped behind her for the phone on the wicker coffee table and yanked it into her lap. Staring at the buttons on the phone, she frantically tried to remember the number for 911.

Dumbly, Nell nodded.

Numbly, Olivia dialed.

"Nine-one-one operator," the nasal voice buzzed into the room mere seconds before a handsome man—looking like a hapless bronc buster on a runaway mustang—rode his bucking pickup through the glass wall and into the sunroom of Hattie Hopkins's boarding house.

If you enjoyed *Say Uncle . . . and Aunt,* check out
Barbara Jean Hicks's *An Unlikely Prince!*
The following is an excerpt from Hicks's first
book in the Once Upon a Dream series.
Available in stores October 1998.

1

And they lived happily ever after."

With a satisfying snap, Suzie Wyatt closed the cover of the storybook and used it to rap gently on her nephew's red plastic fireman's helmet. "Good story, huh?"

Gordie rolled his eyes. "Them fairy stories are all the same," he said disdainfully. "All *mushy.*"

"*Those* fairy stories," his mother automatically corrected him as she stepped into the playroom, doffing her paint-spattered work shirt.

Gordie hopped out of his chair and began to race around the room with his arms out to his sides. "Vroomm, vroomm-mm!"

If ever there was a prototypical imp, four-year-old Gordie was it: carrot haired, freckle-faced, gap-toothed, perpetually in motion. He'd already made more trips to the emergency room in his short years than Suzie had in thirty—though he still had miles to go to catch up to his father, Suzie's brother Simon.

The red hair and freckles he got from his mom. Suzie still

remembered the first time she'd met Priscilla, the summer before first grade when the Cornwells had moved next door.

But probably not as well as Priscilla remembered it. Suzie had been certain her new neighbor's curly orange hair was a wig and much to Priscilla's consternation had tried to pull it off. Still, somehow, they'd ended up best friends—and eventually, family.

Suzie raised her voice over the noise of Gordie's airplane simulation. "How's the painting going, Pris?"

"Almost done. One more coat around the edges." Priscilla draped her shirt over the back of a chair. "I told Dad I'd meet his new tenant at eleven-thirty. Shouldn't take more than ten minutes to do a walk-through with this guy—the place is tiptop. Simon put more hours into that old house this summer than he did the entire time he and I lived there."

"Can I play with Woof now?" Gordie interrupted, already bored with playing airplane. "Huh? Can I?"

"*May* I play with Woof?" his mother corrected him again, absent-mindedly.

"Sure!" he said magnanimously. "We can both play with him, Mom. Aunt Suzie too."

Laughing, Suzie joined her nephew at the screen door and scooped him up in a hug.

Gordie wriggled and wrinkled his nose at her. "Did I make a funny?"

"You *are* a funny," she said, setting him back down and tweaking his nose.

She turned back to Priscilla, who was surveying the room with a bemused expression. Every square inch of table and counter space was piled high with books, puzzles, reams of construction paper, plastic tubs of safety scissors and fat crayons, and jars of poster paints. Giant rolls of butcher paper in jellybean colors leaned against each other in one corner. Cardboard boxes filled with toys, games, and dress-up clothes sat shoulder to shoulder along the walls.

Priscilla sighed. "And I thought the whole idea of Labor Day was to *rest* from our labors. Are we really going to have this place organized by tomorrow?"

"If we don't, we're setting up business at your house," Suzie answered cheerfully. Simon and Priscilla's house on Bramble Ridge was brand-new. No way was Pris going to hand it over to a gaggle of preschoolers. Not even if that meant she had to work through the night. "I think your family room would make a good—"

"Never mind. We'll get it done," Priscilla interrupted wryly.

"Did you leave the paint out in the other room?" Suzie asked. "I can work on that while you're gone."

Priscilla looked doubtful. "And leave Gordie alone in here?"

"Aw, he'll do fine." Suzie knocked her knuckles against Gordie's fireman's hat. "Won't you, sport?"

"You never said if I can play with Woof," he pouted.

The black-and-white mongrel lay dolefully on the stoop outside, his muzzle resting on his front legs and his tail thumping at the sound of their voices. Woof had proved much more trainable than Gordie had, his mother claimed, though sometimes under Gordie's influence he still reverted.

Suzie raised an eyebrow at Priscilla.

"After lunch," his mother told him, apparently deciding he was safer inside than out. Unfortunately, fences were more challenges than obstacles to Gordie. "Okay, Suze, I'll be back in a jiff." She knelt in front of her son and looked him straight in the eye. "You listen to what your Aunt Suzie tells you, hear?"

"We'll be fine, Priscilla, really." Suzie made sure the screen door was latched and locked as she waved her friend across the yard. "Don't forget. I want a full report when you get back," she called.

"Oh, don't you worry about that!" Like many a happily married woman before her, Priscilla was always on the lookout for eligible men for her friends.

Forty years old, single, and a doctor—that was the scoop they had on the tenant so far. That and the fact that Priscilla's father was delighted with him. "Perfect" was the word he'd used, Priscilla had said.

Who knew? Maybe the good Lord had decided it was time to answer her prayer for her very own happily-ever-after.

A girl could dream anyway.

"Didn't I tell you, Blue? Didn't I tell you it was the perfect spot for my sabbatical?" Professor Harrison Hunt allowed the thinnest edge of excitement to creep into his voice as he pulled into the drive of the lovely Tudor-style cottage on Hokanvander Street.

He braked to a stop. The boxes piled in the backseat shifted forward and then back again. "*Just* the place to write a book on the history of Tillicum County. Just the place," he said.

Blue, despite his cramped quarters in the wide-mouthed gallon jar strapped into the passenger seat of the Volvo, flipped over in a joyful somersault.

Conventional pets had never worked for Harrison, who was horribly allergic to dander. He'd made a place for a fish in his life last year, however, after reading that aquarium watching could lower one's blood pressure substantially. Not that his blood pressure was especially high, but one could never be too careful.

He'd never expected a fish to be such a delightful companion. Blue was a marvelous listener. Unlike the majority of students in the history classes Harrison taught at San Juan University in Seattle. Sometimes he even practiced his lectures on Blue, who had never once interrupted a discourse with a rude noise or a smart-aleck question.

Blue was a *Betta splendens,* better known as a Siamese fighting fish. Two in an aquarium could rip each other's delicate fins to shreds, but Harrison didn't plan to give his pet the opportunity. The closest Blue ever got to a sparring partner was his reflection in the mirror attached to the side of his tank.

He wasn't strictly blue. In fact, at present, he was rather a muddy brown. When the mirror in his regular tank tricked him into thinking he had competition, however, he turned beautiful shades of turquoise, green, and purple, with streaks of red in his tail and fins; the overall effect was blue. As the Latin name implied, in fighting form he was truly resplendent. Even at peace he was lovely, especially when he swished the fins along his back and belly and flicked his long, flowing tail, as he was doing now.

"I know—I can hardly believe it myself," Harrison answered. "After fifteen years. Twelve *glorious* months away from the classroom." Goodness, he was almost giddy with delight! "Nothing to do but read and write," he added. "And soak up the atmosphere. You'll love it, Blue. The town. The neighborhood. The house."

A quiet little house on a quiet little street in the quiet little town of Pilchuck, Washington. The *sleepy* town of Pilchuck, one might even say.

Harrison stepped out of the car, glanced up and down the empty street, then gazed raptly at the cottage. That he would be living on Hokanvander Street! Granny Grace had been a Hokanvander. He'd taken the name of the street as a sign.

He'd checked out several other houses on several other streets in several other towns in Tillicum County. None of them suited the way this one did.

It was a vintage 1930s house, built in a style as old and elegant as Will Shakespeare himself. One could almost imagine a thatched roof sitting atop the half-timbered whitewashed walls and candles flickering in the diamond-paned windows at dusk.

Moreover, the cottage came furnished. Charmingly. With his large cherry desk, his ergonomic chair, and extra shelves installed in the second bedroom, he'd be quite comfortable. *Quite* comfortable.

The neighbors were tailor-made for a man with serious work to do. On one side, the Reginald Wyatts. A delightful retired couple, longtime friends of Harrison's new landlord. On the other side, a graveyard.

What could be more peaceful?

Directly behind the house, on the other side of an arched garden gate, sat the Pilchuck Public Library and the Pilchuck Historical Society, both of which had resources Harrison was positively salivating over.

The Pilchuck Post Office, the Apple Basket Market, Manny Mo's Variety, and the Roadkill Café were all within walking distance—not that he had much hope for an establishment called the Roadkill Café. But the market and whatnot shop looked promising.

Most important—and this point he had researched with particular diligence—no one on the entire block was under sixty-five years of age.

"When we lived there, of course, there were children everywhere," William Cornwell, his new landlord, had informed him when he signed the lease six months ago. Mr. Cornwell was the registrar at San Juan University.

"Seven children right next door at the Wyatts," Mr. Cornwell said. "Of course they're all gone now. All grown up." He sighed, as if growing up were somehow a lamentable experience.

"My daughter Priscilla married one of the Wyatt boys," he added. "You'll meet Priscilla. She and Simon lived in the house till they finished building their own six months ago, and I've asked her to manage the property for me. Hard for me to fix a leaky faucet from Seattle. Not that you'll have leaky faucets," he'd hastened to add.

Harrison looked at his watch. Priscilla Wyatt should be here any minute.

"Not a single child buzzing about the neighborhood," he murmured with satisfaction. "Not even on a holiday."

Children! he thought with distaste. He'd never understood children. And quite frankly didn't approve of them. How did parents bear the little creatures, with their noise and their runny noses and their endless questions?

Parents! Parents were the problem, of course. Parents and the educational system. Encouraging childhood as if it was some necessary stage of human development. Didn't they realize childhood was simply an invention? And a relatively modern invention at that?

Whatever happened to the days when children were expected to be *useful?* The way he had been? Granny Grace had always been so proud of him. Her "little man," she'd called him.

He opened the passenger door, unbuckled the seatbelt, and carefully lifted the glass jar out of the seat. Blue darted nervously around its perimeter. "No need to get excited, Blue," he said. "No need even to *think* about children. Or adolescents. Or even young adults. Didn't I tell you I'd find us a quiet place to work?"

"Dr. Hunt?"

A pretty redhead appeared around the corner of the house.

"Oh!" As usual when confronted by a pretty woman, Harrison felt flustered. Befuddled. Thoroughly disquieted.

It was a handicap he'd dealt with all his life—feeling self-conscious in the presence of pretty women. It might have been a debilitating handicap, considering that females—many of whom could be considered pleasing to the eye—made up roughly half the population. And appeared with quite provoking regularity in faculty meetings and classrooms, not to mention libraries, banks, doctors' offices, restaurants, stores, *et cetera ad infinitum*.

Harrison's "Method for Dealing with Desirable Women" was almost automatic by now. The "Less-Dangerous-Category Method," it might be called. The moment a pretty woman hove into view, his brain started clicking through the categorical possibilities: *Colleague. Student. Service Provider. Salesperson.* Anything but *Pretty Woman.*

Property Manager, he settled on for the redhead without too much fuss and flurry. He shifted Blue's jar in his arms and reached to shake her hand. "Mrs. Wyatt?"

"There's nothin' to do in here!" Gordie said to Suzie.

"Nothing to do! Gordie, my boy, are you blind? Try another picture book or a puzzle. Or—" She tapped a cardboard box next to the back door with her foot. "There's some fun new stuff in here." Buttoning Priscilla's work shirt over her T-shirt, she added, "Don't open any other boxes unless you ask me. And you stay put, you hear?"

Without answering, he peered into the box at her feet. "*Way* cool!" he said and dumped out its entire load of interlocking, wooden racetrack pieces.

Suzie eyed him warily. Maybe Priscilla was right about not leaving him alone. As much as she adored her nephew, she'd spent enough time with him to know Gordie played by his own rules.

But the door was locked, and the racetrack should keep him occupied. *Better here than in a room with open cans of paint,* she thought, shuddering.

She watched him for a moment longer as he pieced the wooden track together, smiling at his concentration. She did adore him. Face it—she adored *kids.* Why else would she have put up with poverty-level wages for the last six years working for the JumpStart preschool program in Seattle?

Why else would she and Priscilla be opening their own private preschool and daycare center, right here in the very house in Pilchuck, Washington, where she and her six brothers and sisters had kept the neighborhood hopping? Living in a thatched hut somewhere in the jungles of Papua New Guinea for the next two years would be a piece of cake for her mom and dad after raising seven kids as wild as the Wyatts.

"Vroomm-mm!" Loud engine noises broke into her thoughts as Gordie zoomed a car around the racetrack.

"You hear me, Gordie?" she asked again. "You stay put."

"Vroomm-mm!"

She took that as a yes and retreated to the room where Priscilla had been working—though if she'd had her druthers, she would druther be sitting on the floor, racing cars with Gordie.

Simon teased that she'd chosen her career as an excuse to play. "Like you didn't?" she retorted.

Her brother was principal of Pilchuck High School. The kind of principal who slam dunked with the kids on the basketball court, played the part of the villain in school plays, invited students to practically drown him at the Fall Fair every year, and once had made an utter fool of himself in front of the entire town singing karaoke at a district fund-raiser. Talk about an excuse to play!

"At least *I've* advanced to high school," Simon needled.

Priscilla was lucky, Suzie thought as she climbed the stepladder and reached for a paintbrush. How many guys out there had the perfect combination of playfulness and dependability Simon had? None that she had found—and not for want of looking, either. The playful ones wanted her to take care of them, the dependable ones were frightful bores, and the one time she thought she'd found both in the same man, he'd turned out to be a liar and a cheat.

"Maybe you're too picky," Priscilla had suggested not long ago.

Suzie glowered. "Easy for you to say when you're married to your Mr. Wonderful."

Priscilla sighed. "Simon *is* pretty wonderful, all right . . ." Absolutely starry-eyed still, after eight years. Both of them.

Suzie dipped her brush in the paint tray and started where her friend had left off. Maybe Pris was right, she thought. If she was ever going to get married and have babies of her own, maybe she was going to have to settle for a Harry Humdrum . . .

No, she told herself firmly. She wouldn't give up. She wouldn't settle. Someday—

Someday her prince would come.

"Hopefully before I'm old and gray," she muttered as she carefully slid her paint-soaked brush along the wall where it met the ceiling. It wouldn't do to spatter the Blueberry Milkshake wall paint onto the freshly painted Vanilla Cream ceiling.

Suddenly an ear-piercing siren shattered the quiet. Suzie's hand jerked, and the pristine ceiling was no longer pristine. Neither was Suzie's face. Drat! She'd never get used to that stupid new fire siren the city council had installed.

WOOoo-WOOoo-WOOoo-WOOoo!

Woof was barking his head off, of course, and Gordie was yelling, "Far! Far!" and probably racing around the—

She heard a door slam.

"Gordie!"

She scrambled down the ladder. The paint tray, poised precariously on the ladder's shelf, teetered dangerously. As she grabbed for it, Blueberry Milkshake splattered across the front of her shirt and down the Vanilla Cream doorjamb.

Drat!

WOOoo-WOOoo-WOOoo-WOOoo!

By the time she got to the playroom door, Gordie was disappearing through the garden gate and into the neighbor's yard, headed straight for his old back door with Woof yelping and nipping at his heels. She should have known the kid could unlock the door.

WOOoo-WOOoo-WOOoo-WOOoo!

"Gordie, get back here this instant!" she yelled, dashing after him. "Woof! WOOF! Come here!"

But obedience wasn't high on Gordie's list of priorities. Nor Woof's at this point. Not when adventure beckoned.

And for Gordie, Fireman of the Future, chasing fire trucks was the height of adventure.

Dear Reader,

We hope you enjoyed this romantic comedy from A Time for Laughter . . . and Romance. Thousands of years ago, King Solomon acknowledged that "there is a time for everything," including "a time to laugh" (Ecclesiastes 3:1,4). But as popular humorist and author Liz Curtis Higgs points out, "Christian women today don't give themselves the time for laughter." Congratulations on giving yourself the opportunity to laugh—and love vicariously—with these lighthearted romances.

If you would like to read more books in the line, ask for these titles at your local bookstore.

Suzy Pizzuti
Halo Hattie's Boarding House Series:
Only God could take hard-of-hearing Halo Hattie's fervent prayers for the wrong things and make them right!

#1 Say Uncle . . . and Aunt: Sean Flannigan and Julia Evans, two high-powered executives, are suddenly on baby-care duty and unexpectedly fall for more than the baby.

#2 Raising Cain . . . and His Sisters: Olivia Harmon is struggling to heal after a tragic loss. Only the arrival of Cain and his sisters can bring her out of her shell again! *Available June 1999.*

#3 Saving Grace: Everything Grace touches or tries turns out badly. That is until she meets Ryan Lowell, the handsome bachelor who helps her realize that with God's help, anything is possible. *Available Spring 2000.*

The Salinger Sisters Series:
Meet four sisters, each of whom has her own escapades while falling in love.

#1 Love on the Run: Cat Salinger wants one thing: the big new ad account. Her chief competition (and major distraction in the love department), Jonas Riley, proves to be more than Cat bargained for.

#2 A Match Made in Heaven: Lucy Salinger is a fantastic matchmaker. But will she find the cute new doctor a wife—or keep him for herself? *Available February 1999.*

#3 The Perfect Wife: After her husband divorces her, Felicia begins a new life. But her new male housekeeper cares for her more than she dreams! *Available October 1999.*

Barbara Jean Hicks
The Once Upon a Dream Series:
Fairy tales retold in modern times!

#1 An Unlikely Prince: A professor rents a quiet cottage in a distant town to accomplish his writing goals. Little does he know that his lovely neighbor is running a day-care center for seven imps! *Available October 1998.*

#2 All That Glitters; Coming in June 1999.
Book #3; Coming in Spring 2000.

In 1999 . . .
Annie Jones
The Route 66 Series:
Meet some incredible characters at the Double Heart Cafe—along historic Route 66—who'll steal more than your heart! *Available February 1999.*